The Possessor of the Seed

Book 1
of
The Prophecy of the Seed

By Michelle LaVigne-Wedel

Sweetgrass Fiction
P.O. Box 1862
Merrimack, NH 03054

A division of Sweetgrass Press

Library of Congress Card Number: 00-191704
Michelle LaVigne-Wedel.   1962-

Possessor of the Seed / Michelle LaVigne-Wedel

Editor: Paul Wedel

ISBN 0-9702630-5-8

COVER DESIGN: The Electric Wigwam

Printed in the United States of America

Address all inquiries:
Sweetgrass Press
P.O. Box 1862
Merrimack, NH 03054-1862

Prologue

Touchea looked out her bedroom window at the orange, dusk sky and sighed. Many things had changed since her first life, so many generations ago, but she was pleased that the beauty of the sky as Kai slipped out of sight wasn't one of them. There was a chilling nip in the air so she reached over, picked up a light blanket and wrapped it around her. It felt soft and warm on her bare shoulders.

She held the blanket tightly and thought for a moment. There was another thing she was happy hadn't changed. She was pleased her people never developed the annoying habit of covering their bodies in layers and layers of clothing. She found the limits of a physical body annoying enough. She didn't need fabric surrounding her skin, reminding her of how finite the world around her had become.

As the generations passed since her first life, the women developed the curious custom of allowing their hair to grow very long. As a matter of fact, it had become the fashion for a woman to let her hair grow as long as possible, even to her ankles, as a symbol of power and command over the men in her service. After all, it took well trained and devoted consorts to maintain such hair. "Such a bother," she thought half out-loud.

Touchea looked at her own long silvery locks and the golden chain that braided them into a smooth even fall. The chain was also a symbol of power. Power greater than any other that existed. It told all who saw it that she was an Exoltaire, the highest of the stations of power.

In fact, Touchea was the highest Exoltaire alive and the head of The Council. In the entire world there were only twenty-eight Exoltaires. They made up the remainder of the Council along with the highest-ranking Regime as a representative for the people from the lower stations of power. The Council made all the decisions of importance for the entire world. After all, their holdings formed the entire world. Each Council member owned a large Habite made up of smaller parcels of land operated by lower ranking women of her clan. Each Habite was an independent and complete world in itself. Trading and other social interactions outside the Habite seldom occurred. Aside from sessions of Council, interaction between clans never happened at all.

"Clans," Touchea sighed as her mind drifted to another flow of thought. "Corays and Sheens," she whispered to herself, "such fools you are."

During the first generation of awareness, the time of Touchea's first life, the Corays and the Sheens were the peacemakers. They were the ones who brought together a world of separate, nomadic cultures into one united people. They, together, built Lumdon Hall — the great place of meeting. They, together, established the etiquette of Council and the ways of order. But there can only be one master in any situation, and though they worked together, they were never truly united.

Both clans kept their bloodlines clean of the other's "inferior" stock, and both envied the power and property of the other. Yet, the only true difference between the clans was the color of their hair and eyes. The Sheens were of dark hair and dark eyes, and the Corays were of light hair and eyes. Otherwise, they were virtually identical as a race. They were both smooth skinned with little body hair other than what was on their heads. They even shared the same narrow facial features. After all, both clans could trace their line back to a common root. They were more alike than different, but they didn't see it that way.

For many generations the two clans bickered back and forth only keeping the peace through elaborate formalities in etiquette and carefully worded insults. But even that precarious peace wouldn't last forever, as Touchea was well aware.

The pressure was building up too fast now to be vented safely, and the power of the people too great to be released. That's why Touchea was alive again. She was there to continue a prophecy she had foretold generations ago. She was there to help her people make the transition into chaos. It is not what she wanted to do, but it was necessary.

A warm glow filled the room and the Exoltaire walked away from the window.

"The time of The Seed has come," she thought.

"It's up to them now, my dear sisters," she said aloud to the sky. "I've set the cogs in motion. Now I can only sit back and watch them turn."

Chapter 1

As the heat of the day rose, the Sheen clan left their houses and fields and entered the cool shelter of the cavus. The dark was soothing and the air smelled of the herbs and wild flowers that grew along the smooth stone walls. It was a comfortable, cool place. The perfect place to go to escape from the high heat and get some rest. It was also a place to meet and talk about the morning's chores. Many people were doing just that, sitting and talking over the morning's events.

In the far corner of the cavus, Seth, the leader of the animal Keepers, was talking to one of the house-hands. In his arms he held a young equis colt only a few hours old. He brought it into the cavus with him despite its mother's objections, because he knew the midday heat this time of year would be too much for a new colt.

"I don't think Tammeia will like having an equis in the cavus," a servant said when he saw the animal.

Seth looked the young equis over. "I don't think she'll mind. I couldn't leave him outside to die."

The servant shrugged and walked away.

Seth adjusted his hold on the colt then leaned back against the wall. His shoulder length hair hung like black strings off his head and over his wrinkled, blue robe. Compared to the others in the cavus, he looked rather rough and messy, but that didn't really matter to him. All he was concerned with were the animals in his care. He had their respect no matter what his clothes looked like.

Like all Keepers, Seth could talk to animals. But unlike most, he became kin with the creatures in his care. They trusted him and listened to him. He gave them his full attention, often putting them before everything else, including what Regime Tammeia, the leader of the Habite, might think.

Seth looked around. A few more people entered the cavus and sat down. It was almost time for Tammeia to come and make the daily announcements and give the morning blessing. Seth yawned and stroked the equis absently. "I wonder what's new today," he said to the animal. "It's been quite a while since she's had some real news to tell us."

The equis fidgeted. Seth was going to put it down, but a group of small children lay asleep on the ground near his feet. Instead, he adjusted his grip on the animal and again yawned, then closed his eyes.

On the other side of the cavus, the child, Alana, also yawned, but refused to close her eyes. Instead she rubbed them and stood up. She didn't want to fall asleep before her mother arrived. She rubbed her tired eyes one more time and looked around.

"There's never anything to do in here," she thought. "I hate the heat. It lasts forever." She brushed her long dark hair out of her face and smiled. At six years old time often seemed to stand still. She danced across the cavus and poked at one of the sleeping children hoping to wake a willing playmate, but he barely stirred. Alana tried again. Convinced that it wasn't going to work, she gave up. Besides, she could tell by the way the people stopped talking and started to whisper, that here mother was finally coming. Again she brushed the hair from her face, straightened out her clothes as best as a child could, and ran through the entrance hall to her mother's side.

"Alana, little one," Tammeia greeted as the child took her place on the right of the Regime. "Are you ready to go in?" she asked.

Alana nodded. "I'm ready."

"Good." The woman looked at her nine consorts and took a deep slow breath.

"Are you alright, Lady?" One of them asked.

"Yes. Let's go," the Regime said after a slight pause and another deep breath.

Since the blessing in the cavus was a formal occasion, the men took their places in formation behind Tammeia. No one showed any sign of emotion. Alana giggled and beamed a smile towards them hoping to get a reaction. She knew it was part of their duties to act so rigid on formal occasions, which made her try even harder to get a response. Usually, someone would smile back or wink a reward for her efforts, but not today. There was no wink, smile, or even a second glance. All became silently still when the procession entered the cavus.

Warm light filled the room as they entered. It gave blue and gold highlights to Tammeia's hair. Colorful flowers that hung from depressions in the stone walls seemed to dance in the light. All the people of the house, Carlafs and consorts alike, lowered themselves to a kneeling position with their heads resting low in respect for the leader of the Habite. Seth knelt with the colt still in his arms; his head bowed as low as his situation would allow. The Regime Tammeia Sheen's consorts shifted into their places to form a semi-circle around her, and Alana took her place at her mother's side.

From where she sat, Alana could see the light sparkling off Tammeia's long, black hair. She watched the reflections dance off the woman's hair as it contoured itself to her pale body. It draped over her head and fell to her ankles as softly as if it were fine silk. "When my hair grows that long, I'm going to let it hang loose down my back," Alana dreamed. "The day I have my own Habite." Alana was so engulfed in her daydream that she never noticed the solemn look in Tammeia's eyes and the silver tinged tear that ran down her cheek.

The lady stood silently for a long moment, then looked over to her consort Jgar and back to her people. "My Clan," she spoke softly at first, gaining sharpness with every word, "I've been in meeting with the High Exoltaire and the Council. We believe we've found a solution to our peoples' dilemma. The answer, however, will be at first very painful to the people of every clan and Carlaf." Her voice seemed to falter a few syllables, but she didn't continue. Tammeia paused a great while.

"The Carlafs of this Habite are to meet with me when Kai's light has faded to dark," she paused again and swallowed hard. "Palray, consort to the Dominion Sharl, the Keeper Seth and my daughter Alana are to be taken from this place tonight and brought to a place where they'll be trained to carry out this solution."

A mild uneasiness passed through the cavus.

"Leave here? Why do I have to leave my home?" The thought made Alana shiver; the fear made her dizzy and weak.

She began to quiver. Her face felt hot and tears welled in her eyes. "No, I can't leave. I don't want to go anywhere."

A hand reached down and touched her shoulder. Its tender warmth caused her to raise her tear-filled eyes. The hand belonged to Tammeia's consort Eisen, a tall man with soft features and hair as black as Tammeia's. His eyes held an inner quiet that Alana seemed to be able to draw from his touch.

"Little one, your actions are not worthy of your station," he whispered. His words were scolding but his message only a gentle reminder. "Let's show some respect for your mother." He motioned for Alana to stop fidgeting.

She looked at herself uneasily. Only then did she realize she'd been quietly mumbling. The child recomposed herself and looked over to her mother. The Head Regime stood in tall perfect form, steady and immovable. Her perfection of body was only challenged by the aura of truth and wisdom that seemed to radiate from her being. Tammeia lifted her right arm and began to sing a blessing that echoed through the cavus. Its tone and pitch carried a sedating quality that helped erase the tension caused by her prior announcement. Even the colt Seth clutched, drifted to total passiveness. The song ended with the traditional invitation for all to rest.

Seth's hold loosened cautiously as if the breaking of the embrace would rob him of his power to stand. He lowered the animal to its feet, then sat himself on a rock with a gingerly motion which was unlike him. Alana tucked herself neatly into a nearby corner she had claimed as her own. She closed her eyes, but couldn't sleep. Her mind was in no state to rest no matter how long a time she tried.

"Who could want me to go away? Why do I have to go?" Alana tossed the questions back and forth without finding an adequate answer. Then, with an agitated jerk, she rose to her feet.

Eventually, the heat of the day passed and the air began to cool. Soon the servants were outside watering the roads so they could be walked on. Tammeia again sang and the people readied themselves to leave the cavus' shelter and return to their homes and jobs.

Alana was one of the first outside. She bolted from the cavus as if its darkness trapped her and its cool air tormented her.

Sola's light was bright and Kai was descending. Alana had to pause to let her eyes adjust before she ran to help the servants pour water from the canals built along the roadside onto the glassy white roads. Other children joined in and soon the chore turned into a game of water fights and splashing. For the moment, Alana forgot about the task that befell her.

"Alana, come on now. We have to get ready," Eisen said. He grabbed her arm. His touch was void of the compassion she'd felt earlier.

The bucket fell from her hand and her smile dropped.

"I don't want to go," she said. "What if I go away and never come back?"

"Let her play," Seth insisted, "today she's still a child." He put the equis colt down and watched as the animal hurried back to its mother's side.

Alana broke loose from Eisen's grip and ran to Seth. Her wet hair left a trail of water droplets like rain.

"You don't have to be afraid, Alana. I'm going on this mysterious journey with you, and I'm not even an heir of the Clan, as you are, but I'm not afraid. Why should you be?" Seth turned away to avoid meeting Alana's scrutinizing gaze. Even though she was only a young girl, she possessed the intuition of a woman. Seth knew Alana would tell from his eyes that he lied. He did fear. Of what, he didn't know. "Your mother would never place us in danger."

Alana looked at him indignantly. "I'm not afraid of danger. I just don't want to leave here."

"We'll return soon. I promise you. This type of thing never lasts long. They'll just bring us some place, and the people there will show us some things, like your reading lessons, then they'll send us home.

"Go see what Eisen wants now, child. I'll see you tonight. If we leave together you can ride the mare I trained for your mother."

"The one as black as the night?"

Seth nodded. Alana's eyes opened wide.

"Now, go and get ready." He gave her a gentle push and she ran into the building. Seth sighed as he lost sight of her.

"What's so important that such a young girl must be taken from her mother? And for how long?" Seth wondered as he walked off towards the woods. He and Alana shared the same questions, and in many respects, the same fears. He felt strangely satisfied with himself; with the fact that he was able to hide his apprehensions from the child.

The Keeper set his sights on the wood and stone barn beyond the trees. As he walked, he hummed a song to himself. Its words eluded him, but that didn't matter. The tune and the barn were all he let fill his head.

What seemed like a small stone hut from the other side of the trees was actually a three-story structure of white stone and elaborately sculpted, bluish logs. Seth started up a stairway that came off the left side of the dwelling and entered to a walkway. Below him, the first floor was separated into stalls. All of them empty except for the people who cleaned them. The animals that were kept in the stalls roamed loose during the day.

"Come upstairs. I have to speak to all of you," Seth called down to the workers. His voice echoed off the walls. "Hurry, there's not much time." He closed the door and continued up the stairs to a hall. Many doors lined its delicately painted walls. Each one was identical in its design to the next, and all were made of the same wood that decorated the outside walls. The hall turned to the right. At the end of this new expanse, stood two large doors of rich red wood. Seth paused a minute to straighten out his loosely tied robe and noticed his hands were dirty from the work he'd done that day. He didn't think of washing them until now. His workload had been too heavy, and as if only to add to his troubles, an equis chose this morning to give birth. He rubbed his hands together and opened the door.

"Lady, may I come in?"

"Yes, come here, my consort," a voice replied from within the daylight filled room. Seth walked in slowly. His Carlaf, Hella was sitting quietly. She didn't speak until he closed the door behind him.

"I was told you spent the heat at the main anhabit," she said.

Seth nodded.

"Then you already know," she continued.

He nodded again.

Hella gave him a half-hearted smile. "Gather your people, to prepare them for your absence."

He looked at her face. A moist cheek and red eyes gave away her secret. Seth realized she had been crying. "She feels it too," he said to himself with a nervous sigh.

Seth shifted anxiously. "Hella, what's this solution Tammeia spoke about? For that matter, what's it a solution for? Where are we going? Why was I chosen to leave? It's the beginning of foaling season. I have equis to breed. Are you aware that there are more than one hundred and seventy mares on this Habite! And more than half of them will be bearing foals this season! Doesn't Tammeia know how much work there is to do? I just don't have any time for folly. Can't she see that?" Seth started to fidget nervously. "Besides, I don't want to leave you. If I do, I'll never see you again." The words flew by his lips almost uncontrolled. Their content betrayed him.

"I know you're upset." She tried to smile. "I wish you didn't have to go. But, you must. Tammeia didn't tell me why yet, but I'll find out tonight. When I return from the meeting I'll tell you everything that I know. So, don't ponder on it. Instead, decide who'll take your place until you return. And you will return, though I fear it will be a long time."

"I know it will," Seth said with a sigh, then tried to change his tone. "I'll miss you, Hella." His voice shook.

"There'll be time to say good-bye later. For now, we have to prepare." She kissed him then walked away.

"No, don't leave me yet." Seth grabbed her and held her tightly against his chest. There was something he felt he should say, but his mouth couldn't form the words. There was something he knew in his soul, but it was impossible to express.

"Our time is limited." The lady pushed her consort gently aside. "Go now, Seth. The Keepers are assembling for you."

He cleared his throat and stood straight. "I'll take my place at the meeting now, with your permission, Lady."

"Choose wisely."

He left and didn't look back to see Hella staring out the window at setting Kai.

The Keeper stopped just outside the woman's door. "Good-bye, Hella," he whispered with all the finality he felt in his soul.

"Well," he said to himself out loud, "better get it over with." He hurried back down the hall until he got to the place where the other Keepers were assembled. He took a bracing breath then entered.

"People." Seth walked to the front of a small podium. On all sides of him were candles made of a yellow wax. The fire they bore gave a warm, orange tone to the windowless room and rounded off the hard features of its roughly finished interior. The people he spoke to sat on the floor in small groups, about seventeen people in all. They were quiet, their attention given only to him. "As you may already know by now, I'll be leaving tonight. For how long, I don't know. I'll most likely be gone through this summer's breeding season and the foaling, and my duties must be taken care of. Therefore, I'm appointing a new leader of the Keepers who will maintain this Habite until I return."

The crowd shifted. A slight rumble of voices rose then faded as Seth went on. "Marc, I leave my chores to you to distribute as you see fit." Marc got to his feet and joined Seth. The head Keeper untied a green sash he wore at his waist and tied it around the other mans waist. "Take this and wear it proudly. You're to be the new Head Keeper while I go on this journey."

Seth turned his attention to the others. "I give Marc my position and title as Head Keeper of the Habite of the Regime Tammeia Sheen. Respect him as such." Seth knelt and kissed the palm of the new Head Keeper's hand, then got back to his feet and handed Marc a large smoothly polished staff made of the same blue wood that garnished the building. A cold sweat broke over Seth's entire being as his inner senses cried that it would be the last time he'd touch the staff, the last time he would set eyes on his people.

Marc grabbed the staff. The presence of his hand cooled the feeling of the warm wood slightly. The sensation caused Seth to wake suddenly from his world of inner thought. He pulled his hand away sharply.

"Seth?" Marc said with surprise. "What's wrong?"

Seth took an uneasy breath. "You have work to do, Keeper. I'll leave you with your people," he said quietly.

Marc looked at him with confusion. He didn't know where to begin. Seth did his best to smile, but his eyes held a disturbed expression. He turned and walked out of the meeting hall. He was glad no one noticed. How could he explain what he felt when he didn't understand it himself?

Chapter 2

In the house of the Regime, Tammeia Sheen, Alana took her favorite dolls and placed them in a leather sack. After all, she couldn't go away without them. The last light of Kai was fading and the sky outside her window was bright orange. Her stomach rolled with hunger and her head swam with a dull ache. Alana sniffled a bit and wiped her nose. The seemingly endless tears that ran from her eyes had all but dried up. For now, though, her only priority was which of her toys she would bring with her. She sat on the floor with her stuffed dolls in her arms. Her heavy eyelids closed and she drifted into sleep. It was a quiet sleep, only disturbed by one dream:

She stood at one end of a large wooden bridge that spanned a dark ravine. The sky was all orange and the ground was dusty loose dirt. She backed away from the cliff and floated into the sky. Suddenly, below her, she saw a group of wild equis. She wanted to get down to the ground and see them better, maybe touch one, but her body wouldn't move forward. The more she tried, the faster she floated upwards.

The animals raced onto the bridge, their hoofs pounding on the wood with a sharp hollow tone. The sound disturbed Alana. She knew the bridge was going to collapse, so she shut her eyes hoping not to see it. The pounding grew louder and louder. The moment she knew the bridge collapsed she felt the sensation of falling to the ground.

The child opened her eyes to find herself surrounded by her toys. The sky was dark and someone was knocking on the door.

"Alana, little one, you must come eat now."

She stood up and assessed herself. She was awake now and very hungry. "I'm coming Meem." Alana opened the door.

An old woman with graying hair and warm brown eyes walked in. She was dressed in a plain green robe. She held out a small tunic obviously dyed from the blue wood that was abundant in the area. "Put this on, Alana. The darkness is cool."

"Meem, I just dreamt about equis. Big black ones. They were running wild."

"You think of equis too much, young lady. Come quickly before your food gets cold."

The old woman grabbed Alana's hand and they walked together through the hall till they came to a room filled with people. Every wall of the room was covered with a decorative etching or painting. The smell of meat teased Alana's appetite. She broke from Meem's hold and ran to her place at the longest table. People from each table left and returned carrying large plates of vegetables and fruits. The meat that smelled so good was on a table of its own in the center of the room. Eisen stood next to it, carving knife in hand. He tapped on the table and the people quieted down, then Meem stood up and sang a prayer of thanks for the food.

Alana got up quickly, her eyes opened wide. "Why is Meem singing the blessing? Where's my mother? She's supposed to sing?" Alana's mind raced faster than her darting eyes. There were no Carlafs in the dining hall except Meem. "Where is everyone?" The tension Alana felt turned to the same sense of panic she had felt in her dream. She ran to Eisen.

"Alana, you must be very hungry to run. Meem's song hasn't ended," he leaned over and whispered. As he did, the song ended.

"All the Carlafs are gone. Where's my mother?"

"At the meeting. Don't you remember?" He cut a piece of meat and offered it to her. "Where's your platter?"

Alana lifted her empty hands and looked at him absently.

"I have it," someone said from behind her.

"Here then, take this meat for your table. May you eat well." Eisen gave the meat to a young boy.

"Come on, Alana." The boy nudged her as he passed by.

She followed him to the table and sat down in her usual chair. The absence of people made her nervous. Every table in the room seemed half-empty, especially the one Alana sat at. It was usually filled by Tammeia, her consorts and Tammeia's Head Nylla, Hella and her consorts. But only a few of each ladies' men were there tonight. The empty chair on Alana's right reminded her of the feeling she got when her older brother became of age and was given to the service of a Carlaf. That was the only other night in all of Alana's memory when she sat by an empty chair at mealtime.

She was given a full plate of food, which she ate almost mechanically. When she was finished, Eisen approached her.

"Little one, you must come with me. Your mother wants you to be ready by the time she returns from the meeting." He picked her up and carried her out of the room to the main hallway. When they got to the bottom of the stairs, he put her down.

"So, are you ready to go?" he asked with forced enthusiasm.

She nodded. "I'm not afraid, Eisen, but my dolls are. They think I won't come home again. But I will, won't I?"

"Of course you will, you're only going for a short time. I don't understand why you worry so much. At your age life is an adventure not a toil." He brushed some stray hairs off her cheek. "Can't you think of anything exciting about your trip?"

"Well..." she said dragging out the word as she thought. "I'm riding the black mare tonight. Seth promised." She pointed to a window. "She's as dark as the night sky."

Eisen followed her finger to the window. The sky was indeed dark and the night clear. The stars shoned like crystals. "A beautiful night," Eisen thought. "It should be a good night for traveling."

"You see, it's not all bad." He grabbed her hand. "Come on, Alana, we don't want to be late." They hurried down the hall into the darkness.

Chapter 3

A bright yellow light filled the assembly hall. It seemed to be coming from all sides of the great chamber, filling every crack and corner with its warm glow. The hall itself seemed to shine, not only with light, but with a different kind of energy that at times seemed as one with the people who stood in it.

Every woman from every house of Tammeia's Habite was there. Each accompanied by at least one consort. The last light of Sola and Kai had faded and the few windows that were opened were like portals to the vastness of deep space. The dark of the night sky seemed to envelop the hall and its occupants in a different time, or perhaps a different dimension. The interior light flickered, as if fighting with the dark for its own existence. The air was cool and sweet with the scent of wild flowers. A door opened on the forward left side of the hall and Tammeia walked in followed by four of her consorts. She was clad in a sheer white veil and had small white and blue flowers braided throughout her ebony hair. Her eyes caught the light with a sparkle and reflected it like a prism. Her movements were sleek and even. She acknowledged her people and took her place on an oversized sculpted chair.

"Please, sit comfortably. We have much to talk about." The crowd seated themselves and Tammeia began.

"I've been meeting with the Council of Exoltaires, and we believe we've found a solution to our people's dilemma.

"As you know, the joining of souls in the outer realms of being, the reality nearest nonexistence, causes great pleasure. But it does far more than this. This melding creates a new and unique mind. A consciousness as real as yours or mine, yet it's without flesh, without direction. These unwanted children of our souls spin off into other realms where they make easy prey for ill forces. And as you all know, they have in the past caused, and continue to cause great problems in the realms of projection and absence. Even so, people indulge in this practice again and again with no concern for the by-product of their actions.

"Even though this practice is forbidden, and the realms where it can take place relatively secured, there are still many people suffering from its abuse. These are the people we're concerned with. When they can be dealt with properly the balance of the system will be restored.

"In hope of achieving this balance, we've chosen several worlds which the Exoltaires feel have a pre-sentient animal population that can be adapted for use as host bodies for the homeless children of our minds. This will be accomplished in various ways."

The faces of the crowd hung with confusion and amazement as Tammeia continued.

"A few people from each Habite on this side of the river are to be taken to the Habite of Exoltaire Pouchetia Coray. People from her Habite will come here in return. The choice of who will be going was based on skill, potential and inbred characteristics that could be useful to the cause. Once there, they'll undergo intense physical training as well as mental conditioning for their journey. By the time their training is over, we should have vehicles ready to take our people to the worlds the Exoltaires have chosen."

"Vehicles? Are we really talking about vehicles to leave this world?" a woman called out from the back of the room. "That's ridiculous."

Tammeia continued without acknowledging the interruption. "Ours isn't the only Habite involved. All Habites on all parts of the world have to train and send people.

"When the people are ready, they'll leave in groups of about fifty. Their mission will be to find and develop any primitive life that may be suitable for our people to utilize, and to return with these animals to use as host bodies."

The mumbles of the audience grew so loud that the Regime had to stop.

"Animals! What kind of madness is this!" another shouted.

"I know you have questions, and I'm sure you're confused but please, let me continue."

The people quieted down.

"The length of each mission will depend largely on the distance of the planet and the stage of evolution of its animal life. The Netrins will provide the transportation. They, interested in obtaining new sources of raw minerals and fuels, have made an agreement with the Exoltaire Council. We give them the location of planets near our system that are rich in the fuels they require, in exchange they take our people with them when they explore these worlds.

"Netrins?" Hella said with surprise, "Regime. They can't be trusted. All through our history they've proven that time and time again. How could we make a deal with them concerning something so important?"

"It's already decided," Tammeia said flatly.

"But Tammeia, the Netrins are the most wicked, passion driven people in all of creation."

"Hella, you forget, they are our mother race." Tammeia gave her a stare, and carefully tuned her mind to Hella's. "Stop this line of questioning now," she said with a thought only Hella could hear.

Nylla Hella nodded. Tammeia turned back to the women of her clan. "Are there any other questions so far?"

A young woman with braided sable hair raised her eyes to meet Tammeia's. "Lady?"

"Stand, Sharl. What's your question?"

The girl stood and so did her consort. "Regime, where are these worlds, and how do we know they have different types of animal life than we do? I mean, what if there's nothing to find on these other worlds? What if the journey's all for nothing?"

"I don't know the locations of all these worlds. Only the head of Council knows them all at this time. But the Council has deliberated a long while to make the final choice. And I have no doubt in the seeing abilities of the Exoltaires. If High Exoltaire Touchea says we'll find what we need, we will find it."

Tammeia looked deep into the Dominion's soul as she looked into her eyes. "Sharl, don't fear for the life of your consort Palray. He'll be safe."

The Dominion pulled her gaze away from Tammeia's. "Could I go with him? I could help the effort." Her soul seemed to pour from her dark eyes to the cold floor.

"No, your part in this effort is here, Sharl, with your other consorts."

"But he's my consort too. I..." Again Sharl's eyes made contact with the Regime's. She fell silent.

"Sharl, if you wish it, we can talk about this later. You're too upset just now. When your mind clears, come and see me."

Sharl sat down. Her face blushed slightly and an uneasy feeling filled her stomach. She was relieved that Hella stood up and captured the crowd's attention.

"Regime, if I may," Hella asked. "Tell us why the sudden interest? There have been homeless minds wandering the world of realms for a long time. Why now? What's changed?"

"Yes," another added. "Why now? Especially when the laws against creating more minds are finally starting to show some results. Why now?"

"All I can tell you is that it's important we do this." She paused for a short moment to try and create a rational explanation. "You see," she said with some uneasiness, "if we don't do this, then I assume things will get worse." She fumbled over her words, then took a deep breath and released it slowly. "As you probably can tell, even I don't have all the answers yet, but all I know I'll share with you."

Hella nodded again. "Then tell us, if you can, are we in any immediate danger? Has something happened to make the bodiless a threat?"

Tammeia smiled. "No. There's no new danger."

"Then why such a rush for a cure?" the woman in the back shouted again. "Why not let the laws take care of things and let nature run its course?"

"I can see I have a lot of explaining to do. I only wish I had all the answers. Some things you'll just have to take on faith."

The people's questions went on long into the night. Finally, when she found she was only repeating the same answers over and over again, Tammeia stood up to dismiss the assembly.

"There's just one more thing that must be said before you can go. I'll need eight volunteers to ride with the chosen to the Coray's Habite, to insure their safe arrival." She looked out across the hall. People began to stand. Tammeia chose four women and four men. Including the Dominion Sharl. "The eight I just named, please stay. The remainder of you may leave."

The hall emptied quickly, revealing its great size.

The lady turned her attention to the remaining eight. "You will prepare yourselves to ride tonight. Already, food and clothing have been packed for the journey. It should take you ten to twelve days one way. And, I wish you would refrain from any projection travel until you return here."

The eight agreed.

"Go and get ready."

They left, and the hall was empty except for Tammeia and four of her consorts. "Jgar, will you ride with them tonight? I'd feel better if you were there to watch over Alana and see that she arrives safely." The woman looked up at the Regimitive's long thin face and curling dark hair.

"I will." He kissed her forehead. "Don't worry."

She rose to her feet and walked through the hall to the door in the rear. Her consorts followed behind her. "Come, the night air is too cool for us to delay." As they walked out of the hall, its warm light faded into darkness.

Chapter 4

An unexpected mist hung in the air and the night was getting cooler. Seth bent over a leather pack, grabbed a strap that ran its width and hauled it up over his shoulder.

"Is that the last one, Seth?" Jgar asked.

"No, there are three more." Seth lifted the bag onto the back of an equis. He wrapped the strap around the animal's stomach and buckled it tight.

"The last three are full of clothing and personal items. The packs of food and water are already loaded." Seth went back to the canopy covered shed to get another sack. He tied it tight and carried it outside. "I think that's all this equis can carry." He put the bundle on the same animal he had strapped the last one to. "The journey will be long and I don't want to overburden any of them." He tightened the sack and checked the girths on all the animals.

"We're ready. I'll get the last two packs. You can get the ladies. Tell them the animals are loaded and waiting." Seth finished loading the equis. Soon everyone was assembled and ready to leave. The group consisted of twelve people and nineteen animals.

Tammeia and Alana stood under the canopy. The woman looked down at her daughter. Somehow, Alana seemed so much smaller than she had just a day before, so much younger. Tammeia didn't want to let her go. "My little Alana, take care and be a good learner. Always remember to be strong." She bent down and gave her daughter a hug.

Jgar picked Alana up, carried her to a tall black mount and put her gently down on its saddle. "Ride carefully," he whispered as he handed her the reins. They were made of a soft thin hair. She grabbed them tightly, clenching her fist around them. "I'll be right at your side if you need me." Jgar mounted his own equis. The assembly was ready to leave.

"Ride swiftly by night and you should reach the river by the heat of the day." Tammeia raised her right hand. "Be well, my children." She sang a quiet prayer to herself as the band rode slowly into the darkness.

The mist was still falling. Alana wiped her face and kicked the sides of her mount until it picked up some speed. The air was dreadfully silent and not one of the riders dared to break free of the shroud it created.

Still, the night seemed to pass quickly. Soon, a bright yellow glow appeared over the horizon. The light brought with it warmth. Alana looked far into the countryside. The land was flat and clear and the grass shined with the mist of the night before. It went on for what, to Alana, seemed like forever with only the hint of hills in the distance.

"When do we rest?" Alana was very tired. Her robe sagged loosely around her shoulders, still wet with the evening's rain.

"We have a way to go yet, little one. I'll carry you if you want to sleep." Jgar rode his equis close to her side.

"No, I'm alright," she said halfheartedly.

As they rode on, the air got warmer. Alana wanted so badly to wrap herself in it and close her eyes. "The river can't be much farther," she tried to convince herself.

The caravan moved steadily forward for what seemed like forever. The air was heavy with the sweet flavor of the green and red berries that covered the blue tinted shrubs that blanketed the plain.

As time passed, the vegetation thickened until they entered a sparsely wooded forest. Thick green moss grew between the trees. It created a lush carpet, moist with dew. Streams and mud bogs etched themselves into the ground like flaws through the endless green.

"The river is just past these woods," Jgar shouted back to the rest of the party. "We should be there in plenty of time to ready our camp and get some sleep."

The light of both Sola and Kai was getting brighter and the ground under the riders began to dry. Soon the moss stiffened and solidified. Once a dull muffled splash, now each step of the equis sounded sharp and clear.

Alana peered ahead through the trees. The hint of a lake, daylight reflecting off the water, danced through the branches.

Soon the water was in clear sight and the group began to move faster in answer to its call.

The break through the trees was like a release from a nightmare. The weary travelers began to wake. Some even cheered out loud. Alana's insides trembled with the sight of the water's edge. The river looked so calm. A swirling pattern in its center was the only flaw in its mirror-like surface.

"Come on. We have to find good ground and make our camp," Jgar called to his people. "The angle of Sola's heat will be intolerable from here. We'll be cooler under that ledge." He pointed to a large stone cliff that hung above the water. "It'll give us shade." They followed him farther down to a bend in the river.

Jgar turned to Seth. "Unload the animals quickly, Seth. Bring them to the water's edge to drink." Seth complied.

Alana began to dismount but her body shook and she lost her grip. She dropped to the sand. Stunned, she waited for a moment then stood up. Her feet were numb and her legs felt like liquid. Never had she ridden for so long. When she was sure her legs would hold her, she walked stiffly towards the others.

Sharl greeted Alana with a gentle hug. "Are you well, child?"

Alana's dark eyes scanned the surrounding riverside. She didn't answer.

"You must be hungry, Alana. We'll be eating soon."

Alana turned to Sharl as blankly as if she'd never spoken. "I've never seen a river before. It is big, isn't it?" Alana was talking rhetorically and didn't wait for an answer. Instead she walked to the water's edge. Four of the party were filling large leather sacks from the river. They passed Alana, one by one, as she stood looking into the ripples they left behind. The water they carried was for a large pit the others had dug and were now lining with a sticky yellow substance. They continued to make trips to the river until the water filled the trench halfway.

"I'll get the vegetables. I know what pack they're in," Seth said. He looked over the packs until he found the right one. "Sharl, can you give me a hand?"

The woman took one last look at Alana. The child seemed to be lost in her own world. "Safe for the moment," Sharl thought. "Alright, Seth." She hurried to help the Keeper. "I'm coming."

Seth and Sharl carried bags of vegetables to the pit and scattered them loosely in the water. Next, several pieces of glassier were fitted together to make a large translucent cover. It was placed on the top of the pit. The clear polished finish would amplify Sola's heat and cook the food.

The animals were herded into the woods for cover. A few chose to stay and wade though the tall river weeds. Already the heat was getting uncomfortable.

"Alana, come. We have to get to the shelter." Sharl returned to the river's edge where the child still stood. "Alana?"

The child's eyes were fixed on the shining river. Her ears didn't hear.

"Come, child," Sharl shook Alana's arm gently. "Don't you feel the heat?"

Alana snapped back to reality and they joined the others who were already gathered for shelter beneath the shade of the nearby cliffs in the water's safety. The river would keep them cool. Almost everyone took this time to relax after the night's ride and allow the water's slow current to ease their stiff bodies.

"Jgar, how long will we rest?" Sharl asked. She was obviously uncomfortable with the fact that he was consort to a woman of a higher station. He looked back at her, meeting her gaze. This put Sharl on edge. It was considered a great insult for a man of any station to look at a woman directly in the eyes without her permission, but Tammeia had placed Jgar in command of the expedition and that gave him the permission to do as he pleased. There was no room in his purpose filled mind for social formalities.

"Do you see that hill?" he said, pointing to a stone pillar jutting into the sky. "When darkness covers it from your view, we'll be ready to go on." He turned and faced the sky to his right. "Kai's rising quickly. So there's no use in trying to travel until it's setting. We have shelter, so I've decided we'll sleep through Kai's light and again travel by night and early morning.

"No other night's ride will be as long as the one past us." He dipped his hands in the cool water and wet his face. "We'll be traveling by the river's banks for most of the next four days. Then we'll stop at the Torta Habite to rest. When we're ready, we'll continue our trip along with the travelers from that Habite. They're also going to Exoltaire Coray's." He paused as if reviewing the entire journey in his head. "The return trek will be harder. By the time we see these banks again, we'll have traveled a long way and our equis will be strained by the distance, yet our longest night's ride will lie ahead of us. It's a trail that will afford us no shelter if we don't make the distance before the day's heat." His eyes softened. "But that's days ahead of us now."

Sharl didn't say a word as Jgar spoke. Her expression never changed. Her eyes still showed the uneasiness she was feeling. "What do you think of this long and useless journey?" Sharl was, as always, blunt.

"Useless journey? Why do you think it's useless?" Jgar seemed amazed that Sharl doubted their purpose. "Do you feel that the Council was wrong?" His words were said almost laughing in anticipation of what her answer would be.

"Jgar, why must we ride for so many days when realm transfer would be much quicker? It would save more time and there's no danger involved."

He looked up at her questioning eyes. She turned away uncomfortably. They were talking about different aspects of the journey.

Jgar cleared his head and started to answer Sharl's question. "Realm travel is not convenient for several reasons." He sounded like a child reciting a well-learned lesson. "Tests of endurance must be done on each. This would be hard to do with one's body in another place." The condescending tone of his voice cut into Sharl's pride. Jgar knew this, but he didn't stop. He never really liked Sharl and felt it was a good time to let her know it. "And if the realm travelers used the bodies of the people already at the Coray Habite there would be no one left to tend to its up-keep. Besides, it's also a mission of good faith. A pact between the two family clans..." Jgar cut his words short. Had he spoken more than he should have? Tammeia went out of her way to avoid that point the night of the meeting. But there were none that didn't know about the cold war the Corays and the Sheens had kept well fed for so long. Generations had lived and died with it over their heads. There was supposed to be a peace between the two clans but the war of ill feelings and dislikes was still going strong. Its beginnings were lost to all but a few, yet its effects shrouded the whole world in tension. It was a tension that kept it fresh in everyone's mind. There were none who had not felt it. Somehow, Jgar knew it was not the content of his words that made him question, but rather, the tension inside of him; the tension of being a Sheen.

"A mission of good faith? So this is just a way of bringing peace to the houses of the Sheens and the Corays?" Sharl asked. Her eyes opened wide.

"No, it's not *just*, it's *also* a peace mission." He cleared his throat.

"This thing really bothers you, doesn't it?"

Jgar sighed. "I'm not sure."

Seeing Jgar falter somehow healed the woman's pride. She stood up and looked deep into Jgar's eyes. "How do you think the Corays will feel, having us from the Sheen Clan in their Habite?" Her question dared him to answer.

His soul shook for a moment as the tension inside of him tightened. "They'll treat us as what we are, People of Tigrin." His words were rigid.

"Yes, yes, but how will they feel? Do you really believe that we're welcome there?" Again she tried to look deep into his dark eyes, but they only reflected the image of her face.

"Jgar, you know better than I do that the Corays would just as soon kill you than look at you. And what about Alana? You're going to have to leave her with the Corays. What will happen then?" She paused. "What then, Jgar?"

He stood silently without an answer. Sharl, knowing she had said enough, waded away toward Palray, who sat half-asleep leaning against a rock on the shallow water's edge. She sat next to him then turned to look at Jgar. He was still standing quietly, his mind deep in his thoughts. She closed her eyes and a small smile spread across her face. She knew she had won.

The heat was still rising and soon the air was too hot to play any longer. The group settled themselves for rest. Even the water around them began to warm. Jgar wasn't worried though. He knew the spring that feds the river would keep it cool enough for protection. Its warmth was relaxing and the lapping sounds of its motion lulled almost everyone to sleep.

Soon, the smell of warm food drifted on the wind. Alana opened her eyes. Kai's light had passed through the glassier and cooked the vegetables to tender perfection.

Everyone ate quickly that day, then bedded themselves down on a large mat in the shade. There they slept until dark took rule of the sky once again. It was the end of the first day.

Chapter 5

The past few days since the riders left were the longest days Tammeia could remember. By the time Sola's light passed through Tammeia's bedroom window on the eleventh day, she was already very involved in the preparations of the day's events. The Council had sent a group of Corays to her for training, although she protested saying, it would be easier to train her own people. But Exoltaire Touchea insisted, saying that it would be better for everyone involved if they exchanged trainees. She would explain no further. So, despite Tammeia's objections, the Corays were coming.

There was so much to get ready. The Corays were to have the best she could offer them, however unwelcome they were. There was no room for anything less than perfection in their care. After all, Tammeia didn't want any Coray to have even the slightest grounds to complain, especially people from Exoltaire Pouchetia Coray's Habite. The Regime knew that Pouchetia would take the slightest transgression in etiquette and twist it until she made Council see it as an act of war of Tammeia's part. She shuddered with anger at the thought of Pouchetia's face and then with fear at the thought of her little daughter, Alana, in that woman's care. Tammeia shook the thoughts from her head and went back to business.

Her guests would be tired when they arrived, so their sleeping chambers were readied first. The two rooms she set aside for them were cleaned and furnished. Fresh fruit and cured, red meat were placed just inside each door. Tammeia looked into the larger room. Across the floor against, the far wall, was a tall pitcher of water and smaller one of a sweet dark red juice. A mural on one wall showed a forest filled with many different animals. On the opposite wall, two large windows over-looked the approach-road to the house and the Sheen family emblem, proudly displayed in the front landscape. Tammeia looked out the window at the road. The light reflected off the shining rocks that embossed her clan's mark into the ground, making it glow like Sola itself.

"Maybe the Corays wouldn't care for such a view," Tammeia thought as she gazed out the window. "It is the best room available, and it is close to all the house utilities."

"No," she spoke out loud to herself, "this room will do fine."

"What, Lady?" Meem walked in unexpectedly.

"Oh, Meem." Tammeia turned. "I didn't know you were there. What do you want?"

"Regime, you haven't eaten yet. Would you please come and have something?" The old woman walked to Tammeia.

"I'll eat later. I'm much too busy now." Tammeia took a last look around the room.

"Tammeia, you must eat. You'll be ill if you don't. Come now." Meem grabbed the Regime's hand. "Your morning meal is waiting for you."

Tammeia smiled. "You'll always see me as a child, Meem."

"And a child you'll always be." She returned the smile.

"Alright, I'll go. But I must hurry. I have to meet with the Council soon." They walked out of the room together.

Tammeia's meal consisted of a piece of red meat, a few vegetables and a large chunk of doughy bread. She ate alone this morning. Everyone else was either busy or still asleep. After she was done, she retired to her bedroom. The time of the Council was nearing and she had to go.

Tammeia sat down on a pile of pillows. She closed her eyes and began to breathe deep and steady in order to ease her body into a deep relaxation. She heard no sounds. Soon the Regime's body fell limp. She wasn't in it anymore.

The break into the astral plan was easy. She was greeted by Eisen and a Nyllative called Rojer Torta.

"Tammeia," Eisen said as his Carlaf appeared. "You know Marlisa's consort Rojer." The man bowed in greeting. "I need his help with a few things. If you have no objections, he'll be using your body today."

"No. That's find," she said without much thought. "I have to go. Council won't wait."

Eisen and Rojer nodded, then vanished from the astral plane to the physical one, before Tammeia broke into the next one, herself.

This was the realm of projection. While on this plane, the pure thought energy that made the Regime's being could be projected from place to place as easily as the wind travels over the ground. Though she couldn't actually see, Tammeia could sense colors. These colors surrounded her. She could feel them penetrate her being. The color she felt now was a cold sharp blue. It gave Tammeia an uneasy feeling. "Not again," she thought. The blue wasn't just the color of a realm. It was hiding something. As she traveled, it became clear. "Homeless consciencseness," Tammeia confirmed. It sensed Tammeia passing and grabbed her. She felt as if it were trying to mesh with the energy of her mind, like it was attempting to flow into her being. She was almost overcome by its extreme feeling of *want*. It wanted everything.

The Regime recomposed herself and raised a small circle of power. The homeless mind that clung to her was distracted by the glow given off by the new energy. When Tammeia released the power and sent it spiraling away, the homeless creature followed it. Tammeia sensed the mind leave. She was free to continue her journey.

The woman readjusted and propelled herself into a yellow light. This light felt hot and Tammeia had to make a few more readjustments to keep her momentum. Soon she came into a bright orange zone. It was the light of Lumdon Hall, and of the Council. A light Tammeia knew well.

She stopped herself and pushed into the next realm. This plane took much more effort to enter. This was the plane of Absence — one of the few realms that transformed matter into energy and energy into matter. When she entered this plane, Tammeia's mental energy took on physical form. A smooth bare body bearing a definite resemblance to her physical self, Tammeia's absentenial self was tall and dark eyed.

There was no great noise or flash of light when she entered this realm. She just appeared. The journey, an everyday thing for Tammeia, took only a few seconds.

She looked herself over once and began to walk toward the great hall. Two sentries guarded its heavy, deep red-brown wood doors. The man to her right bowed low as she approached. The one on her left opened the doors. Tammeia walked pass silently. Just inside the door, she came face to face with an Exoltairetive named Rovear. He was on his way out. She glanced at him, then walked past into the hall's vastness.

Lumdon Hall was very large indeed. Eight of its ten walls were made of thick glassier, the same glassy rock that windows and food pit covers are carved from. They were polished to a smooth, milky finish. When light passed through the clearer areas of the translucent walls, it was broken down to its elemental parts, filling the great hall with rays of different colors. The two remaining walls were on the side of the hall Tammeia had entered by. These walls were made of rich, dark wood. The hall's doors, when closed, met at the seam that joined the two remaining walls. Portraits of past heads of Council lined both walls from about waist level to the ceiling.

The floor was covered with thick, fur rugs that were remarkably white and plush. Tammeia enjoyed their feeling beneath her bare feet.

She sat herself at the far-left end of a large oval table. The Exoltaires sat closer to the middle. Any observers or guests would sit on the surrounding rug. In the center of the table was an open area where those addressing the council could stand. A row of auburn colored beads enclosed this stage. At one time the beads held the power to isolate the speaker from the thoughts and influences of any others in the hall. If their power were still strong, Tammeia didn't know, for in all the time she sat in her position of nobility they were never put to the test. It was said they held other ancient purposes too, which Tammeia had never learned. These original meanings were lost from centuries of idleness. The beads were only ornamental now.

Tammeia looked around the table, twenty-five women sat quietly waiting. There were three empty chairs. Not everyone was there yet. "Good," Tammeia thought with a sigh. "My little problem didn't make me late." Tammeia gazed though the milky walls to the light beyond them, her eyes not truly focused on anything clearly enough for her to see the landscape beyond the hall's light. She turned her gaze to see the inside decorations of Lumdon Hall itself. The beauty of its shining walls was only rivaled by the elaborate carvings on the bending beams that supported the hall's dectagonal structure. Each carving depicted a time or event in the people's history. Tammeia remembered each story as she looked at the different columns.

The column closest to her told the story of the Netrins and of how the first pioneers left that world and came to the unseen planet. They named the planet Tigrin, which meant Freedom. It told of Tarshaw and of the dreams he had that Netrin was seeded by an evil that would overcome all. He dreamed that the people who had faith would find a vast valley and be free. The column remembered the struggle of the one thousand five hundred settlers on the new world. The air was different, the soil was different and the heat was killing. It also listed the names of the one hundred and twelve who survived the first year. Not one of those names meant a thing to Tammeia.

The next column told of a great plague and the terror that it brought with it. The plague was the worst disease to strike in all of history. It seemed to only attack the woman at first, killing most of them and driving the others mad. They became like wild animals, dangerous and unmanageable. The column told of how the men had to drive them into the forest, away from the settlements. It told of the roundups in the forest when the men would catch females, sedate them and breed with them to keep their race alive. But the plague brought with it a few more unexpected turns. It caused sterility in many of the men, and even with a potent stud and a fertile woman, conception was seldom achieved. Often, when a girl child was born it would not live. Boy children seemed to have a better chance of survival, but most of them would not grow to father children of their own. Not only this, but the woman began to develop strange abilities. Their psychic skills seemed to strengthen with every few generations. Soon one man could no longer control a wild woman. It took several. The column told of how the men studied and developed a psychic system of their own, but one man was still no match against one woman. Thus, a woman's strength was tested and the men were assembled whose combined strength would equal the woman's. These men were responsible for keeping her clean, healthy and, if possible, pregnant. This was the beginning of the consort system still in use today.

The third column told of how the power of the mind brought with it clear understanding to the possessor and over time this wisdom raised the women from their primitive ways and sent them on their way to a civil state.

Tammeia snickered silently, "Civil state indeed."

The column also told of the development of the stations of power and the creation of Lumdon Hall.

"Somewhere on this column," Tammeia remembered, "it's written that a cure was found to stop the plague and not one more shall be struck with the madness." She shrugged and gave another snicker, this one very bitter. She had lost her first daughter to that cure. "Not one more shall go mad, but some will die," she thought with pain.

The hall's doors opened again and drew Tammeia's attention away from the column. The last of the Council was now arriving. Tammeia turned towards the table's center. The meeting would soon begin.

Chapter 6

Far across the river, as the darkness gave way in favor of the eleventh day's light, Jgar knew that the Coray's Habite was not far away. He wiped his brow and sat well forward on his riding pad.

"Nylla Marlisa, come here please," Jgar called back to an older woman who lead the people that joined the Sheens at the Torta Habite. She rode up along side of him. "Are you well, Marlisa?"

The woman motioned a reply.

"Good, ready your people. We'll be arriving soon."

The woman tightened her grip on the smooth equis' reins. The animal turned in a tight circle.

Even though Marlisa Torta was an older woman, she still possessed the beauty of her clan. The Torta were bred originally from Coray roots and the Coray colors were prominent in Marlisa's body. She looked unusually strong and vital for an old woman. Her eyes were a light sky blue, at times seeming almost translucent. She gave the illusion of being carved from the shining glassier rocks. On each hand she wore a ring. A black stone on her right represented her rank, High Nylla of the Torta Habite. On her left she wore a yellow stone, the color of her clan. These rings also gave her leadership over the others of her clan on the journey.

She held her hand up and called a halt to the travelers. Jgar stopped and dismounted, then whispered something to Marlisa. Alana, who had been sleeping in Seth's arms most of the night, began to stir quietly and rub her eyes.

"Awake at last, little one." Seth lowered her to the ground and stretched his arms.

Alana looked around. The morning mist hung heavy in the air. It was going to rain. The ground was soft and muddy under her feet. In front of her spread a moss covered plain, to her right, lay the flat plateau from which they came. In the distance to her left lay a great stone wall. It looked like a thread over the gray blue landscape to prevent the morning sky from seeping in and becoming lost in the ground.

"Another cold wet day," Alana thought. "Why does it have to rain so much?"

Marlisa sat quietly and when all seemed in order she began to speak. "People, we're near our destination. That wall in the distance marks the beginning of the Habite of the Exoltaire Pouchetia Coray. We'll be arriving there soon. When we arrive I expect every one of you to conduct yourself in a civilized manner." A cold breeze made her stop for a moment and shudder. "You are to treat the Corays with the respect you would give any of your clan. All or your inner hostilities must be put aside and..." Once again a cold wind stole her words.

"Come, let's move on. I fear there'll soon be a storm."

"A storm is what I fear too," Sharl whispered across to Jgar. She was obviously trying to be sarcastic.

"Don't fear the wind, Sharl. For that's a child's game. Fear instead the storms that blow from inside your soul." Jgar smiled as he spoke.

Despite the weather, the company resumed on foot to stretch their muscles and give the animals a rest; all except Marlisa, who's age allowed her a mount.

What once looked like a small thread on the horizon was now a very large wall made of single blocks of stone, each at least seven equis long and eight men high. The wall stretched to both sides of them until it became a thread again. When they got to its base, a party of people appeared on its edge.

Alana felt uneasy, as if she were being watched. She was. She tried to look at the people standing on the rim but the movement of the clouds over the wall made it seem like it was falling forward on her. If she tried to adjust herself she began to fall backwards. Alana wobbled.

Sharl's instinct made her stand at rigid attention with her hands readied in striking position. She watched Jgar as he mounted his equis and paralleled Marlisa.

"Come, Lady Torta. Let's greet our host." He turned to the group. They stood uneasily in the bitter wind. "Wait here. Walk no farther until we return."

The tension in the air was as heavy as Alana's tired feet. A feeling of uneasiness overcame all. Alana grabbed the side of

Seth's robe and pulled it close to her cheek. "Seth, I don't want to go in there," she whispered to the Keeper.

"It'll be alright," he put his arm around her and held her close. Jgar and Marlisa rode off toward the wall.

The knot in Jgar's stomach tightened as they drew nearer the gate of the Habite. The tension grew in his mind until it felt like an electric current was running through his arms and legs. Sharl's biting question echoed in the back of his mind, 'how will they feel?' The journey had been long, yet now the wall and what lay behind it was far too close for Jgar's liking.

The gates began to open as he and Marlisa neared. The deep, black polish that covered the immense wooden doors gleamed brightly despite the lack of Sola's shine in the sky. Jgar came to a quick halt, Marlisa just behind him. She dismounted with an ease that seemed unsuited to her age and looked through the gate, unconsciously reaching her right arm up to Jgar whom still sat astride his mount. He got down, his muscles tight with anxiety.

"Hello!" he called to the people who lined the wall's edge. They ignored him. "Hello!" he yelled even louder waving his arms above his head.

"Riders are coming. I count seven. They bring with them fresh animals." Marlisa said. The woman motioned for Jgar to stand at her side. "They must be coming at a great speed. They're splashing up mud from the ground under them."

Jgar looked toward the reception party. Mud splattering from the beating hoofs and the steady mist in the air made the figures seem almost spectral. As best as he could tell, there were three women and four men. He looked behind him at the rest of his people standing in the now pouring rain.

The hoof beats came to a stop. Jgar turned. Three women clad in sliver and red draping robes captured his eyes. Yellow / white hair, wet with rain, lined each face like a delicate frame. Even in the gray afternoon, it glistened. Jgar had never seen anyone like them before. Their beauty rivaled his imagination. The pitch-black equis that bore each woman added to his vision of splendor.

"People of Torta and Sheen?" the woman in the front questioned, blank of feelings.

Marlisa nodded.

"Good. Come with us. We have fresh equis and clothing for your people." The woman gave a look back at her companions. Jgar knew they were talking with their thoughts, but their minds were so finely tuned, he couldn't pick out any of the ideas being transmitted between them.

A tall consort with the same coloring as the women, brought two fresh equis from the pack he led forward. Jgar and Marlisa mounted then returned to the rest of the company across the muddy plain.

Jgar noticed blue-green vegetation sprouting in the mud. The shoots grew so fast he could almost sense the stems stretching to the sky and life giving rain. A long time ago he had heard of such plants. They lived on plains that were barren and dry most of the year, except when it misted long and hard. Only then would the plants bloom with a few short days to live their lives, shed seeds and finally die.

"This field will bloom soon," Jgar thought to himself.

"Yes. It comes to flowering once in the cool season and once more during the mid season's rain," the blond Coray male replied to Jgar's thoughts as if they were directed to him. The man's deep green eyes disturbed Jgar. He found it hard not to stare at them. "The colors are impressive to see. My Carlaf had hoped you would've arrived one day later, then you would have seen them in full bloom upon your approach." He sensed Jgar's uneasiness. "I hope your thoughts weren't personal."

"No, they weren't. I welcome the conversation." Jgar covered his embarrassment.

The Regimitive began to get edgy. "What if I'd been thinking something wrong, something that would have offended the man?" he worried. He couldn't let others hear his thoughts so easily. He felt awkward about putting up a mind field so that others wouldn't know his thoughts, but he decided he must. He didn't have to do it very often at home, but he decided his mind images would be a curiosity among these people. If they were to find out the fears and apprehensions he harbored about the Corays, he would have more to explain then the reason for a simple mind shelter. Besides, he didn't want to embarrass himself again.

Jgar tried to clear his mind of anything other than a present pattern of thinking. First he cleared his mind of all things except a color — the color red. Red like the robes the Coray women wore. Red like the sky, like the ground, like his skin, like all he could see. Even the blue moss below him seemed red to his mind. He filled every corner of his thoughts with the color red until the color was more real to him than anything around him. It was everything around him. Red was now his sanctuary. When his normal pattern of thoughts exceeded what he felt was shareable with others, he could think of red and anyone who attempted to see his mind images would see nothing more than the color red. He felt a little safer.

As Jgar worked on his mind shelter, the reception party reached the rest of the people. The rain had just about stopped and it was beginning to warm up. The four Coray consorts dismounted and unpacked dry clothing for the Sheens to change into. After everyone was dressed in dry robes they were mounted on the equis the Corays provided. These animals were much larger then the Sheen's animals, which seemed rather stocky when compared to them.

"Have all your people arrived safely? Were there any injuries?" The question came from the same Coray woman who spoke before. Her tone was still as blank.

"No, there were no injuries," Jgar said. His reply was totally ignored by the woman with the yellow hair.

"There was no one hurt," Marlisa said quietly.

"This is good. Will any of your people be needing special accommodations or foods?"

"No, Lady. They're content with your hospitality and will need nothing else." Marlisa glanced back at Jgar. He seemed somehow lost among the others. He didn't want to be noticed.

Sharl noticed him, though. She rode up along side of him. "Too soon the winds change. Your words mean nothing here." She beamed a sarcastic smile at him, reminiscent of the smiles he often used during the journey to poke fun at her.

"Dominion, my winds have yet to change." Jgar's eyes met Sharl's directly, causing her to feel uneasy again.

"Mind your place, Jgar. Here you are once again a consort and I'm a Carlaf." She sat back on her mount and the animal slowed.

"Ah, yes. Sharl the Carlaf." Jgar was tempted to sneer back to her but he knew it wouldn't be received well with the company around him. So he held his tongue.

All eyes were upon the riders when they entered the gates of the Habite. All those who were working behind the great wall, Consort and Carlaf alike, stopped what they were doing and watched as the party rode passed. Jgar was amazed by how busy the area behind the gate was. People were running around getting ready to harvest the sweet blossoms that were soon to grow outside of the wall.

As they rode farther into the Habite's, boundaries there was no one to be seen, the great wall was just a memory and the open plains gone long ago. They rode through a thick forest. The air around them was very warm and Jgar thought it must be the heat of the day, but the trees sheltered them from the daylight so well, he had no way of telling.

The lead woman turned to her companions. They spoke between themselves with their thoughts. "Very well, Renia," the yellow headed woman said aloud. They turned to face the travelers and a different woman spoke. This Carlaf was much more frail then the first. She seemed little more than a Child.

"Which of you is the Keeper?" Her voice was so soft it was almost lost in the air.

"I am, Lady Coray." Seth bowed his head as he replied.

"Keeper, free your equis. They'll be sheltered by the trees and there's plenty for them to eat here."

Seth untied the trailing animals and the journey continued.

Jgar was wrong. It had not been the heat of the day earlier, for the air was getting hotter and harder to breathe. Sola's light was starting to break through the thinning canopy of tree branches and Kai's light lay ahead of them on the horizon. It shone through the tree trunks and low ground bushes. "Kai was just rising, the heat was yet to come," Jgar thought with surprise. The Coray women showed no signs of feeling the rising heat, and even less of stopping for shelter.

The Coray men rode to the back of the pack. Jgar looked behind to see where they were going. They stopped behind the rest of the riders and resumed the trail pace. Jgar looked forward again counting all in the party. There were twenty-seven in all, twelve Sheen, eight Torta, and seven Coray, riding in rows of three and four. He wondered why the Corays weren't preparing for shelter. They had been riding for more than half the day and in their exhausted condition he doubted if anyone would survive the full day's heat unsheltered.

Jgar rode parallel to Marlisa. "Nylla, why don't we stop for the heat?" he questioned her verbally at a whisper. He didn't want anyone else to hear him.

Marlisa looked at him with a half smile. "Don't be concerned. Our guides know this land better than we do." She looked away.

Jgar wasn't really satisfied with her answer but he didn't question her further.

The lead woman took a sharp left turn that led to a clearing. Before reaching the open field, the Corays stopped.

"We must ride quickly if we're to get to Nylla Christance's anhabit before the heat reaches its apex. It's not very far from here, so we've decided to ride now rather than wait for the heat to pass. Our chances of reaching the Nylla's anhabit are greater than the chances of some of you surviving the full of the heat this time of year." The Coray woman paused and looked at Marlisa. Are you well enough to ride in this hot air at a quickened pace?"

She nodded.

Seth sat straight, in his arms he held a sleeping little girl. Alana hadn't slept since they first reached the Habite. She was exhausted. "Lady, the child sleeps. Will you wait so I can wake her?"

"Don't wake the child. Rovear will carry her."

The man with the yellow hair and green eyes that Jgar had spoken to at the gate took Alana from Seth. She didn't stir. Rovear cradled her gently but firmly.

"It's best the child isn't aware of the task besetting us," the woman said. She looked at her companions, and with a nod of her head, gave the signal. The party started, full gallop, into the open, heat-drenched field.

Each running equis filled the air around it with dust from the dry ground. Every breath was filled with the hot ash-like soil that stuck to the wet faces and clothing of the riders as they persisted full speed to escape the heat. The animals foamed with sweat and huffed loudly as they took each long stride. Jgar looked down at his hands. They were red with the heat. Beads of perspiration ran down his bare arms and off his fingers.

The speed of the equis the Corays had furnished was considerable. Their long legs gave them the ability to stride nearly twice the length of a normal equis. It was no wonder why they were bred so tall. The speed of an equis could mean life or death for its rider on this terrain.

The surface of the ground became very dry and began to crack in places, causing gaps; most of which were very large. Jgar watched as each equis, in turn, stepped over or jumped the cracks with a sure-footed ease. One misplaced hoof and both animal and rider could be killed. But the equis didn't miss a step yet, and they seemed used to the terrain. Jgar reassured himself with that thought.

He looked over to Seth who was on his left. Seth's face was covered with sweat. His eyes looked straight ahead of him and didn't turn to acknowledge Jgar's stare.

The Keeper looked at the ground and the gaps in its surface. The cracks were coming more frequently now, and his equis' stride became very uneven as it danced over them. Finally, he turned to his right and looked at Jgar. There was a brief pause then they both returned to the job of watching the gaps fly beneath them.

Jgar looked at the man who was holding Alana. Somehow Rovear was able to hold her securely without losing his grip on his running equis. The child was still sound asleep. He wondered how she could sleep through such an ordeal. "Surely she's under some kind of spell," he thought. For whatever reason, he was relieved that she was unaware of what was going on around her.

The equis Jgar rode bobbled, causing him to turn forward to maintain his balance. He looked to the distance and thought he saw a building. Then he thought it was just the light reflecting off the rocks and playing a trick on him.

Kai was steadily rising.

The pace quickened as the animals reached the top of the hill they were climbing. The wind that blew on Jgar's face was no relief, for it was as hot as fire.

When they crossed the top of the hill, Jgar saw a crack in the world. It was far too large for even an equis ten times the size of the Coray animals to negotiate. A heavy wooden structure bridged it.

The animals were running faster than ever down the far side of the hill toward the bridge. They ran faster than Jgar thought possible. The equis ahead of him stumbled and he saw its rider fly forward over its shoulder. She grabbed its neck and steadied herself. Jgar felt it was only a matter of time before more equis faltered and someone was seriously hurt.

When the riders bolted onto the bridge, Jgar realized that the other bank was much farther away than it seemed from the hill's ridge. The bridge, that first looked very narrow, was actually wide enough to accommodate the riders who still rode three and four abreast. Hoof beats thundered as they strode onto the bridge. The whole structure shook as if it were about to fall apart.

Jgar looked to the side and shuddered. The bridge had no side rails. No matter how hard he tried, he couldn't see anything past the bridge except the sky. For a brief moment, he lost himself in a dark thought. He imagined the bridge twisting, throwing him off and sending him flying down into nothingness. The thought made him glad he rode in the center of the pack, away from the unprotected edges.

Jgar looked cautiously over his shoulder to check on the rest of his people. They were all still in the pack. He looked at the Coray, Rovear, who carried Alana. A cold chill ran up is back making him clench his teeth even tighter. His heart seemed to jump up into his throat. Rovear rode so close to the edge of the bridge that Jgar was convinced an unexpected move of the equis would surely cause the Coray to drop Alana into the emptiness beyond the edge.

"It wouldn't take much. Just one mistake," Jgar said to himself. He thought about the animal Rovear rode. It didn't spook. "It must be able to see the drop off the bridge from where it's running. Maybe," he concluded, "it too, is under a spell, like Alana."

The trip across the bridge seemed like it would never end, and when Jgar's mount finally strode on firm ground again he was grateful. There was a building on the horizon and the land on this side of the ravine was of a different kind of soil. There were no more cracks to jump over. A hot wind blew across Jgar's face and he was again aware of the heat. It was still rising. Nevertheless, the party continued without casualty, at a fast gallop to the anhabit of Nylla Christance Coray.

Chapter 7

The light of Tigrin's two burning stars heated Lumdon Hall to an uncomfortable degree long before the heat of the day, yet the Council was in session and wouldn't recess for such a trivial thing. The consorts of the Exoltaires lowered the wooden shades that hung from the walls of the great hall. The sides of the shades facing out were dyed bright white and the other sides were coated with a waxy type of material. Not long after they were lowered, the temperature returned to a comfortable level.

With the shades fully closed, the hall gave the appearance of a honeycomb chamber, and it was as busy as one. No one spoke verbally here, but the silence was only physical, for the realm around the table was very noisy with the thoughts of the Council members. Their mind transmissions flew back and forth so rapidly they seemed to cause a friction that could almost be tasted in the air.

Tammeia fidgeted from side to side. A mask of frustration hung on her face. Her gestures were becoming less nervous and more angry with each passing second as she tried, once again, to make her thoughts heard. Someone was blocking her. She stood up quickly.

"This is senseless!" Her voice ripped through the seemingly silent air.

"Sit down, Regime." The order was firm. Exoltaire Pouchetia Coray meant sit down now or else.

"Are you all blind? It's senseless!" Tammeia addressed herself to the rest of the Council and not to Pouchetia. There was urgency in her voice. "Why should we bother with a mission. We should just kill them now and get it over with!"

"Sit down, Regime!" With this order Pouchetia stood up.

"I will not! Not until I've had my say. You can overpower my thought images, but not my words." She stood in the center of the table surrounded by the beads. "I may only be a Regime, but I'm still a member of the Council. I have the right to speak in this Council and I'm taking that right now!" Her voice bordered on a shout, her actions on hysteria. When she was convinced that all eyes were on her, Tammeia continued in a quieter fashion.

"You've all heard the reasons that Exoltaire Coray uses to commend this mission. She said it will cure realm overpopulation, for when the colonies return, they'll bring back animals to be used by the bodiless. What she forgets to tell you is this technology we are receiving from the Netrins is not as perfect as we'd like to believe. And the chances are slight of a safe arrival to these other worlds. The chances of return are even slimmer," she paused for only a few seconds, not long enough for anyone to comment or stop her. "My consort, Eisen, studies the stars and he's calculated the time of some of the journeys by their distance. Most will take more than one lifetime to reach. If our children and loved ones do return to this place, we won't be here anyway. For that matter, neither will the homeless minds. Since we have secured the realms of creation, it's impossible for our people to make any more homeless. The ones adrift now will die off long before anyone returns from these missions.

"This is if we can trust the Netrins at all. Who knows what will await our children in their hands. To put them through all the possible dangers and probably death, for what? Because no one had a better idea!"

"Sit down, Sheen!" Pouchetia shouted. She didn't try to hide her anger. For a Coray to address a Sheen in the tone of voice Pouchetia used was degrading and a call to challenge.

Tammeia turned to Pouchetia. "You have no better ideas so you choose to kill our children." Tammeia's voice cracked but she didn't cry. She was too fired up for tears. She left the center of the table. "You, Pouchetia. You choose to destroy children."

"You forget, Lady Sheen," Pouchetia's tone was quieter. "I'm sending all three of my own children on this mission."

"All three males!" Tammeia snapped. "Worthless sons. You're taking my only daughter, the heir to my Habite." Tammeia's voice bordered on panic.

"You won't have your Habite long if you keep disgracing yourself in front of the Council, Tammeia," another voice from the table said. A hand reached out to her. "Come, let's go for a walk." The offer came from a short thin woman with hair as black as the Regime's.

"No, Breyan, I don't wish to leave. I must hear what other tales Lady Coray will spin."

Tammeia was returning to her seat when Breyan grabbed her arm. "You're just upset, Tame. Come with me into the fresh air, away from all this commotion." Breyan called almost everyone by a nickname.

"No, let her stay." Pouchetia walked slowly away from the table to the open vastness of the room. "Have you anything else to say to me, Sheen woman?" She grinned.

"Pouchy," the Exoltaire Breyan Sheen whispered, "don't do such a silly thing. She's only speaking from a painful heart."

Tammeia's heart did pain, with the racing blood that pumped through it now three times faster than ever before. She knew if the Exoltaire decided to attack and strike her, she would be defenseless. She knew very well that Pouchetia's mind energy was stronger than her own and she did not have more than a slight chance that any of her strikes would make contact with Pouchetia. Even if they did, they would be nothing against her mind fields and protection realms. The Regime's chances of winning the conflict were near to impossible. Tammeia was angry enough to try the impossible.

"If Tammeia wishes to speak, let her talk to me," the Coray woman said. She pushed her hair back and tied it in a knot out of her way. Tammeia reached slowly and steadily down the side of her leg. She opened her hand to reach for something, the knife that would have hung by her side in the physical plane, had she needed it. While here, her nude body offered her no material weapon. She reached one last time — nothing.

A sudden surge of pain seared its way through the Regime's body. She felt her knees collapse below her. That Pouchetia had struck her hard without warning was her only thought. Then she realized she was not really hurt and tried to get up.

Tammeia stood slowly, expecting to be struck again. But it didn't happen. She looked across the hall at her opponent. Pouchetia was also just getting up off the ground. Tammeia was confused. She knew she had not hit her.

"Enough of this. Will you both sit down? Lady Sheen, Lady Coray, please. We have a lot to talk about in a short time.

Come and rejoin the Council in peace. If you can't, then please leave now." The woman who spoke, Touchea Coray, was the Highest Carlaf on the Council. She was the Highest Exoltaire in the world. Not even Pouchetia would question her. Pouchetia returned to her seat.

"If there's any more foolishness I will strike both of you again," Touchea said.

"Tammeia, please. Come and sit down." Breyan held Tammeia's hands between her own. She looked at the Regime with concerned eyes. "Please come in peace." She returned to the table coaxing gently for Tammeia to follow.

"No, I don't think...I..." Tammeia lost her words. The anger was wearing off and she felt ashamed.

"We'll understand if you wish to go," another voice from the Council said.

Breyan offered again, "Come with me Tame. I know Jobb would enjoy a visit from you." Breyan's eyes lit up in an inviting way. "Everyone misses you. You haven't visited in a long time."

"No, Breyan, I don't feel like seeing anyone. I just feel like being alone." The Regime held the Exoltaire's hands. "I must understand all this. It must sit straight in my mind."

Breyan nodded her understanding and Tammeia excused herself and headed toward the door.

"Wait."

The Regime stopped and turned to see who called her.

"May I come with you?" Touchea asked in a friendly tone.

Tammeia was momentarily filled with indecision. "What could she possibly want with me?" Tammeia's mind raced. "What do I do now?" She wanted to be alone, yet she felt too intimidated by who was asking for her audience to refuse. While Tammeia's mind was still weighing the possibilities for such a request, her mouth replied, "If that's what you wish."

"It is," Touchea said then left her place at the oval table.

"What is this? Touchea!" Pouchetia was stunned.

Touchea said nothing. She walked past Pouchetia and took Tammeia's hands in greeting. The two walked out of the hall.

Chapter 8

The cool air of the cavus felt like a blessing from the gods. Its darkness was comfort to put any soul at ease. Entering it was like entering another world; a world far from the searing heat outside its shelter. Jgar took a deep breath of cool air and wiped the dust from his eyes. Breathing was once more a pleasure. His flesh stung when touched and the drastic change in air temperature made him shiver with cold. He didn't mind though. It felt so good. He sat down against the cool rock wall and looked around him. At first he saw nothing except the flames of the candles that hung on the walls. Slowly, his eyes adjusted. Marlisa lay across the lap of one of the Torta men. he was unconscious. Someone was attending to her with cool water and herb paste. Everyone else seemed all right. They were tired, and many had skin burns, but none were seriously hurt, except Marlisa.

Jgar instinctively counted his people. Eleven Sheen and eight Torta.

"Eleven Sheen!" His first thought was Alana. He looked for her. No, Alana was on his right. A young Coray boy was putting some kind of salve on her red face.

Jgar looked toward the shallower end of the cavus. "Seth," he realized. "Have I lost Seth?" Jgar peered through the dark to all sides of him.

"Consort, where is the Sheen Keeper?" he questioned the boy who tended Alana.

"All the Keepers are with the equis, I believe." The boy's answer was obvious. Seth's concerns were with animals not himself.

"Where are they?" Jgar forced himself to stand. "I must find my Lady's Keeper." His worry was easy to see.

"I was told that all arrived alive. Your Keeper is well." The boy held up a dish filled with a blue colored, herb paste and a clear salve. "Let me dress your burns. This will help you to heal," he said referring to the herb paste. "And this will take away the pain." He put some salve in the palm of his hand.

"Attend to the others first." Jgar again looked into the depths of the cavus. Seth wasn't there.

"If anyone should look for me, I'll be back shortly," he said to the boy. He bent over and looked at Alana. Her long hair hung string-like with perspiration. Her burned red face shone with the soothing salve. She opened her eyes and looked up at him silently. No words could have expressed the feelings that spread through the man's soul as he reached down to hold her outstretched hand.

"I'll be back soon, little one. I'm only going to find Seth." He gave her hand a gentle squeeze. She said nothing in reply. Jgar got up and walked into the darkness of the hall that led out.

The light at the end of the passage hurt Regimitive's eyes and the heat hung dead in the air. The hall widened to a shaded area just before the ground surface. Jgar found Seth there.

"Seth, why haven't you come into the cavus?" Jgar asked as he walked up to him.

"The equis must be walked to cool after running so long. If not, they will die." Seth led two equis out of the shade.

"Friend, let someone else tend to these animals. You need some water and rest." Jgar followed Seth into the glaring heat. The memory of the cavus' cool comfort was stolen from him by its harsh light.

"Take these animals," Jgar said. He took the lead ropes from Seth and handed them to one of the others who was walking equis.

"Now, come on. You've got to get something on your burns."

Seth gave a last look back at the people leading equis in a circle, in and out of the shade.

Jgar pulled aside the great door that lead to the inner room of the cavus. The cool air hit the Keeper's overheated body with a hard slap. He passed out onto the dirt floor. Jgar picked him up as best he could and carried him into the cavus.

"He needs water." Jgar put Seth down and motioned to the boy who now sat idle. Marlisa still lay motionless.

"How is she?" Jgar questioned the man cradling the Nylla's limp form.

"She hasn't moved since our arrival. Nothing done to revive her has helped." He wiped the woman's forehead with a damp cloth. Jgar touched Marlisa's face. Her skin was as hot as fire.

"Her life force still dwells in this body. It's strong. She will get well," Jgar said.

It was true that Marlisa Torta's life energy was still in her body, but it was very weak. Jgar doubted she would recover, yet he didn't feel it was his place to tell the man, Stephen Torta, that his mother was dying.

Jgar took a place next to Seth. "Rest easy, Seth," he said quietly.

The Keeper turned his heavy head. "And you, also." Seth put his blistered hand on Jgar's shoulder and fell asleep.

Jgar didn't know if he slept at all. If he did, it was sleep filled with just a continuation of the same thoughts that plagued him in his waking state. But, he must have slept, because when he opened his eyes, Seth was no longer at his side. He got to his feet.

"How is Lady Marlisa?" he asked her son.

"She still breathes, but not steadily. They're getting a cot to bring her to the house. They've sent for the mender. He should be here soon. She'll be fine." Stephen looked at Jgar. The young man's eyes were filled with hope. Jgar knew he had misled him.

"Stephen..." Jgar attempted to tell him of his mother's true condition.

"What?" Despite the red burn that covered his face, Stephen looked quite pale. Jgar couldn't bring the words past his lips. "How soon till the heat ends?" he said instead.

"The heat is past. Even the roads are cooled by now. I'm still here because I'm waiting with my mother until a place is ready for her inside. Jgar looked around. Except for a few people who were cleaning, the Torta woman and her son, the cavus was empty. He said nothing and headed for the surface. As he walked out, he was passed by someone carrying a stretcher.

Chapter 9

"Tammeia, come with me. I know a place where we can talk undisturbed." Touchea led Tammeia into the realm of projection. They traveled in this mental energy state for quite a while before Touchea stopped. Tammeia, who was trailing her, felt the energy fluctuation and stopped also. Touchea broke into a realm of a different polarity and resumed her absentenial self. Tammeia soon followed.

"No one will bother us here," Touchea announced.

She began to walk. Again, Tammeia followed. Tammeia was disoriented by her surroundings and walked slowly and cautiously. She had no idea where she was. The realm was virtually undeveloped and there was not much to be seen. All around her, including over and under her, was a white emptiness. The ground was indistinguishable from the sky. They walked, but seemed not to get anywhere.

"Where is this place?" Tammeia's eyes were wide with wonder. "I've never experienced anything like it before."

"It's nowhere. It only exists for as long as we choose to let it."

Tammeia looked puzzled.

"I let this place exist for our privacy only. It has never been, nor will it ever be again." Touchea smiled at the Regime. "We are enclosed between the dimensions of reality. We are truly no where."

Now Tammeia understood. It wasn't hard to conceive. Not now that her nerves once again allowed her clear thought.

Touchea continued, "I know you have delicate questions and this is the best place for us to talk. We won't be interrupted and I'll give you any answers you require." She motioned for Tammeia to come closer. "Well, Tammeia Sheen, what do *you* wish to know?" Her emphasis on the word *you* was tremendous.

"If these missions are useless and doomed to failure, why are we going through with them?" Tammeia's question was to the point. She knew that if she wanted real answers she would have to ask real questions.

"This mission isn't doomed to fail and it's far from useless. Actually, it will fulfill its purpose quite well," The Exoltaire continued. "What is this purpose? Well Regime, the true cause has been displaced by what most would reason to be the obvious one. You're correct. The development and propagation of a suitable primate life forms is near to impossible. And again you're correct in assuming that this development, if possible, would take more than one lifetime. It will take many more than one. To risk the lives of so many on such a venture would be foolish.

"Tammeia, you're well aware, I trust, of the hostilities between the people of our clans. There's no real reason for the streak of cold hate that runs deep in both Coray and Sheen for each other. Even yourself, a woman of Council position, feel some prejudice toward Pouchetia Coray, yet she's never done you real harm.

Tammeia interrupted. "My dislike of Pouchetia has little to do with her origins."

"Maybe so. Yet it's always easier for you to become angry with her, a Coray," Touchea paused, "as you did today," she added, if only to make a point.

"She blocked my mind images. I was denied my right to express my views," Tammeia defended, although she knew it was useless.

"The Council was aware of this. You're right. Pouchetia was wrong in stopping your images. Yet, I believe you could have handled it in a better way than you did. Your actions were no more commendable."

Tammeia fell silent.

"But enough of that. I'm mot here to correct your actions. Only to answer your questions."

The Exoltaire resumed with her answer. "This hatred between clans must end. Our world faces a great peril. There are too many people here with the ability to do too much. And many of them let their hatred fog their judgment. Many more enjoy the empathy hatred brings with it. I don't ask you to understand my reasoning, but this is the answer. This world and her children must be united. If it cannot be united in joy, it shall be untied in loss.

We will all feel the pain of loss, and we will all survive," she paused. "We will survive it as a people."

"But we're talking about children. Innocent children," Tammeia argued.

"No, Regime. We are talking about everyone. Every Carlaf, every consort and every child."

"But my Alana is my only daughter. There are others who have more daughters. Why my heir?"

"Tammeia, you know the answer to that." The Exoltaire moved her hand and the area around them took on a more natural look. "Lady Sheen, of Alana you should not be selfish, you should be proud."

"It hurts too...I..." Tammeia paused. "I am proud of Alana, that's why it hurts." The woman verged on tears.

"Be aware that others feel the same sense of loss. Also remember that suffering bonds unlikely ones together."

"Won't this suffering draw us apart? I can feel its pull already." Tammeia couldn't help but find fault in Touchea's reasoning. She knew there was something else; some other reason Touchea wasn't telling her. "It's all so strange. I mean, am I the only one who does not understand?"

"No, Tammeia you're not the only one who doesn't comprehend. There are only a few others who see it all fully, as I do. Please don't fear. You will see it soon. There is a true solution in what now seems madness."

"But why all the unanswered questions? Why all the secrets?"

"There are no secrets. It's all written out for all eyes to see."

"What do you mean? I was never given anything to read. Where is it written?" Tammeia asked anxiously.

"It is, as with all prophecy's, written in the books from the past," Touchea said.

"I'm still not sure," Tammeia said. She began to fidget with frustration.

"Not many on the Council are," Touchea confirmed.

"Then, if I'm not the only one who doesn't understand, why did you choose me, a Regime, to explain it to?" Tammeia became more confused.

"I never promised to explain it to you or bring you to an understanding. I merely decided to answer your questions." Touchea smiled impishly.

Tammeia finally understood. She returned the smile. "Then, tell me Lady Coray, will my Alana return home safely?" Tammeia's heart stopped beating as she waited for the answer.

"Yes, Alana will return. Of this I am sure." Touchea held out her hand to let Tammeia touch her palm. Tammeia reached toward Touchea's hand. This was a sign of truth. For when Tammeia's palm made contact with the Exoltaire's, she would know for sure if what Touchea said was true or if the woman only humored her to put her mind at ease. She stopped just short of touching the Exoltaire's hand. If Touchea was lying she didn't want to know it.

"I accept your words as true. I need no proof." Tammeia began to walk again.

"And all your questions?" Touchea walked along by her side.

"Answered as thoroughly as I require." Tammeia bowed, giving Touchea the customary thank you.

"Then let's go back. The Council awaits our return."

Chapter 10

Jgar bent over and touched Marlisa's face again. He checked her life force many times since they brought her inside. She was steadily slipping away. He was sure she was too far for any cure. It was only a matter of time before her body joined her mind in death. The thought of the Lady's passing saddened him, but not as much as the grief he felt for Marlisa's son. Stephen sat applying cold water to the forehead of his mother's lifeless body.

Jgar felt a strange chill go through his body. He checked her life energy again. She was gone. Soon, her body stopped breathing. There were no last words, no last embrace. She simply stopped being Marlisa Torta. He put his hand on Stephen's shoulder.

"Stephen, she's passed over," Jgar said. He stood silently for a moment, hoping that some great words of comfort would come to him, but he couldn't think of anything else to say. The Regimitive sighed and slowly walked out of the room. He was met in the hall by a short, rather stocky, old woman with amber hair and the same green eyes as her son, Rovear. She had to look up to see Jgar's eyes.

"We all felt Marlisa leave. Her pain is over now." The woman extended her hand to Jgar. He stood numbed by Marlisa's death for a moment, then he began to bow in front of this woman, as formal etiquette required.

"Please, get up. One should not grieve on his knees."

Jgar stood straight.

"Your name, Consort?"

"Regimitive Jgar Sheen," he replied.

"You're Jgar. The one Tammeia sent?" She smiled and looked him over. "I'm Nylla Christance Coray. But, to you, I give permission to call me Christance." The little woman was trying to cheer him up, so she spoke in a tone that seemed inappropriate to Jgar for such a time. He tried to turn away so he wouldn't meet her gaze eye to eye, but that just made him more uncomfortable. He stood nearly twice her height. When he lowered his eyes, they met hers. He really couldn't help it. This made him ill at ease.

The awkward moment was broken as Stephen walked out of the room behind them, and stood in the hallway. He didn't speak.

"Jgar, go and tell your Carlaf of this tragedy," Christance said. Jgar nodded and closed his eyes. The old woman reached out to Stephen. "Your mother has passed over into death. It's in the nature of all things to die. Even people. Please don't weep for her."

Stephen swallowed hard and forced back his tears. "I know," he said quietly. "But it didn't need to be."

Thud!

Christance turned. Jgar's body had fallen to the ground. She watched it long enough to make sure his involuntary muscles would force his breathing to begin again. When she was sure his body would breathe without an occupant, she took Stephen's hand, gingerly stepped over the shell that usually housed Jgar, and led him off to join the others.

Eisen's hands were full when he felt the strange pull on his eyes. It was as if they were being tugged from behind or inside his head. Someone was calling him from another realm. He knew it wasn't his Carlaf and he had more important things to do than chitchat. The Nyllative Rojer had blacked out while he was in Tammeia's body. Eisen wasn't only concerned about what might have caused Rojer to pass out, he also had to stop the bleeding from a gash that Tammeia's arm had sustained in the fall. So, he ignored the signal.

He felt the pull again.

"Go away. I'm really busy," he conveyed back to the unwelcome visitor.

It pulled once more.

"What is so important!" Eisen shouted with frustration. He was sure it was one of his brothers and none of them would have anything to say of importance. That is to say, anything that couldn't wait.

Rojer was waking. He began to mumble something but Eisen couldn't make out a word of it. The pulling happened again. Eisen was getting annoyed. "Damn you," he cursed. "It better be something important or someone's in trouble." He gave Rojer a quick check to make sure he couldn't hurt himself further then eased himself into the absentenial plane to find out what was going on. When he arrived, he was surprised to find that the pulling had come from Jgar.

"What are you doing here? You were told not to come like this," he said, refering to Jgar's traveling in projection.

"I have news for our Carlaf. Where is she?" Despite his even tone there was urgency in his voice.

"She's in Council. What's the problem?" Eisen's brow wrinkled in consternation.

"Do you know when she'll be back?"

"I don't..." Eisen began to answer him when his mental energy jumped. "I've got to go back. Rojer Torta passed out ill in

Tammeia's body. He seems disoriented." Eisen's mind reached back with a probe to the physical plane.

"Did he just black out a few minutes ago?"

"Yes. We were on our way to the garden with some work tools when he said he didn't feel well. Then, without warning, he fell. It was a good thing we were almost at the bottom of the stairs. Still, Tammeia's body suffered a severe cut which I was attempting to heal when you came by." Eisen was eager to return. "I don't know if what happened is because of him, or if there's something wrong with her body."

"Let me treat Tammeia's injuries," Jgar said as he and Eisen both entered Eisen's body. Jgar took physical domination while Eisen was only a mental occupant. For a short moment, Jgar savored the feeling of cool, smooth skin. His own was burned and peeling. Rojer mumbled incomprehensible syllables as Jgar stopped the bleeding and dressed Tammeia's wound.

"The cut looked worse than it really was. Her body will heal," Jgar said as he returned physical control to Eisen.

"What about Rojer?" Eisen tried to return control to Jgar so he could treat Rojer. Jgar refused to accept it.

"I can't cure him. His Lady died today and his is the rare case where his blood-bond with her didn not release itself at the time of her death. Their bond must be broken or he'll stay like this until her joins he in death.

"Remove him from Tammeia's flesh and return him to his Lady's Habite where they can care for him. I must find Tammeia." Jgar left Eisen and headed for the plane of Lumdon Hall.

The Hall's doors were opened when he got there. "Good, they must be in between sessions. I better hurry before they close the doors." He ran into the hall. He knew he had to hurry because if Council resumed sessions he would have to wait until it recessed again.

He was met at the door by the Exoltairetive guards.

"What do you want in the Council?" Jgar was questioned both verbally and mentally.

"I must see my Carlaf, Regime Tammeia Sheen," he answered in both modes.

Breyan saw him at the door and came quickly. "What's the matter Jgar?" She motioned for the guards to let him pass.

"I must see my lady. I have a message of importance."

"She's not here."

"When will she return?"

"If there's a problem, you can tell me. I'll be sure Tammeia hears of it."

Jgar looked back at the guards. They stood as still as stone, watching him. "Tell my Carlaf that the trek across the plains to the Coray's is complete with one loss." He again looked around. It was the first time he had ever stood in the Council hall. Although his Carlaf was a council member, she was only a Regime and her consorts were never given the honor of guarding the hall. He paused to take its beauty into his memory. Soon he realized that all eyes rested on him, waiting for the news. He took a breath then continued. "The Nylla Marlisa Torta died not long ago. A victim of exhaustion and the day's heat."

As he spoke, Tammeia and Touchea walked in. "Jgar why are you here?" Tammeia knew the answer was trouble.

"He brings the news of the passing over of Nylla Marlisa Torta. She succumbed to the heat," Breyan explained.

"Were there any others hurt?" Tammeia asked nervously. "How is Alana?"

"Alana is well, Lady. Only Marlisa was killed. Some of us were badly burned, and all of us are very tired, but we'll all heal." He paused briefly. "No thanks to our Coray hosts. They choose to..."

"Council will resume now," Touchea announced, cutting him off in mid-sentence. "Jgar, you must go."

Jgar embraced Tammeia and vanished. When he became aware, he was in the plane of projection. His soul ached to go back and cradle Tammeia in his arms. He hadn't seen her for nearly twelve days and he felt the separation.

Before long, the women of Lumdon Hall were again occupied with debate. This time the discussion centered on the immediate effects of their master plan. The ultimate results didn't seem as important as they once had. Tammeia knew this death was only the beginning. She made sure the rest of the Council was aware of it too. When Council adjourned, Tammeia stayed behind, staring at the shining glassier walls.

After a while, Breyan returned to the hall and to her daughter's side. "Tame, why don't you come home with me. I'd really like to have you stay a few days. You know, get away from all the problems."

"No, I don't think so," Tammeia sighed. "I'm too tired to think. I guess I just need some sleep."

"Well, you won't get much sleep at your home. Come home with me and I'll have my people make you your favorite supper. And after a good meal and a quiet sleep, everything will feel much better. What do you think?" Breyan smiled broadly.

"No. Thank you, I have work to do." Tammeia got up and walked away.

"My offer is always good," Breyan reminded.

Tammeia turned back and smiled a thank you, then she left the realm of Lumdon Hall and returned to her own body.

She was greeted by Eisen. He also had news for her.

"Lady Sareen and her party have met the Corays. They're inside the Habite's boundaries. They expect to be here in one more day. He offered her some cold red juice. She refused it.

"Tell Sareen they are to stay at Kara's anhabit for Tomorrow's heat." She looked absently at the bandage on her left arm. "Make sure they only ride by dark." She lifted her arm and looked at Eisen quizzically.

Nyllative Rojer Torta blacked out and fell." He held her wrist in his palm. "It should be healed in three or four days."

She looked into his eyes. "One more annoyance. Come on. Let's get something to eat." She left the room quickly, leaving Eisen to follow.

Chapter 12

Dark fell over the anhabit of Christance Coray five times before Jgar's people were ready to continue. The past few days had gone without incident and though the death of the Torta woman was still fresh in everyone's mind, there was a job to be done. The equis were loaded and the riders mounted. There was a new rider among them. The young Coray boy, Gabriel, who had attended to the Sheen's wounds. He carried with him herbs and lotions to treat the severely burned who still hadn't healed fully yet.

The eldest of the three Coray guides was talking to Sharl. After a short moment Sharl turned and called to Jgar, "Come here, Regimitive."

"What is it?" He was mounted, so he prodded his equis over to her.

The Coray woman said, "The passage from this point is a simple one. You may, if you wish, start on your return ride now. We'll pack trail animals with more food, water and medicine. I can provide a guide for you to the gates of the Habite." She motioned to Rovear. He nodded.

Jgar turned to Sharl. "It would save us days of riding." He was obviously anxious to return home.

"Can our people's safe deliverance be assured?" Jgar questioned.

"Of course."

"Sharl, do you wish to depart now?" Jgar's eyes darted back and fourth between the two women.

"The decision is yours, Jgar. I don't care for long drawn out good-byes." Sharl looked at Palray. He returned her gaze forlornly. "You do understand?" she asked.

He nodded.

"Then bring us fresh animals and supplies. We'll begin our return today," Jgar said quietly.

He gave Alana a slight smile. "Be good, little one. Make your people proud." Alana said nothing. She just stared silently at him. He lost himself in the child's gaze and stood for a long moment fighting off the urge to grab her and take her back with him.

The silence was broken by the Coray woman's voice. "The safety of the darkness won't last forever," she said. "We better get going."

"You're right. We have to leave now," another of the Coray guides said. The three women looked at each other. With a final nod they resumed the trek into the heart of the Habite. Jgar watched until the animals and their riders disappeared beyond the edge of the horizon. Tears ran from Sharl's cheeks and landed on the dust with a silence only rivaled by the stillness of Jgar's eyes. For once they lacked any sign of thought.

Chapter 13

     The first day of the return trip was cold and silent. No sounds were heard from anyone, except an occasional person weeping. Jgar didn't know who it was, but he wished they would stop. The group traveled slowly, resting often so the strain of the journey wouldn't overcome the already physically stressed travelers. By the heat of the next day they had stopped on a rocky hillside and made camp. The Coray guide, Rovear, began to unpack food to lay out in the day's heat. Jgar helped him without saying a word.

     "Jgar, I'd favor your company. Don't your people know how to talk?" Rovear was insulted by Jgar's silence.

     Jgar wanted to reply with something like, 'I'm tired. I want to be left alone' or 'I don't wish your company', but he knew, deep down, he really did welcome the conversation.

     "Forgive me, my mind's been drawn elsewhere." Jgar gave himself a subconscious boost of spirit. "But I have returned..." He looked around him at the rocky wilderness, "...to wherever we are? I don't remember these hills. We didn't pass by here on the way in. Did we?"

     "No, you're right. I decided to come this way so you can witness the Illu-danchant, the lights of the summer's dance."

     Jgar listened with doubt. He knew what Rovear spoke of, but thought it was only a legend.

     "I saw it once as a child, and the memory still lives in me." The Exoltairetive paused. "It's going to happen in a few days from now. We are only about one and a half night's ride from the Illu-Danchant Mountains. The only problem is that the terrain is very treacherous and almost impossible to negotiate in the dark. The further we travel into these hills, the less ground soil covers the rocks. We'd be riding on glassier. One could easily slip." He looked toward rising Sola. "The time to ride there would be between the heats during the daylight."

     "It's too dangerous to ride during the day exposed to the heat on these barren hills. Besides, many of my people are scarred by Sola's burning rays already," Jgar said then paused. "I thought the Illu-danchant was only a fable, a story told to children before they sleep."

"Many believe that, but it's not so. Illu-danchant is real. I've seen it myself." He offered Jgar a piece of dried fruit, and they sat together to eat. "And you'll see it too. If you wish."

"I would go, but I can't force the others to follow on such a journey." Jgar bit into his fruit hungrily.

"This camp is secure, there is water and shade, and there are no wild animals in the area. Anyone who doesn't wish to go can stay here and wait for us. It won't be longer than a few days. Besides, the rest may do them some good." Rovear's offer was inviting to Jgar's sense of adventure.

"I'll ask my people. They'll have the final decision."

Sharl sat herself at Jgar's side. "Final decision about what?" She took the fruit from him and bit it.

"Rovear has offered to take us to see the Illu-danchant. It's supposed to take place soon," Jgar explained.

Sharl looked surprised. Jgar continued before she could comment. "It seems it's not just a myth. It will happen somewhere in these hills."

"Then we'll go see it." There was no question in Sharl's mind. If it existed, she was going to see it.

"I don't think your people would make the distance in time and we'll miss it," Rovear said. He offered Jgar another piece of fruit, which he accepted.

"Then they'll stay here. We have tents for shelter and plenty of food. Only the three of us will make the trip." The woman gave Jgar the pit of the fruit she had taken from him. "I'm going to tell the others." She got up and walked away.

"She's a Dominion, is she not?" Rovear laughed a little.

"That she is." Jgar looked into his hand at the naked pit then tossed it away.

Sharl wasted no time telling the people about the side journey she, Jgar and Rovear were taking. Before dawn, they were well on their way into the Illu-danchant Mountains.

The morning lent itself to rain, but its cool cover was welcome after the last day's passage. Jgar let the cool precipitation caress his body. Sharl, who rode ahead of him, had taken off her robe to bathe in its refreshment. Jgar looked back at Rovear. He seemed to be interested in surveying the surrounding hills. "He must be trying to get his bearings," Jgar thought. He shook his head slowly. "We must be lost." The thought of being lost didn't alarm Jgar. He actually found it amusing. Again he turned his attention to the appealing figure in front of him. Her wet hair dangled down her back, crossing to the front at her waist. Her streamlined figure rocked from side to side with each step of the equis that carried her. His eyes caressed her. His body longed to take her flesh, if only for a brief few moments. There was something alluring to Jgar in Sharl's unrefined beauty. He compared her to his Carlaf, Tammeia.

Tammeia's beauty was one more deep, a beauty that stemmed from her soul and manifested itself in her form. Sharl's beauty was of a much shallower type, one easily grown out of. It was a beauty old age could steal. But the Dominion was far from old and her primitive beauty, and the swaying of her body, made Jgar remember his manhood and what seemed like an eternity away from his lady. Many times during the journey he thought of Tammeia and longed to hold her. Yet today all his bodily attention focused on the frail, wet figure that rode in front of him.

How long he watched Sharl's body and dreamed, he didn't know. The thought of touching warm, smooth skin, the feeling it created in him put him in a daydream state.

"Jgar."

Jgar didn't hear Rovear.

"Jgar," he said louder.

"What?" Startled, Jgar returned to the real world.

"We're here," Rovear announced with a smile that reflected the pride he felt for his efforts. "And we made it in good time."

Jgar looked around him. Rocks. All he saw were hills and hills covered with glassier rocks. "Where?" Jgar wasn't impressed, though Rovear's smile persisted.

"Come here to the cliff's edge." He led Jgar and Sharl to the ridge of a great cliff that over looked a valley of glassier rocks. They shined like stars, reflecting Kai's yellow light through the valley. Four great mountains in the distance were covered with a mist that seemed to dissolve when the light touched it.

Sharl turned to Jgar. She looked amused. "A long ride to see rocks. Don't you think so?"

"They may just look like rock hills but notice how tall they are. Their peaks are lost in the clouds. At the apex of the Illu-danchant when the light of Kai and Sola meet above their peaks, the light dances on them with an energy you've never felt before. Just the sight of the Illu-danchant will enrapture you." He paused to see if his description had any effect. Jgar was silent with thought.

"When does this great event happen?" Sharl's disbelief was apparent in her tone.

"We made good time getting here. We have the night to rest. It will occur at the peak of the heat tomorrow. The apex of the orbit." Rovear stood his ground. He was excited about the Illu-danchant and no one was going to put a damper on his mood — especially not a Dominion. "You'll enjoy it, I promise." He smiled and winked at Sharl.

"It's getting late, we have to find wood and build a fire. It's not safe in these hills at night. The handra-can hunt by dark and we don't want to be their prey." Rovear began to unpack a small bag filled with sacks of salts and dried herbs. He put them on the ground, then slung the empty sack over his shoulders. "Jgar, find a place to set up camp. I'm going to find wood." Rovear started off, down the side of the hill.

"Where do you want to set up camp, Lady? One rock pile is as good as the next, as far as I'm concerned." Jgar extended his hand toward the rocks in a gesture of welcome.

"This place is fine." Sharl sat on a large rock on the edge of a patch of dirt. She watched as Jgar pitched the tent-like shelter and dug a shallow pit in the scant topsoil for the fire.

"Is there any water near here for the equis?" Sharl patted an animal that came to her for food.

"There's water enough for them in that jug," Jgar said. He pointed to a dirt colored container on the far end of the camp. "But watch what they drink. It has to last them until we rejoin the others. I don't think we'll find any water in these hills."

Sharl got up to get the water.

"These are fine animals," Jgar said. He patted one of the lean, tall equis briskly. He offered it a piece of dried fruit.

"Ah, so Jgar has a soft spot in his heart for animals." The lady laid a pan of water on the ground in front of the equis. "That is, if the man has a heart."

Jgar turned his attention away from the animal and looked at Sharl. "If I have a heart, than it was just broken in two by your unkind words." His tone was sarcastic, his face smiling. Jgar's grins always annoyed Sharl and this time was not an exception.

"Be careful with your words, Jgar. I won't put up with your contemptuous behavior forever." She straightened her posture in an attempt to look aggressive. Jgar wasn't impressed.

"Sharl you're a beautiful woman. You don't need force to persuade a man to do your will. All you need is the right tone of voice." He touched her cheek and pushed back a few strands of stray hair that dared to hang in her face. "You have all that would ever be needed to make a man march to his death in your name." His hands felt the back of her slender neck. The feeling of her smooth skin and flowing hair caused his day dreams to begin again. They stirred up sensations. His hands twitched as his mind fought with his manhood for their control. She pulled absently away from his embrace.

"So you have looked at me. I've felt your eyes watch me. I've always felt your want for me." Sharl said. Her tone hinted of a conceited boast, yet she wasn't aware how true her words were. To Sharl they were only tools in a game. To Jgar they were a verbalization of an emotion he was trying to suppress — the feeling of want.

Jgar said nothing. He stood still and staring at the bare breasted woman in front of him. A pulsating feeling started in his stomach and spread through his whole body. She stood proudly, with an arrogance that Jgar found strangely appealing and very sensual.

"Want is a word used when speaking of an object." He put his hands on her shoulders and slowly slid them down over her rounded breasts. "I desire you." He eased the young woman's body to the ground.

"Jgar, remember your place. Stop this." Her words said no, yet she didn't resist him. Jgar stopped and sat very still for a moment. He thought of the wrong that was about to take place, but he couldn't stop himself. His body's cries for satisfaction surged through him. To his surprise, he really did desire her.

Sharl reached up to him "Jgar..."

"Lady, don't talk." He put his fingers over her lips in a gesture of silence, and then he began to caress her. Her skin was so smooth and inviting.

"Jgar," The Dominion's body quaked but she didn't pull from the Regimitive when he lay himself upon her. Instead, she grabbed his shoulders to hold him close to her. The touch of her warm flesh against his own filled Jgar with an excitement that was soon replaced with a feverish passion, that grew larger and more intense with the momentum of his body. Each deepening thrust, a witness to his strength. Each sound from his partner's lips, a testimony of his dominance over her. His passion grew until he could no longer contain it and it burst out of him in a rush of sensations.

The moment past him, the passion over, Jgar regained himself. He didn't say a word to Sharl as she sat up and combed out her hair. He just stood up and walked away. His once uncontrolled hands hung lifeless at his side. His brow was sweaty, his mind deep in contemplation.

That his thoughts were of the delight of what had just passed or of the woman he had just come to know would be doubtful. That his thoughts were of the vow he had given his Carlaf, Tammeia, so many years ago and of the uneasy guilt that grew inside of him because of his betrayal of that vow would be more to the truth. Maybe he feared the wrath of his society. For a consort to take a woman other than his Carlaf was not allowed. Not that it had never happened before.

Actually, it was quiet a common practice for an older woman of status to teach a younger one of her same station the finer points of Carlaf-hood through the "lending" of more experienced consorts. But this was an accepted method of teaching a woman all the skills her position demanded of her. It's very necessary in a social structure where the higher the endowment of psychic strengths a woman has, the more consorts she coordinates. Yet for Jgar, the circumstances were different. His own Carlaf had not given her consent and the act was one of physical lust and served no purpose other than his own pleasure.

The most unacceptable aspect of the event, Jgar knew, was the factor of status. He was a High Regimitive and Sharl a common Dominion, more than two stations below his Carlaf. By taking a Dominion, even if only for passion's sake, was a shame to his Lady's name.

If Jgar thought of these things or of others, he didn't make it apparent. What he thought of was a secret he held only with himself.

Sharl got up and stood behind him. "Jgar," she said quietly.

He turned to meet her eyes. She wasn't naive. She knew what had happened meant nothing emotionally to him. She, too, was well aware of the implications of what they had done.

"I won't tell anyone. What we do is an affair of our own. I wish you wouldn't tell anyone either. If you do, I'll deny it. If I have to, I'll tell them that you took me by force." She looked past Jgar to the hills. "Rovear is coming back. If you don't tell anyone, they'll never know." She started to put up the tent. Jgar turned away and went down the hillside to meet Rovear.

"Don't flatter yourself, Lady Dominion," Jgar thought, projecting the thought to her. He was sure she would understand what he meant.

As he walked down the hill, he thought about how long it had been since he held a woman in his arms. There was no anxiety, no longing in his body, just a reflection, an evaluation of his attitude concerning Sharl. He missed Tammeia's gentle fairness more now than ever before.

Chapter 14

When the Sheens arrived at the main anhabit of the Habite of Pouchetia Coray they were brought directly to a small holding room to await a physical examination. The small room made Alana very uneasy. She had never seen such a small room without windows being used for anything other than storage before. "Seth, do you think this is a closet?" she asked with wide dark eyes.

"I really don't think so," he lied with a smile. "Well at least I hope not."

"Maybe it's the place where they keep their animals." Palray snickered under his breath. Seth just looked at him.

A woman came in and took Alana by the arm and led her away to a room across the hall. This room was brightly lit and had a cot in the center. Many jars and bottles filled with colorful powders and liquids lined the walls.

"Are you Alana Sheen. Daughter of Regime Tammeia Sheen?" The woman undressed Alana as she questioned her.

"I am." Alana's voice was timid and weak. She tried to avoid meeting eyes with the sickly thin woman who was now examining her body for damage.

"Do you feel ill at all?" She poked Alana's abdomen.

"No."

"Have you been ill since your left you anhabit?"

"No. I've been well." Alana's voice cracked with nervousness. For the first time in her life she felt her nakedness.

The nameless woman poked and prodded at Alana's body for quite some time. Finally she gave her back her robe and set her to join the others in the small room without windows. Minutes later the woman returned and took Palray away. Other than the woman, a young girl came in with a pitcher of water and cups. It wasn't until much later anyone else came in to talk to them.

This time the visitor was a man. He was plain of face with no distinguishing features, with the exception of his brilliant rust colored hair. Alana couldn't help but stare. Her people all had dark hair, and up until this point, every Coray she's seen had yellow or white hair. But this man was different. Despite the friendly look on his face, the shining red tint to his hair disturbed her.

"All of you have passed your health test. I trust that you're all in need of rest," the man said. He stood in front of the only door in the room. "Unfortunately, you have already missed the evening meal. If you wish anything to eat, I can have someone bring you something when we get you settled in your rooms.

"Alyx, come here," he called to a young boy who was passing through the hall. The boy came immediately. "If these people require anything you'll see to it their needs are met." The young boy nodded but didn't say anything.

"If you require anything feel free to ask Alyx. He'll see to your wants."

Alana found it odd that the man would assign a boy to serve them. "Don't the Corays have servants?" she wondered.

"My Carlaf has set aside rooms for your use," the red headed man continued, "come with me. I'll bring you there." The man stepped aside to let the Sheen people pass. Alana looked up at him with caution, then darted past him into the hall.

The rooms provided were very large and fitted with what Seth thought must be some of the finest furnishings he'd ever seen. The five of them shared two rooms that were connected by a small wash area. The boys, Alyx and Gabriel would be bedding with them until they knew their way around and could get things for themselves.

The Sheens and Tortas spent the first two days at the house of Pouchetia Coray as days of rest. They were not asked to leave their room and were encouraged to eat large portions and sleep often so they would regain some of their depleted body weight. In this time, Seth learned that Alyx and Gabriel were brothers, Alyx being slightly older. Seth also learned that they were sons of Exoltaire Pouchetia.

All Alana learned about the two boys was that Gabriel liked her, so she became his playmate. Alyx wasn't like his bother at all. He didn't like to play with her. She didn't like Alyx.

On the third day the visitors were invited to share in the clan's group meals in the meeting hall. They were also given freedom to explore the grounds, provided they didn't venture past a wooden fence that surrounded the area.

The fence made Alana uneasy. She had never seen a fence to hold anything other than animals. "Why would anyone put up a fence around such a large building?" It didn't make sense to her, but she didn't ponder it very long.

The next day, when Seth was walking where Alana played, she thought of the fence again.

"Seth, why is there a fence around here? Do they think we're animals?" She looked up at him.

"Maybe the fence is to keep the animals out. I don't think there's anything to worry about," he explained then he paused and looked at the wooden structure that ringed the house. It was built no more than waist high. It wouldn't stop any animals from crossing its bounds.

"Or, maybe," Alana's child mind speculated its own answer, "it's to keep everyone from running away."

Seth smiled. "Do you wish to run away," he knelt down to her height, "and leave me here alone?"

"No, I wouldn't leave you. But I think some people ran away already." She pointed to the building. "My mother's house is smaller than that one, but more people live in it. Gabriel said that many more people lived here before. He said that they just left. I think they all ran away and that's why there is now a fence. So no one else can go." Her logic made flawless sense in her own mind, and she was proud of her explanation.

"That's foolishness. Who would leave such a home? I think you dream too much." Seth tried to explain the fence to Alana in a different light. He didn't want her to ponder on it too long. She may find a reason for the fence that he couldn't disprove. Besides, he felt she should have an innocent opinion of it. "You see, little one, the fence is a decoration. The Corays have always decorated with fences." He got to his feet. "Look, Alana, your friend Gabriel is sitting there with no one to play with." He pointed to the lone boy. "Why don't you go see him?"

Alana nodded and left Seth to join her friend.

The Keeper looked again at the grand structure behind him. Alana was right. It was more than twice the size of Tammeia's residence, but it was virtually void of life. He looked again at the fence and decided to find out, "Why a fence? Who are we being cut off from and why?"

The fire Rovear kindled only minutes ago now blazed bright red against the night sky. Its heat chased away the evening's mist. A wisp of black smoke rose from the end of each fiery peak and filled the camp and the otherwise barren hillside with a heavy musk-like odor.

Rovear's wide eyes were affixed to the fire's dance. He stared blankly into its light as any other animal would. Its heat warmed his face. The sounds of cracking and snapping from the fire were all that stopped the night from being as quiet as death.

Rovear picked up a stick that lay on the ground by his side and poked the burning embers. The fire flared up releasing hundreds of glowing ashes into the black sky. Jgar stood silently behind Rovear, his hands on his hips, as still as a statue. The firelight reflected off his face.

"Jgar, sit down. Share the fire's warmth with me."

Jgar sat next to him and joined in the silent vigil of staring into the brilliant flames. "Your mind is far from this place tonight, Rovear," Jgar said. He decided it was his turn to start a conversation. "What are you thinking about?"

Rovear turned his gaze from the fire and looked at Jgar. "Not one certain thing." He turned back to the fire.

Jgar moved closer. "I can only think of one thing that would pull a man's mind so."

"And that is?" Rovear's eyes returned to reality.

"Who's your Carlaf, Rovear?"

Rovear smiled and thought of his lady. His eyes again took on a faraway look. "My Lady is the wind. She's the color of the dusk sky. She's the cool waters of a rapidly moving river." Rovear spoke dramatically on purpose as was often his way.

"Yes, but what's her name?" Jgar prodded.

"Her name. My Carlaf's name is Pouchetia," he replied.

"Pouchetia. Exoltaire Pouchetia Coray?" Jgar questioned.

"How many Pouchetia Corays do you think live on this Habite?" He smiled. He knew his words surprised Jgar but he didn't know by how much or why.

Jgar cocked his head to the side and thought.

"And your Carlaf, Jgar?" Rovear smiled.

"My lady," Jgar said slowly, "is Regime Tammeia Sheen."

Rovear's smile faded. Here he sat with the consort of a woman who had made it a habit to annoy his Carlaf. It was a well known fact, especially to Rovear and Jgar, that there was no great love between their Carlafs.

"Tammeia," Rovear said after a silence that seemed unending, "is a very beautiful woman. I've seen her at the Council many times." Rovear tried to forget the tension and turn the conversation in a positive direction, but it was no use. Both men's minds were already remembering bitter incidents between the two women. The tension grew.

Jgar tried to ignore it too, and continued the conversation.

"Yes, she is. I've never seen Pouchetia. What does she look like?"

Rovear answered him without much feeling. "She is about Tammeia's height. Her eyes are golden. Her hair, pale yellow. She is..." Rovear stopped.

Jgar didn't even hear Rovear's answer, nor did he notice Rovear had stopped speaking. He was too busy remembering how Tammeia had described Pouchetia when he once dared to ask. "She is," he remembered Tammeia saying, "as ugly as all the hate that lives in her heart." He pictured many forms and figures of ugliness, thinking that Pouchetia could resemble any one them. Finally, he noticed Rovear had stopped talking.

Rovear knew Jgar thought ill of his Carlaf but couldn't prove it. Every time he tried to hear Jgar's thoughts, he was greeted by a wall of red — a mind shelter. Still he couldn't prove that Jgar was thinking ill of her. He just felt that he was.

"You say you know my lady, Rovear?" Jgar finally said.

"Yes, I've seen her many times. It's hard not to miss Tammeia," Rovear commented dryly.

"What do you mean, 'hard not to miss her?' " The tension was building steadily. "Are you saying my Carlaf is a spectacle! An exhibition!" Jgar stood up.

"Not at all," Rovear's tone was still dry. "But you must agree, she has a habit of making her presence...known."

Jgar became angrier. "Do you say that my lady doesn't know how to handle herself in Council!"

"No, I'm only saying that she has caused herself some embarrassment in the past."

Jgar's eyes darted. His fist clinched. "Who has embarrassed herself in front of the Council if not your Pouchetia. It's not Tammeia who is always late for meetings. And it wasn't Tammeia who was suspended from Council meetings last spring for questionable behavior. What did she do, Rovear? Whatever it was, I'm sure it was more than just embarrassing. I bet it was as wicked as Pouchetia herself!"

With Jgar's words Rovear stood up. This was in insult he expected lay waiting under Jgar's field of red. The two men stood face to face, staring coldly at each other's eyes for a long still moment.

Jgar looked at Rovear. A man who was a good friend in the making only moments ago now stood ready to kill him. Anger left his heart and was replaced by sadness. His face softened. He almost smiled. Jgar sat back down in front of the fire and looked up at the confused Rovear.

"I didn't mean that," he said. "Must we get involved in the women's conflicts?" He lay himself on the damp ground. "I'm going to sleep now. If you wish to kill me for you Carlaf's sake, please don't wake me first. I don't wish to know about it." Jgar closed his eyes and tried to sleep. He was unaware that Rovear had laid himself down on the ground just a few feet away.

For a long time after, the night went on void of any sound, except that of the fire. Neither Rovear nor Jgar knew when or if the other had fallen asleep. Even so, they both slept very deeply.

Before the fire burned itself out, the light of morning began to rise. Rovear shook his tired, heavy head and rose to his feet.

"I think I'll get some food ready. Are you hungry?"

Jgar opened his eyes to look at Rovear then closed them again. "No." He sat up stiffly and began to stretch his limbs. He was still very much alive. To him that meant Rovear had decided to forget the night before, as he had already. "Today's the big day," he yawned. "We see this great event today." He smiled at Rovear who stood watching him try to loosen his unyielding muscles. Rovear looked unsure of what to make of him. "It better be all you say it is. I wouldn't want to think that all this was in vain," Jgar groaned. Again he flexed his arms and stretched his torso.

"You shouldn't have slept on the damp ground. Your pain is your own fault, not the Illu-danchant's." Rovear tried his own stiff muscles. "I found a hot spring during my search for wood yesterday. Could I persuade you to join me in a morning swim?"

Just the idea of a hot spring began soothing Jgar's aches. "Don't waste time persuading me. Just lead me to its paradise." He reached out a hand to Rovear.

"Wait," He pulled it back. "I'll go tell Sharl where we're going so she won't worry." He paused, "She may think we forgot about her and left her here to die." Jgar smiled an impish smile. "We would never think of doing that. Would we?"

"Of course not," Rovear laughed. "Not in a million years."

Jgar looked into the tent where Sharl slept. She was still asleep. He contemplated waking her, but decided not to. Instead he closed the tent flap and returned to Rovear. "She's sound asleep. Let's go before she wakes." Rovear and Jgar walked down the hillside together.

The hot spring was music that made their tired bodies dance with relief. The two men sat soaking themselves for a short while. Soon the minerals in the water loosened their tired muscles.

"I believe this is what you needed, friend." Rovear said timidly. He breathed a nervous sigh.

"Yes, my friend. Just what I needed." Jgar slouched in the water until it came up around his neck. Rovear let out another sigh so relaxed that it was almost as soothing to Jgar's ears as the water was to his body.

"This water feels like heaven," Jgar said. He closed his eyes and took a deep breath, releasing it with a sigh that rivaled Rovear's for the verbalization of contentment. "Could anyone do better?" Jgar asked rhetorically and was surprised to get an answer.

"Aside from Pouchetia and a handful of other Carlafs, I doubt it. You'll have to be satisfied with the hot spring," Rovear said with a grin. He splashed water in Jgar's face and swam away.

Jgar chased after him, catching him moments later. The two wrestled playfully in and under the water until finally Jgar had to stop for air.

"Don't you think we should be getting back soon?" He panted loudly between words. "We don't want Sharl to..." He took an especially deep breath and let it out slowly.

"I know. We don't want her to think we've forgotten her." Rovear's breathing was also laborious. "Besides, the Illu-Danchant is not long away." They waded toward the water's edge.

Rovear picked up his robe from the rocky shore and threw it over his shoulder. Jgar stopped to put his on properly. He lifted the robe over his head then stood very still. There was a noise coming from behind a large rock to his right.

"What's wrong?" Rovear called back. He was about thirty paces ahead of Jgar.

"Are there wild animals in these hills?" Jgar slowly slid his robe over his body. He stared directly at the rock to his right.

"No, there are none. That is other than reptiles no larger than your hand." Rovear waved his arm in a beckoning motion. "It was probably nothing. Come on."

Jgar moved cautiously away from the rock. He hurried to rejoin Rovear and they started their way up the mountainside to the camp. Jgar turned back occasionally until the spring and the rocks behind it were well out of his sight.

"What about the handra-can? Didn't you say they live in these hills?"

"They only hunt at night. I was told they can't even see in the daylight." Rovear tapped Jgar's shoulder. "You still feel like you're being watched, don't you?" Jgar didn't have to state the obvious. "So do I, Jgar. But I wager it's only Sharl trying to spy on us."

"Yes. I believe so," Jgar agreed verbally, but he didn't really feel as if he were being spied on, as much as he felt he was being sized up, evaluated by some basic intelligence. He felt more like an atakapy being stalked by a kenya, or like a rodent about to be pounced on by some great bird of prey.

They entered the camp quietly.

"See," whispered Rovear, "Sharl's nowhere to be seen."

Jgar looked around. She wasn't in camp. "Unless," he thought. He looked into the tent. The Dominion was there, sound asleep. Jgar cleared his throat. "Lady, get up." Sharl stirred.

He left her and returned to finish the conversation he was having with Rovear. "Are you sure they only hunt at night?" Jgar sat down near where Rovear stood peeling fruit.

"Who?"

"The handra-can. What are they?"

"Oh, the handra-can. They're large flesh eating animals. I was told they have the strength of two strong men and can rip a person apart." He paused to make his description more impacting. "Some say that they can think just like us, and that they even look like us only they walk on four feet. But I know better. They're only dumb cave dwelling animals, seldom ever seen and often misunderstood. They live among these rocks, hunting by night, eating reptiles, small animals and an occasional traveler that may pass here unknowingly." Rovear executed another dramatic pause. "They're no threat to us during the day. They won't even bother us by night. We're safe," his voice became ominous, "unless they hunt in packs. Then they could easily over power us. That's why I built such a large fire last night. I was assured fire keeps them away."

Jgar looked around cautiously. He still felt uneasy. "They won't hunt by daylight. Are you sure?" Jgar felt certain something was watching the camp, waiting.

"Some claim to have seen them hunt by day. But none can prove it. They're creatures of the night only."

"What do they really look like?" Jgar looked around expecting to see whatever Rovear described.

Rovear was growing weary of Jgar's questions. "They're big, four-legged creatures with snarling teeth and gaping jaws. What do you want me to say? I've never seen one either."

Rovear placed some of the peeled fruit on a platter. He tossed the extra few to Jgar. "Enjoy your breakfast," Rovear said. He walked to the tent with a plate of food for Sharl. A strange feeling edged up his spine. He stopped mid-stride. "All this talk about handra-can is making me nervous," he thought to himself. Rovear ignored the feeling that he was being watched and entered the tent with Sharl's breakfast.

Chapter 16

The past few days were busy for Tammeia and many times she found her patience near its end. Cooperation on the part of her Coray guest seemed to be lacking, and the morale among her consorts was getting lower. It was their job to make the Coray's feel welcomed, which they tried to do, but the Corays didn't respond to any of their courtesies. It seemed the harder they tried, the more obstinate the Corays became. They ate all their meals in their rooms and they talked almost exclusively among themselves. What worried Tammeia most was their lack of feeling. They seemed to be totally apathetic to their situation. The little interest they did show was directed to how long it would be before they were allowed to go home and nothing else. Sometimes she wondered if they knew why they were there at all.

Tammeia sat in a sunlit parlor with her eyes closed thinking about them when Eisen came in. He looked at her, assumed she was in another realm and turned to leave.

"Eisen, what do you want?" She opened her eyes and startled him.

"Oh, Tammeia, I didn't know you were here." He took a breath. "Lady, there's trouble with the Corays."

"Trouble? What kind of trouble?"

"The Corays have disrupted the morning meal. They came in during the blessing and grabbed Hella and Meem," he explained as he helped her to her feet. "They have weapons."

"What kind of weapons?" They hurried out of the room.

"They have cooking knives and heavy pieces of wood. It looks like they broke apart the furniture in their room."

"Eisen, have you alerted anyone else?" she spoke softer as they approached the dining hall.

"No, I haven't had time. I came directly to you as soon as it happened." He stepped lightly so not to make noise.

"The first chance you get, go and alert the Habite's Carlafs in case I need their help." She thought for a moment the said, "Eisen, you go in first. Make a loud noise to distract them. When you do, I can enter by the side door unnoticed. I must get a good look at their placement so I can decide what course of action to take. Keep all attention on you. When I have a plan, I will enter and take care of them." Tammeia ran swiftly but quietly down the corridor to the side of the hall. She hoped she would come up with a plan.

When Eisen was in position, he swung the hall's main doors open and proudly walked in. "Hey, what's going on?" he said loudly but casually. He faced the head of the hall where the Corays stood with their captives. "Hey, what do you think you're doing?" All eyes flew to him.

A large Coray consort came running at him. Eisen raised his hands defensively as the aggressor neared. The Coray man threw himself at Eisen. The two men, locked in a bizarre embrace and flew backwards to the ground. There was a short struggle for dominance, which ended with Eisen on his stomach and his opponent on top of him. He struggled to his knees in hope of gaining the advantage only to be greeted by a stinging blow from his Coray opponent. He fell back down, dizzy. The man raised his fist again.

"Stop," the word was spoken softly. Tammeia didn't need to raise her voice. "Let him go." She walked into the room from the side door. One of the Coray girls nodded and Eisen was let go. He staggered to his feet.

Tammeia addressed herself to this young girl who seemed to be in charge. "Lassen, why do you do this?" She turned to a young man who held the old woman Meem at knifepoint. "Is there something you want that's too great to ask for? Or have we wronged you, our honored guest?" The Regime said with a very diplomatic smile even though her heart was steeping with anger.

"Please, sit down and be at peace. I'll have the morning meal served." Tammeia calmly sang the morning blessing as the Corays stood nervously trying to anticipate her next move. "Please sit. They bring our food now."

The Corays still did nothing. Tammeia looked at Meem and her captor again. The woman was pale and her age let her fear show easily. Tammeia glanced at Hella who was also being held at knifepoint. For that second, their minds met. Hella knew Tammeia's plan and returned her gaze with a slight smile. Tammeia looked to the back of the hall at Eisen. His body leaned, resting against the back wall trying not to be noticed. Eisen himself — his mind — was gone. He had left to alert and assemble the other Carlafs of the Habite. Tammeia knew this and stalled for time.

"Why don't you join me. We'll eat together and discuss your problem," Tammeia offered then sat down in her usual chair at the head of the table.

"We have no problem any longer." Lassen's lips shook with fear as she spoke.

Tammeia found it hard not to feel deep pity for her. She wasn't much older than a child.

"But you do require something from me?" Tammeia said. "Come, we can talk it over."

"What we don't require is talk. What we do require," she emphasized with a sarcastic sneer, "are trail animals and food for our journey back home. Which you will supply." She swung her hair over her shoulder defiantly.

"Haven't we extended our best to you? Do we treat you poorly?"

Lassen didn't answer.

"No," Tammeia continued, "I can't give you what you wish. You must stay here until Council orders otherwise." She again glanced at Eisen. He hadn't returned yet.

"The Council has nothing to do with this. And as I see it, you have no choice. Either you do what we want or they die." She pointed to Meem and Hella.

"No one will die, and you won't leave here until Council says so." Tammeia sat back in her chair. She noticed Eisen's body moving again. He had returned. "Now stop this foolishness before it becomes too much for you to handle."

"I'm giving you one final chance to obey me." The Coray girl ordered then stamped her foot. "I don't want to kill, but if it's worth our freedom I will."

"Restore civilized order to your people or I will." As Tammeia spoke she reached out with her mind to find the women Eisen had hurried into absence to aid her. They filled the realm that passed through the one Tammeia now stood in. The circle of power their united minds created was ready to be extended at the Regime's call. Tammeia thought, for a moment, that her young opponent would be no problem to handle by herself, but decided to use the offered help. It would be neater, not to mention easier. Tammeia felt their presence surround her.

Lassen must have also felt their presence. She became very uneasy and less confident.

"Restore order to your people now Lassen, or I will," Tammeia repeated.

"Your time is up Lady Sheen." Her voice shook and cracked. Tammeia didn't react. "On my signal kill them." Lassen raised her hand ready to give the signal.

Tammeia was surprised that Lassen would choose such a drastic move so soon, but she wasn't taken by surprise by it. With an opponent as inexperienced as this young girl obviously was, Tammeia knew she couldn't expect anything logical. This whole attack wasn't logical as far as Tammeia was concerned.

Lassen lowered her hand. Tammeia reached into the other realm to tap the circle of power. The signal was given and the men drew back their knives to strike their captive. Hella and Tammeia's eyes met. Meem shook with fear as a shining knife descended to meet her flesh. There was a brilliant white flash.

Tammeia sat at the head of the table — her usual seat. Hella stood by her side. Meem ran to her consorts. All the Corays lay on the floor, unmoving.

"Do you think they'll listen now?" Hella looked at Tammeia then at the unconscious young Coray girl. "I think the hate in her is too strong to give up."

"The hate, Hella?" Tammeia looked at her quizzically. "I only sensed need," she paused. "A need to survive."

"Their people misunderstand, or more likely they were misinformed. Either way, it will do no good to punish them." She shook her head slowly. "We'll have to try to clear any misunderstandings, correct any misinformation."

The Regime called her consort. "Eisen, please thank the women you assembled for their help, then gather your brothers. I must speak to you."

"Jgar too?"

"No, Jgar must not be disturbed. If he needs to know, I'll tell him when he returns."

Eisen again shed his body in favor of a different realm.

"Hella, get someone to bring our guest to a place where they can sleep undisturbed but closely supervised," Tammeia said. She picked up the kitchen knife that had once rested on Hella's white neck. Like all the metal in the hall at the time of the flash, its blade was all twisted and gnarled. She tossed it to the floor. "And have someone come clean up this mess. I have to go see Breyan. I'll be back soon." Tammeia walked out of the hall silently.

Chapter 17

Seth looked out the window at the star-lit sky, tightened his loosely knotted belt and took a deep breath. In the far away hills he saw the flickering of light, or maybe he saw nothing. It was hard to tell at this distance. What he felt were fires of a settlement might actually be only the reflections of the stars on nearby moist leaves. It was hard for him to judge the distance across the vast field in front of him. The hill may not be too far away, then the light would be mere reflections or the plains could go on forever and the hill would be a mountain a considerable distance away. Then the light would be roaring fires. Either way, Seth was soon to find out.

He carried a knife that he appropriated from the kitchen shelves and a container of water in case he was still out when the day got hot. Once again he looked to the stars, then quietly, he climbed out the window.

The Keeper paced himself at a slow trot, making sure to stay in the shadow of the building as much as possible. When its shelter gave way, he slowed his pace and lowered his body to a crouching position. Slowly, he neared the fence.

There had to be an energy field of some kind running the fence's length. There must be some kind of alarm or trap to stop intruders. He remembered a few days after their arrival, an equis was frightened off by some over enthusiastic kenya and it jumped the fence. The kenya ran under the fence and taunted the equis, but no one crossed the fence to retrieve the animal. Instead, they walked the great distance to the front of the fence where it was open to the road. He found it awkward that they would take such a long route to a panicking animal.

"Maybe then, only people were susceptible to whatever power the fence had. After all, the equis and kenya crossed it safely," he pondered for a short time. He picked up a hand full of dirt, sifted through it for a rock and stopped. If he threw the rock he could set off the alarm system. If there was an alarm system, then what would be his excuse? Caught out in the dark, far from the house with a knife in his hip pouch.

"No, not a good idea," he thought. He put the rock down and began to walk the perimeter of the fence toward the front gate, then stopped. "There'll be someone watching the front," he said to himself. He turned around and headed back to where he dug up the rock. Seth scooped up another handful of soil and dropped it slowly into place as if salting the ground below him. He scooped it up again. "Digging," he said quietly.

Then it dawned on him. The equis jumped the fence and both kenya slipped under it through the small clearance. They both crawled, slowly and belly down as flat as they could.

"They never touched it. Even though it would have been much easier for them to climb. They never touched the fence!" He smiled broadly. "They couldn't know about an alarm," he reasoned. "There must not be an alarm. Some sort of painful punishment more than likely, but no alarm." The Keeper sifted restlessly in the dirt for a rock. He found one and lobbed it over the waist high fence. Nothing happened.

He sat quietly for a moment, holding his breath. No lights went on in the house. No one was coming. "There is no alarm," he concluded. Seth brushed the dirt off his hands. "Now to cross it."

The man got down on his stomach and examined the amount of clearance the fence would give him. It was not nearly enough. He thought about digging, but gave that idea up. It would take too long and he had wasted enough time already. Seth backed up about seven paces. "I should be able to jump the fence without difficulty," he thought, but wasn't sure. He'd never had to jump a fence without touching it before.

The Keeper gulped hard and ran full speed towards the fence. His take-off was timed beautifully, but during the three seconds he was in the air he noticed that his left foot didn't have enough momentum and was crashing down towards the fence. In an effort to stop that from happening, like lightning, he pulled his body into a tight ball. The ground felt hard and cold against the side of his face. He had made it over and his foot had cleared.

In the front of the building, by the gate of the fence, Jerami was working on the gate watch again. This was the third night running that he watched the gate. He tried to keep his eyes open. Not getting caught sleeping was the only way to get out of gate watch. He yawned a little and tried to spruce up his tired face with a brisk rub, but it didn't help much. Jerami was tired and his eyes knew it. He began pacing to keep awake, talking to himself in a low rumble. "What a useless job to lose sleep over. No ones going to come at night."

"The gate must be guarded and you know why," he said in a mocking falsetto tone.

"Jerami was caught sleeping when he was supposed to be watching the gate, Lady," he mocked the one who turned him in.

The Lady's only response was Jerami's sentence for the crime. He would have to watch the gate every night until he could do it without falling asleep.

Jerami's head slowly and steadily fell forward as he slipped into the surrounding thoughts. Something inside of him became aware that he was asleep. "Huh?" He bolted his head upward and opened his eyes wide. "Wake up," he said out loud to himself. He stood glossy eyed and stiff legged. His eyes started to close again. This time he slept deeply.

Not far away, Seth got to his hands and knees, then to his feet before he noticed that the fence behind him was glowing slightly and there were lights on in the house. "Damn!" he thought. "There was an alarm after all." He contemplated whether he should make a run for it across the plains or give himself up with a good excuse and an apology.

The field was far too long and flat. A person standing even quite a distance away would be seen easily and he couldn't even begin to think of a reasonable excuse. His instincts told him to lay low to the ground and be still and maybe he would not be seen. The Keeper pressed his body hard to the ground and closed his eyes so that the lights wouldn't reflect off them, then he waited.

"Wake up, Jerami you fool," Artin shouted and shook him. Jerami startled and bolted to his feet. He looked at his brother with still sleepy eyes. He said nothing.

"You tripped the fence alarm when you fell asleep. You must have brushed up against it."

Jerami straightened up. "Did any of the ladies hear it go off?"

"No."

Jerami sighed, "Thanks."

"No brother," Artin grinned, "thank you. Tomorrow was to be my night for gate watch."

<h1 style="text-align:center">Chapter 18</h1>

Three figures stood on the mountain's edge, silhouetted against the purple sky. The Illu-danchant was about to begin. Rovear was seldom silent but now he and Jgar were wordless in anticipation. Sharl looked around her. The two men who stood on her right seemed far away. She sat on the ground and gazed into the valley below her dangling feet. The sky was becoming a deep rich purple and the air was getting hot and hard to breathe.

Kai and Sola were both over the horizon, left and right to each other. They were rising in an arc who's apex would be directly above the mountains with smaller brighter Kai in front. The stars began to eclipse and the valley filled with yellow light. It mixed with the purple and dissolved into fiery violet. The light reflected off the shiny rubble of the basin and glared up as if reaching for the stars that gave it life.

Jgar heard a very low hum, or maybe it was very high. He couldn't even tell if he really heard a sound at all. His head did, but his ears heard nothing. It was like the sound somehow passed his ear drums and attacked his audio nerves directly.

The large center mountain of glassier turned from glowing white-yellow to a brilliant blue. Lights of every spectral color burst out of it in all directions, reflecting off the valley floor and up into the sky. The two stars overlapped perfectly. The two side mountains of the Illu-danchant blazed in magenta and violet streams. The light from them more brilliant and dynamic than the center one.

The tone in Jgar's head was rising in pitch, or maybe it was volume. He still couldn't tell. The fourth and largest mountain shined yellow, then white, then it seemed to burst into a wheel of incredible color and intensity that poured out some kind of energy. Jgar could feel it flow through him, lifting him up. Were his feet on the ground? Was he flying?

He didn't know, nor did he care. All he knew was the power and the excitement. His mind floated in the light. His body quaked with more sensation that any physical encounter could give him. He had hit his peak and beyond and he was staying there.   It was like he had no restraint, no measure. He was everything.

For a moment, he wondered if the others felt as he did, then realized he really didn't care. Suddenly, he remembered the sound in his head and felt like screaming. It had grown more intense than he believed possible. A flash of searing pleasure, or maybe it was pain, at this point there was little difference, and Jgar felt the ground again. He fell on his back, but didn't open his eyes. He didn't have time to before he passed out.

Jgar might have slept for days if he hadn't been awakened by a cry for help coming from behind him. He opened his eyes and bolted to his feet.

Rovear again yelled for his help.

"Rovear!" Jgar looked around him for a weapon. All he found were small rocks. He looked over at the things that were attacking the Exoltairetive from four directions. "Handra-can," Jgar said with amazement.

The animals nipped and pawed at Rovear with their large claws as if they were trying to make sport of the man before they killed him. Jgar gave one more quick check for a large rock or weapon and once again found nothing. Then, with a yell as primal as the beginning of time, he ran head on into the pack of beasts.

His scream drew the animal's attention for a split second. That was all Rovear needed to make his move. Following Jgar's lead, he shrugged his shoulders then jumped on the nearest animal's back.

"Jgar! Rovear!" Sharl screamed frantically from the security of a large, high rock roost. "Here! Catch!" The Dominion tossed a silver knife, handle over blade at Jgar.

Through some kind of luck or God-gift, the knife landed squarely in the back of one beast's neck. The animal fell to the ground. Jgar made a dash for the knife, but Rovear reached it first. With a foot on the bend of the helpless beast's neck, Rovear pulled the knife up. There was a loud snap. The handra-can stopped moving.

Rovear turned his attention and his blade to the three remaining animals. One struck out a Jgar. He jumped back. It struck out again. Warm blood poured from his arm. The animal stopped to lap the warm liquid off the ground. Another loud snap resounded through the rock hills when Rovear's full body weight, plus all the force he could get centered on his right heel, made contact with the lapping animal's spine, his knife to its neck. The animal screeched then let out a few low, vocal groans before it died.

Jgar took off his waist sash and fumbled to tie it tightly around his arm. He was feeling light headed and dizzy. He knew he had to stop the bleeding before it was too late.

Rovear got a few deep jabs at the remaining animals before they ran off back to where they came from. He stood still for a moment to make sure they were really gone and not just regrouping. Satisfied that they were gone, he turned his back to the hills.

"Jgar, are you all right?"

The Regimitive leaned to one side. He looked very pale.

"Jgar." Rovear ran to him, making sure not to step on the carcass of the beast he just slaughtered. "Jgar, let me help you." Rovear grabbed the sash and began to twist it tighter and tighter.

"Were those," Jgar asked between labored breaths, "visitors," pause, "handra-can?" Jgar asked. His teeth clinched tight to hide his pain.

"We're the visitors and the handra-can obviously don't like company." Rovear smiled awkwardly trying to hide his alarm. Jgar's wound looked bad. It was worst than Rovear expected it to be. The gash covered almost the whole length of the man's upper arm. He was losing blood fast. Rovear had to do something for him.

First of all, he had to get Jgar and Sharl to shelter. He helped Jgar to his feet. The Regimitive wobbled dizzily then fell. Rovear lifted him and carried him to their camp.

"Sharl!" he shouted.

She stood cautiously, looking out into the surrounding hills.

"Sharl, watch him. I have to make a fire before the handra-can come back." Rovear rushed off to get wood. When he had a raging fire going he returned to the tent.

"Look Rovear. His hand is blue." Sharl's eyes were wide with shock. "Will he lose it?"

Rovear loosened the sash a little. The blood started to flow again. "I should hope not. Not for a wound like this." He poked at the sore and Jgar groaned with pain. "It looks bad, but his muscle fibers seem to be intact. Here." He handed Sharl her knife. "Cut me strands of your hair."

"My hair?" Sharl questioned. She wiped the blood off her knife.

"Yes, your hair. Make them long strands. At least twenty or thirty of them," Rovear explained then stared into space as if lost in thought. He knew he had to do something drastic. He could never get help in time, and he didn't dare seek help from his Carlaf and her menders. They'd surely let a consort of Tammeia Sheen die. Rovear ran out to the handra-can carcass and turned it over.

"What could do it? What would work?" he wondered. The man stood, staring in thought for just a moment longer, then he returned to the tent.

"Sharl, give me the knife again." Rovear grabbed it and ran back to the carcass. He cut the beast paw off and turned the skin inside out. Using the knife with meticulous skill, he cut through the tendons and fibers to the paw's ivory bones, still warm from their former life. He chose a strong straight one then cut it free at its cartilage covered joints, then he placed the bone on a flat rock. He hit it hard with the ball of his hand. It splintered.

Rovear picked the three best shards and with the point of the knife placed a small hole at their widest points. He got close to the fire for better light. There he shaved the edges of his newly born needles until they were smooth and finely pointed. He thought for a moment then ran into the tent.

"Your hair, lady," he said.

Sharl gave him a pinch full of her long brown strands. Rovear put them carefully down at his side, picked up three together and pulled them. After a slight effort, they snapped.

He tried five, then ten. No use. Her hair wasn't strong enough.

"The equis tails. Their hair should work." Rovear ran to the back of the camp to the place were they had tied the equis. Only one animal was left standing. Its bright white hair stained with mud and the splattered blood of its companions. The other two equis lay half eaten in a bath of blood. "The handra-can have been here too," Rover remarked to himself. He was disgusted but not alarmed. He had other things on his mind. He cut the tail off one of the corpses and returned to the tent.

"Rovear!" Sharl gasped. She was shocked to see what her carried.

"No. I didn't." He waved the tail. "It seems the handra-can had lunch before they attacked us. That's probably the only reason we're still alive.

"Are they all..."

"No. For some reason, one is untouched. The other two are dead."

"Untouched?" she questioned. "I wonder why they didn't kill it also?"

"I don't know. Maybe it didn't look too tasty." Rovear pulled at the equis tail hairs. They didn't come out. He cut a few and tested them. One would do. Two would do even better. He cut some more off and threaded his needles.

"Rovear, did you say our equis were killed?" Jgar murmured and tried to get up. Rovear eased him back down.

"Yes, but everything will be all right. Does this hurt?" Rovear touched the edge of Jgar's wound ever so lightly.

Jgar cringed with clinching teeth, "No."

"That's what I thought." Rovear gave Sharl a very concerned stare. "I'm going to have to try to close your wound. Do you understand?"

Jgar moaned.

"Jgar, take some deep breaths for me." Rovear had never done anything like this before, but breathing deep seemed like a good beginning. Rovear took a few deep breaths of his own then got started. He pierced the skin to the right of the wound and sluggishly pulled the needle through. Jgar bit his bottom lip and shook. Rovear caught the skin on the left side and pulled it. Jgar let out few gasps and some half audible sounds. Rovear tied the ends of the hair together so they wouldn't slip, then pierced the right side of the wound again. As he drew the thread up taunt, the agony on Jgar's face met with the nervous fright on Rovear's. Jgar tried to smile. Rovear pulled on the thread and knotted it again. Jgar's eyes rolled back into his head. He had fainted. Rovear felt relived that Jgar fainted. It stopped most of the pain, not only Jgar's but also his own.

When his stitching was complete, Rovear took the knife, cut a strip away from his cloak and wrapped it loosely around Jgar's wound then removed the sash that he had used as a tourniquet. He took it and all the other pieces of clothing that were covered with blood and tossed them into the fire. The blood scent in their clothes would attract the handra-can, Rovear was certain.

While Jgar rested, Sharl and Rovear skinned the four carcasses and cut away the meat they would need as food. The remaining parts were cut up and tossed into the fire.

"Rovear, will they be back?" Sharl asked nervously.

"I don't know. I don't think so, but we'd better move on as soon as Jgar is able. That shouldn't be too long from now," Rovear said without looking up from his work.

The woman looked around, hugging her bare shoulders. "I hope not. I don't like this place." She shuddered.

Rovear stopped his work and looked at her. "Did you enjoy the Illu-danchant?" He said changing the subject. "With all this confusion I almost forgot about it. Wasn't it wonderful?"

"I didn't think it was that great," she shrugged.

"What?" He looked surprised, then shocked when he realized she was serious.

"All that happened to me was my ears began to buzz and my eyes were watering because of the bright light," she paused. "So, I hid behind that rock over there." She pointed to the rock she had been on top of earlier. "As soon as I did, the sound stopped. So I thought I'd just wait there until the whole thing was over. I must have fallen asleep. I woke up to your yelling for Jgar." She looked up at Rovear. "I couldn't have missed very much. After all, I can see colors in the sky almost every morning in the Nylla's arc."

"The Nylla's arc," he huffed with disbelief. "She compares the Illu-danchant to the colors made by the light shining through the morning mist." Rovear shook his head slowly. Her ignorance and arrogance annoyed him.

"What did you see?" Sharl's tone was flat and mocking.

"Only some colors in the sky," he replied in the same tone.

"You mean you didn't see a miracle," she laughed.

Rovear didn't answer.

"No angels from the heavens with golden robes and fiery torches?"

He still didn't reply.

"Or maybe you saw your Carlaf with her teeth falling out and her hair in knots and mats," she laughed.

"Watch your words, girl child," Rovear replied.

"Or maybe you saw nothing at all, like I, and you're too afraid to admit it." She laughed louder and danced around him. "That's it. Isn't it? You saw nothing."

Rovear turned to face her. "Dominion Sharl, I saw infinity. And there is only on thing larger. And that is your stupidity." He walked away from her and returned to the fire.

Rovear pulled out an equis bone and cut the meat away from it. It was cooked on the outside but the center was red with its own juices and would be full of the nutrients and vitamins Jgar needed to replace his lost blood. Rovear brought it to Jgar. The Regimitive ate as best as he could. After he was done, Rovear cleaned away the scraps and threw them in the fire to burn.

He stopped to think. "The fire's large enough. It won't burn out before daylight. It will keep the handra-can away," the Exoltairetive said to himself with confidence. That night Rovear and Sharl slept in the tent with Jgar. Halfway through the night, it occurred to him that the handra-can do hunt in the daylight. That was one myth proven wrong. "Maybe they weren't afraid of fire either." With that thought, Rovear got up and for the rest of the night he kept watch. There was no sign of them.

Chapter 19

Seth opened his eyes and looked up. The fence was no longer glowing. Soon after, the lights in the house went out. The danger had passed him. He gave one last look around then headed into the open field. When he felt he had enough distance between himself and the house he began a steady paced run. He kept up this pace for a long time before he reached the loose rock foothills of what turned out to be a considerably large mountain. The hillside was covered with loose rock and shale making it a difficult climb. But with some effort, Seth was able to use shrubs and small trees as handholds and made his way up its steep grade. When he felt comfortable with his progress he sat down in some berry-covered shrubs and closed his eyes to rest.

Sola was just beginning to peek over the horizon and the sky behind the now tiny Coray anhabit was warm pink. He knew he would be missed soon but it was too late to turn back.

Seth pulled out his knife and cut down a sapling gorlifm tree that was about twice his height, and carved away all its bark. He selected the best section of the bluish wood tree then cut the two unwanted ends off. The remaining rod, which he lay on the side of the hill to dry and become hard, would stand only slightly taller than himself.

The Keeper ate some of the red berries from the bushes around him, then collected a few handfuls and put them in his hip pouch. Seth looked at the ground under his feet. Even though the soil was firmer and less rocky, it wasn't that much better than the ground at the hill's base. It was going to take some thought to pick out the best way to climb. So Seth decided to take some time to look at the terrain ahead of him.

The land beyond the small plateau where he sat sloped upward as far as he could see. It would take time to climb to the next plateau, but the slope behind him was a worse climb by far. The soil was loose rubble and the grade steep, but he had managed through it. All of the walking and riding he had to do to get to the Coray's Habite had made him stronger. Seth knew it wasn't going to be a very hard climb, just a time consuming one.

Sola was well above the horizon now. "By now they know I'm gone. But I should still have some time," he spoke out loud to himself. "No doubt they'll react like children and assume I've run home. Maybe that will buy me some time to make my climb." He looked across the plane to see if anyone was coming but the building that once looked so large was so small in the distance it was impossible to really tell. Hoping to throw any who followed off his trail, the Keeper, staff in hand, began his assent not up the hill face, but around to his right, going a little higher every few paces until the anhabit was well out of sight. Then he started his direct climb up.

When nightfall neared, he stopped in a cave formed from loosely fallen boulders of a long time past. He gathered brush and small branches and built a fire then sat down to eat his berries. He was so hungry that he could have eaten them all, but he stopped himself. They were the only food he had seen all day and they might be the only food he would see tomorrow. He tried to forget his hunger and get some sleep. After his climb, he did need the rest.

Chapter 20

"Breyan, I wish to speak to you." Tammeia's request for audience was only a formality, for as she asked, she pushed her way into the body of one of Breyan's consorts. He gave it up to her without a struggle.

"Tame." Breyan gave Tammeia a long hard stare. "Are you here to take me up on my offer or is it something else?"

Tammeia flexed the arms of her newly acquired flesh. Everything seemed to be in order. She looked at Breyan. "Well..."

"Well, whatever the reason, you're here." Breyan kissed her daughter's forehead.

"I've come to get your opinion on a problem and some quiet in which to think over your answer," Tammeia explained then sighed heavily.

"What's the matter? Is there something..." Breyan stopped. The question she was about to ask was unnecessary. There was obviously something wrong. "Tell me what worries you?" she decided to say instead.

Tammeia fidgeted a bit. "I've had a hard time with the Corays."

Breyan shook her head. "You and Pouchetia should at least pretend to get along. You share the same world. If women of your stations can't overcome these..."

"It wasn't concerning Pouchetia," Tammeia interrupted before Breyan got too involved in her lecture.

"Not Pouchetia? Who then?"

"The Corays at my anhabit disrupted the morning meal and threatened two of my Carlafs at knife point." She continued with the details of the whole event. When Tammeia had finished Breyan spoke.

"You say everyone is fine?"

"Yes. The Corays were stunned but they're unharmed. Though when they wake up they're going to be furious."

"I'm sure. What about Meem?" Breyan was especially concerned with Meem. For many years Meem had been guardian to Breyan's children. She helped raise Tammeia and her brother, and when it came time for Tammeia to have her own children, Meem cared for them as well.

"Meem was shaken terribly. I'm afraid her strength isn't what it used to be. She may be ill for sometime. But I think she will recover with some peace and quiet," Tammeia said then stood up and started to pace nervously.

"What do you think provoked this attack?" Breyan motioned for her daughter to sit.

"I'm not sure. I can't help but think they believe we are holding them hostage or prisoners of some kind. It was almost as if they had to escape or die."

Tammeia sat down. Breyan's expressions turned to one of deep thought. She was still and unmoving. Tammeia began to fidget with a wisp of her hair, twisting it and untwisting it nervously. The Regime hated to bring her problems to her mother. It made her feel somewhat incompetent. It seemed to Tammeia that Breyan could solve any problem with just a moment's thought. Whether it was a problem Tammeia contemplated for minutes or days unending, Breyan could always come up with its solution in no time at all.

The look of contemplation on Breyan's face was slowly being replaced by the look of confusion. "The Corays arrived with no real problems? They didn't give your people a fight?" she finally asked.

"That's correct. Though they isolated themselves from us, they didn't offer any resistance," Tammeia explained, "at least at first."

The Regime looked at her mother. Breyan seemed perplexed by the situation. Tammeia felt strangely satisfied. For once she didn't feel like she was wasting the Exoltaire's time. This time she had a real problem, and a real reason to ask for help.

"The only ones who were involved were the ones who came from Pouchetia's Habite," Tammeia added. "And..."

"And they seem to be set on returning there," Breyan finished.

She cocked her head and looked at her daughter. "Do you think it's wise to keep them against their will? Or do you think you should grant their wish?"

"Breyan!" Tammeia exclaimed. "What do you mean, grant their wish? They wish to leave. What about the Council?"

"Tame, calm down." Breyan stood and put a hand on Tammeia's shoulder. "You're getting all worked up over nothing."

"Nothing!" Tammeia became more agitated. "I don't want it said that I was the only one who couldn't fulfill her part of the mission."

"But it's only the Corays who would leave. You'd still have people to train and send. Let them go."

The older woman walked to the window. "Come here, daughter." Tammeia joined her. A shinning white star glowed bright in the morning sky and Sola's orange light danced off the ripples of a near-by lake. "Tammeia, look at the morning star and the reflection on the water. They are both free. The plants and birds, the very world that gives them life can never really be possessed. Mortals cannot control them. It's not the High Exoltaire Touchea that makes the morning light come. It's not she nor I, nor anyone else who keeps the world moving through space, yet these things are controlled. The morning will always come." She looked into her daughter's dark eyes briefly then returned her gaze to the window. "There is no one to teach the birds to fly or the plants to grow toward the light, yet birds do fly and plants reach for light.

"You see, Tame, one lesson you have yet to learn is that of patience. There is a natural order in the world. Everything, living or not, is a loyal subject of this order. And all that exist must obey the plan or pattern creation prescribes for it.

"You can't tell water not to flow. By its nature it must flow and it will. Yes, you can hold it back temporarily but eventually it will flow past your hands to its freedom." She looked at her daughter. Tammeia's eyes were wide and dark.

"Yet nothing is entirely free. The same laws also bind it. Water has no choice. It is water, therefore, it must flow. Just as you had no choice. You were born to be a woman."

"But I do have choice. I'm alive. Water has no life and therefore no choice," Tammeia interjected.

"All things that live have control of choice in small ways. But the things that are the most important to life are not among those choices. Your mother, your birthright, your health, even your soul were not your own choosing. If all could choose these things, wouldn't everyone choose to be the highest Exoltaire."

Tammeia's mouth began to open in reply, but Breyan cut her off before she had a chance to say anything.

"Would you choose to be a slug that crawls on muddy logs or an insect that will soon be killed by the snap of an equis tail?"

Tammeia again opened her mouth to reply. Breyan again cut her off.

"I should hope not! If you were to answer yes, I'd say I gave birth to a fool!" Breyan smiled and poked at Tammeia playfully.

"So you see, my daughter, the same inner law that brought you here also controls the Corays. Let them go."

"Let them go! What about the Council? What of its laws?" Tammeia huffed and walked away from the window.

"Have you ever thought that the Council may have been wrong to send them to you in the first place?"

Tammeia looked shocked. "The Council wrong! Breyan, you have sat on the Council for years. How can you say that?" Tammeia was talking faster and louder. Her high strung disposition was quickly taking over.

"Tammeia," Breyan lowered her tone to almost a whisper in hope that Tammeia would notice and realize that her own voice was quickly nearing a roar. Breyan knew far too well about Tammeia's excitable nature. She also knew that a gentle reminder would be far more effective in calming her than the more direct approach she had tried earlier. "Council doesn't really make laws. We only record the laws of nature. If we were accurate and stated a law the way nature commands it then it is a good law and it works. If, on the other hand, we were more involved in our wants, or of things opposed to nature then we may make a law that's not just the way nature planned it to be and the law won't work." She paused for a moment to talk to one of her consorts who was standing at the door waiting for her attention. She turned back to Tammeia. "Do you understand? The only laws that one can follow are the ones her Creator has designed for her," Breyan said then hugged Tammeia reassuringly.

"Well, my daughter, we'll have to talk later. Daun has just reminded me that I have an appointment soon. I must get ready." Breyan lead Tammeia back to the window. "You can stay here and think if you wish. I'll be back soon."

"Thank you, but I think I'll go," Tammeia said. She called out with her mind to the owner of the body she occupied. Breyan hurried out of the room and down the hall. Tammeia exited the body and set out for home.

Chapter 21

By morning, Jgar's sore was white and yellow with infection. It had swollen terribly, and he was in a lot of pain.

"Sharl, we have to go now." Rovear fitted a bit on the remaining equis.

"What's the rush. It's barely daylight. Are we going to be attacked again?" She rushed to pack their bags of supplies.

"No, it's not that. We have to move on or Jgar will die." He helped Jgar onto the equis. "We have to get to the others."

"We'll never get to help in time, Rovear," Jgar said. His voice was failing. "The best you can do is cut off my arm and hope it doesn't re-infect."

"There's nothing to pack a severed arm stump. Besides, it would only be re-infected by nightfall. Now, be quiet and save your strength."

"Are you ready, Sharl!" Rovear shouted.

"Almost. I just have to pack the tent." She carried three bags of food to him.

"Forget the tent. Get on."

The Dominion shrugged and climbed on the equis behind Jgar. He leaned back on her for support. Rovear tied the bags of food over the neck of the equis. The jug of water he tied to his own back.

"If we keep a steady foot pace, we can make it to the others in just about three nights and four days," Rovear said.

They started down the mountainside, Rovear on foot, the equis bearing Sharl and Jgar behind him. They hadn't been walking long when Sharl called to Rovear, "Jgar is burning with fever. He's as hot as Kai."

"Jgar are you alright?" Rovear called back to him. Jgar mumbled but was incapable of answering.

"He's going to die," Sharl said nervously.

"Here, Sharl. Wet him with this." Rovear gave her the water jug. She poured a little on Jgar's head then stopped.

"More Sharl! We have to bring his temperature down. He'll die if we don't," Rovear urged. "Wet him some more."

"A lot of good that will do. Don't you see, Rovear, he's as good as dead now. I won't pour the only drinkable water we have on a corpse!"

Jgar moaned. Maybe he objected. Maybe he agreed.

"He's not dead yet!" Rovear said. He fought with Sharl for the jug. She didn't let it go.

"Can't you smell that infection. He's as dead as if he didn't breath." She held the jug fast and pulled quickly to get it away from him. It worked. "Look at his eyes, Rovear. He's just waiting to die."

"That's only the fever. He'll be all right once we reach the others." The Exoltairetive paced with agitation. "He needs the water to keep him cool."

"And what do we, the living, do for drinking water?" She still held the jug tightly. "Tell me that. The only pool of water in these hills is poisoned with salts."

"The mineral springs!" Rovear thought with excitement. He jumped onto the equis' back. The animal grunted with the load. "Hold Jgar as best as you can, Sharl." He kicked the animal and whipped its reins. It ran.

The mineral spring was right where Rovear had remembered it to be. He had no trouble finding it. He dismounted and grabbed Jgar. The Regimitive's body was lifeless and heavy. Rovear stumbled and was sure he would fall, but he regained his footing. He waded into the cool dark water and lowered Jgar until it covered him to his neck. Jgar screamed out in pain when the mineral filled water streamed over his festering arm.

Soon his fire hot skin began to cool and Rovear noticed traces of white, poison, pus floating on the water's surface. Excited and worried, he removed Jgar's bandage. Globs of the infection's poison floated up to the water's surface. Jgar was slightly conscious now and Rovear told him to shake his arm back and forth under the water. With each shake more of the poison fluid of the infection worked its way free and to the surface. The water seemed to be bubbling around the edges of the wound.

"Let me see your arm, Jgar," Rovear asked gently.

Jgar lifted his arm and in place of a pus oozing sore was pink and white skin, neatly cross-stitched closed. Rovear looked at Jgar's lips. They were blue. They had been in the water all afternoon. It was time to come out.

"Rovear, Thank you," Jgar said as the Exoltairetive helped him sit at the water's edge.

Rovear felt Jgar's forehead. He was much cooler. "Rest my friend," Rovear replied. "We'll have to move on soon. The handra-can are around here somewhere." He shuddered uneasily.

Rovear cut several strips off his robe and tossed the remainder of the garment to Sharl. "Take this robe and fill it with the food and tie it as best as you can. I need the leather sacks." He grabbed the sacks and dumped the food out at her feet, then he took the sacks back to the spring and filled them with the mineral water.

"We'll have to keep his wound washed with this water until it's healed all the way." Rovear turned to go get Jgar. To his surprise, Jgar was standing behind him, not in full strength and not ready to run, but he was standing and walking.

"Jgar, get on the equis. Are you trying to get yourself sick again?" Rovear scolded half heartedly. With no reluctance and some help from Rovear, Jgar mounted the animal. Sharl quickly, but carefully, mounted behind him.

"Rovear, thank you," Jgar said again.

"You don't have to thank me for saving your life. You'd have done the same for me." Rovear picked up the equis reins and started to walk.

"My life? Oh, yes. Thank you, brother, for that also." Jgar rummaged through the make shift bag for a tasty piece of food.

"Also?" Rovear stopped and turned around to face him.

"Yes. I was thanking you for showing me the Illu-danchant. You were right. I shall never forget it. It was wonderful." He said and tossed Rovear the remainder of the tasty food, then flinched in pain.

"Now stop moving. You're still sick you know." Rovear turned and started to walk again. He wore a smile from ear to ear.

"What did you think of the Illu-danchant, Sharl?" Jgar asked. He looked as far over his shoulder as he could.

Sharl didn't answer, and infinity felt very, very large to her.

Chapter 22

Tammeia called her consorts into her room for a meeting and they had all arrived by the time she returned from Breyan's. They were restless, if not annoyed, about the morning's events. Eisen sat in the back of the room nursing a sore side.

As she walked into the room, instead of a greeting, Tammeia said, "When the Corays awake, they're to be given supplies and set free to go where they want."

"Let them go?" Eisen's eyes rolled in his head. "I wish you would've thought of that earlier." He looked to see if his remark was deemed entertaining to his companions. Seeing it wasn't, he sat quietly.

"Let them leave? Why?" another questioned.

"Because it's what they wish." Tammeia turned away. "Now go. Get things ready for them."

Her consorts got up, each frowning in his own way, and headed for the door. All except Eisen who stayed, sitting on the corner of her bed.

"What do you want, Eisen?" Tammeia looked uninterested in his answer.

"I just want to stay here for a minute." He slid over close to her. "If you'd like a listening ear, I have two." He put his hand on her soft neck.

"Do you want to take me as a mate?" she asked matter-of-factly with an obvious lack of interest.

"Only if that's your wish. But it seems more likely that your mind needs a mate, not your body." He smiled a slight smile. "Come on now, what's on your mind? What do you want to say?" He nudged her a little. "If you wish to cry, my love, I'd like to hold you. Besides, no one need know." He hugged the woman and she did cry.

"Eisen, what's wrong with me? I feel as if my body is tired and wants to sleep but I'm not sleepy. My eyelids are heavy and my bones are sore, but I'm not sick. But most of all, I feel like my heart is being ripped from my chest. I'm filled with...I don't know what to call it..." The lady paused and wiped her eyes. "I think I'm only making too much of things." She swallowed in a sob and wiped her eyes again. Eisen stroked her long black hair. "Maybe it's only the pressure," she said and tried to smile.

"What is it, if not the pressure? Don't worry, Tammeia. You must just be over tired."

"No, it's more than that, Eisen. I feel as if something is wrong. Wrong with everything. And it's only the beginning."

"The beginning," he chuckled. "Don't be so melodramatic, my lady." He stood up and walked to the window. "I think I should leave now so you can get some sleep. I'll make sure that the others do what you want them to do. Don't worry about anything." He closed the yellow folding blinds.

"But..." she protested.

"At least promise me you'll try and get some sleep." He blew her a kiss and closed the door behind him as he left.

"Tammeia's been working too hard," Eisen thought to himself. "She's going to make herself ill for sure. And it won't be the first time." He thought about the last time.

Tammeia was pregnant; expecting Alana, when Breyan felt it was time her daughter had a Habite of her own. It seemed that one of Breyan's aunts was getting very old and was having a hard time running her Habite. Breyan decided that in the best interest of all, her aunt should come and stay with her where she and her own could be properly cared for. Tammeia was given the Habite by natural succession as well as the council seat attached to it. The original owner didn't have a daughter or an heir.

The trip to the Habite was a strain enough on Tammeia. After all, it was a quarter of the world away and most of that distance over water. Even though it was made without incident, it made Tammeia very weary. When she was tired she didn't reason very well and she would have unexplained feelings. That's what she called her frustration and exhaustion. But instead of admitting that she was just tired and needed some rest, she insisted that something terrible was going to happen. She would try hard to keep busy so she could avoid thinking of things, but that just made her more tired and her condition began to spiral down into depression.

At first, she felt the people of the new Habite, who were loyal to its former owner, would hate her and do her harm. But when that proved wrong — for she was very well received and respected — she displaced the idea with the new life she felt growing inside of her. 'My baby will be born sick.' She would say constantly. As her time grew nearer she changed her doomed forecast to 'My baby will be still born. My baby will be dead.'

Sometimes she would talk about her second child, the one that came before this one. That child was struck sick and died early in life. She kept remembering and reliving those black days. She got so involved in her self-made pains, that she refused to eat or sleep and she became very sick. Her weakness fed her feelings of doom and the doom fed the weakness until Tammeia's condition almost brought her fears to fruition. She became so weak and thin that her body could barely support the own life functions, never mind those of her unborn child. Her womb began to cry the red tears of a dying baby.

Eisen thought of how Tammeia tried to hide the problem and then told Meem about it as if it were nothing. Meem didn't tell the others. Being a birthing-woman, she knew that if the baby was going to die, she could do little to stop it. She had to work on helping the mother survive.

To this end, she hounded Tammeia all or her waking day to keep off her feet. She was constantly feeding her sweet foods. The sweetness often covered up an herb or mineral medicine. She gave Tammeia warm drinks of soothing milks and bid her drink them before they cooled; making sure every drop was gone. Tammeia began to recover her strength, but this didn't drown her feeling of doom. Eisen recalled how she told Jgar she would die that very night. By then, everyone was so used to hearing her songs of death they felt it best to make light of them. He ignored her, not realizing she meant she would die at her own hand. Tammeia had planned to kill herself with poison korfray root that night.

Eisen remembered seeing her double over and fall to her knees in a rush of blood. He remembered thinking that she must have hit her head on the base of the stairs she was passing when she fell. When he reached her, she was already unconscious. He wasn't sure what happened until he saw the pieces of root still in her teeth. Eisen was sure she would never wake up again.

While the woman floated in unconsciousness, her body ejected a child, small and yellow — Alana. She looked so fragile that a touch could rob her of her new life. For five days, Tammeia lay in her stupor, not knowing that the fragile life she gave birth to, nursed on another woman's breast.

Eisen was the first to see Tammeia when she awoke. He remembered how she touched her abdomen and realized she was no longer with child. He remembered how she didn't ask him what happened. She didn't even cry. She just walked past him to the window and made ready to jump to her death.

He cleared his mind of those thoughts. "That was a long time ago," he said half out loud. "She was under a lot of stress back then." He shook his head sharply and turned his thoughts to his work.

He had to work fast. He wanted the Corays out of his Ladies home and out of her life as soon as possible.

Chapter 23

Alana was the first to notice Seth was gone. She had woken up early and looked around for something to do. There was nothing going on in her room, so she went into the room where the Keeper slept, and found that his mat was not rolled up, yet it was empty. She looked around for him, but he was nowhere. Then she noticed the open window.

Alana pushed a nearby chair under the sill and climbed on it. The noise she made caused a few of the room's occupants to raise their heads from sleep. Outside the window a field of mossy grasses stretched beyond Alana's visual capabilities. "No Seth there." She closed the window and climbed down.

"What are you doing up there, Alana?" Gabriel sat straight on his mat rubbing his tired eyes.

"I just wanted to look out." She scurried down to sit with him, but at the last second, almost as if it were an after thought, Alana sat on Seth's mat and pulled at his covers.

"They'll notice he left without rolling his mat," she thought.

"I bet you didn't know I slept here last night," she lied with pride. "I had a nightmare and came in her to sleep with Seth."

The others in the room began to wake up and start their daily routines.

"I bet you didn't even see me come in, or hear me snore," She laughed. Inside she knew Seth wasn't in the house. He had run away. Just like the people Gabriel told her about. She also knew in her heart that she had to keep anyone else from finding out. She really didn't know why Seth had run away, but it didn't matter. He was gone.

"Alana, don't open windows anymore. You could have fallen out," Alyx scolded her. "And Alana," he paused then cleared his throat pompously, "I saw you come in last night. You could've awoken the dead you were so noisy."

She smiled. "I'm sorry, Alyx. I didn't mean to cause you so much grief," she said sarcastically, trying to sound as old as him.

At almost twelve years old, Alyx was cold eyed and stiff lipped. He bore an indisputable resemblance to his mother, Pouchetia. She and her consorts gave Alyx a lot of responsibility, which he took willingly and dutifully. At twelve he was not a man but far from a boy. Alyx, like his mother, was putting up with the Sheens. He had no idea that he would never be away from them again.

"Where is Seth?" a different voice questioned Alana. She turned red and her face felt hot, but she anticipated the question and was ready.

"He said he had to go to the bathroom. He'll be back soon. If he doesn't find something else to do first." She paused to take a much-needed breath. "Maybe you'll see him at morning meal." She rolled up the Keeper's mat loosely and darted out the door.

The morning dining room was full of people. Alana skipped innocently in and grabbed some fruit and a piece of yellow cake. "No time to sit down," she thought to herself, then rambled out of the hall as quickly as she came in.

The first place she looked was the game room. Its long highly polished walls glistened. Even though the room had no windows, it gave the appearance of being airy and full of daylight. The room was empty now because the anhabit occupants were all busy with their morning activities. No one had time for play yet, except for Alana.

She forgot her search for a little while. Instead, she looked around and found a bowl. She emptied the bowl's contents and ran with it to one end of the room and put it down. She turned it and slid it to the right a little. Convinced it was where she wanted it, she ran to a pair of glass doors on the left side of the room. Behind the doors was a small closet filled with game equipment. She fumbled through a few things and found the pieces of a game called lober. She pulled out three heavy balls and turned them until she found the tabs and poured their contents into a dish of sand.

For a little while she tossed the emptied balls at the bowl, trying her best to get them in it. Then when that got tiring, she ran to the top of the stairs, climbed on the banister and slid down. She ran up the stairs and slid down again and again. She ran up the stairs and down the banister pretending she was a pokest running through the trees. When her game again began to bore her, she returned to her search.

He wasn't in the story room. He wasn't in the small room with the blue walls. He wasn't in the front or backyard. He wasn't anywhere in the house. "He's not here," she said to herself. Alana smiled because she had known that already and her search confirmed it.

She returned to the kitchen. Almost everyone had finished eating and her steps echoed in the hall's emptiness. She grabbed another piece of cake and turned to run out.

"Alana."

She followed the voice. "What do you want, Alyx?" She stood leering at him with her hand on her hip trying to look annoyed.

"Where have you been all morning? I'm supposed to look after you!" he snapped sternly.

"I've been here."

"No you haven't," the boy said harshly, but didn't press the issue. "Have you seen Seth?"

"Yes. He was in the game room." Alana pointed in that general direction.

"I'll go get him. You get to the meeting hall. You're going to be put to work today." Alyx walked away. Alana turned her nose up and galloped out of the room.

When Alyx got to the game room it was empty. He decided to make one more thorough check of the house then report to his mother.

The meeting had started by the time Alana opened the door to the hall. She entered quietly, sat down on a fur rug and tried to catch up with what was said. Some woman was speaking of assignments. Something to do with schooling, Alana gathered.

"...The next course of study will be that of physical endurance. You'll be made strong so you can survive through the journey ahead of you," the woman said.

"Journey," Alana moaned. "Not another Journey. I'm sick and tired of traveling unless it is to go home." She allowed herself to drop to her side. "I don't want to be on an equis back ever again."

Alana tugged on Gabriel's sash. "Come on, let's play," she whispered to him.

"I can't," he said shortly.

"Oh, Gabbie, come on. I have a great game. We can pretend we're pokests on the stairs."

"Pokest, you're not a pokest."

"Yes I am," Alana insisted. She imitated the sounds and movements of the animal.

"No, you're not. Besides, we can't play on the stairs. We'll get in trouble," Gabriel insisted

"Oh," Alana whined. "Come on, everyone is here. No one will know."

"But..."

"Shhh. Children, be quiet. I'm trying to hear Regime Renia, not you," one of the Torta boys snapped. Alana got up to leave.

"Alana," Gabriel called in a rather loud whisper. "Don't go yet. Here comes my mother." He pointed over her shoulder. She turned to see Pouchetia walking into the room. It was the first time Alana or anyone else in her group had glimpsed the Exoltaire's bright yellow hair and burning gold eyes. Alana lifted her gaze to see the towering figure above her.

Pouchetia pushed her hard to one side and strode past not even turning to see where the child she shoved landed. The Exoltaire walked to the center of the room, consorts behind her. She turned to the assembled crowd.

"Where is your Keeper, Sheen people?" Her voice echoed. Eyes darted from place to place. No one answered. "Where is the Keeper?" she said again. The air in the room seemed to dance back and forth with agitation.

Alana got up and walked forward. "I saw him in the game room," she said calmly.

"When?" The red headed consort asked.

"Earlier, after morning meal." She cleared her throat and looked at her friend Gabriel then back at Pouchetia. "He said he didn't feel well. Maybe he's gone somewhere to sleep." She turned her eyes away.

"Look for him everywhere in the house," the Exoltaire commanded then dismissed her consorts. They rushed off, each in a different direction. "If he's not found by night fall you will suffer child." Pouchetia took Alana's chin in her hand. The steadily upward pressure she applied made Alana's eyes well up with tears. "If you, like your mother, are a liar, then you will die. I promise." She dropped the child to the ground. No one moved to pick her up. Pouchetia gingerly stepped over Alana and walked out the door.

Gabriel followed her out and grabbed his mother's hand. Her stone set face melted and she smiled when she picked him up. "My brave young man. How are you?"

Gabriel didn't smile back. "What's wrong with Alana?" he asked innocently. "Was she bad?"

His mother put him down. "Yes, love. She is very bad."

"But I like her, mother. Maybe she did bad on accident." He trotted down the hall to keep pace with her.

"Not accident," she thought smugly, "birth defect. Born of Tammeia Sheen."

"Never mind her," she urged her son. "Go outside and get some air before it gets too hot."

Gabriel shrugged and trotted away.

Chapter 24

Seth slept well considering he had no mat to cushion the ground. When morning came, he got up and stretched. There was a stream of water outside the cave. He followed it with his eyes to where it went up the mountainside and disappeared into some rocks. It wasn't very much of a stream and when he cupped his hands under it he almost stopped its flow altogether. He splashed the cool water on his face then filled up his bottle. "Huh?" The Keeper froze. He felt something watching him. He turned slowly to find behind him, a pack of kenya. There were five in all. "Large ones," Seth thought. "Definitely not house pets." He started to move away from the animals. They paced towards him slowly, reflecting the same caution.

"Kenya," The Keeper said quietly so not to startle them. "Brother Kenya," he repeated in the ancient tongue of all Keepers. "You are my brothers. I'm a son of your mother soil."

The animals turned to each other, then back at Seth.

"We are brothers of the soil. Brothers of the hills, we are one." He raised his hands, palms facing forward to the kenya. One animal edged forward toward him. Its tail low. It darted back to the pack. Another reached forward then pulled back. Seth's foot found a loose rock and he stumbled. The animals jumped back and bared their teeth. Their low growling danced off Seth's neck hairs.

"Brothers, brothers," he whispered. The ancient language of the Keepers sounded like mystical music. "Come and be my brothers or go in peace." He dropped his hands.

The animals began to pace and whimper. Then slowly, one kenya made its way to Seth. It laid down at his feet and turned belly up in a gesture of friendly submission. The Keeper patted the animal's underside briskly. Another came to him, and then another. Soon all five kenya were at his feet or on his lap.

A big brown female kept nosing at his hip pouch. He opened it and offered its contents to her. She snubbed her nose at the berries and trotted away into the woods. A smaller tan and white kenya and a slightly smaller gray one noticed she was leaving and raced after her.

"Wait for your babies, mother," he called out.

Seth looked at the remaining two animals. The large black one he named Noir, which in Keeper's tongue meant 'night' and the fluffy yellow one he named Strat. The name Strat meant, "to travel," in Keeper's tongue. Even though the name really didn't make much sense as far as the animal was concerned, Seth found it strangely appropriate.

His new companions watched as he cut down some small trees and fashioned himself a bow and some arrows. He tested three boughs before he found one suitable to make into a bow. Now he just had to find something to use as a cord. There was a yapping sound in the forest and his new companions took off into the woods. "Alone once more." Seth shook his head and half laughed.

After much searching, he found a straight strong vine that he felt might make a good bowstring. He sat down at the mouth of the cave to string his weapon. There was a rustling in the brush. Seth readied himself for a fight but it wasn't necessary. It was mother kenya and her troop returning. Behind them they dragged a full-grown atakapy carcass. Seth was amazed. The animals laid it in front of him and started to tear away at it.

"I guess I won't be needing this today." He swung the bow over his shoulder.

He shared the kill with the pack, then napped with them in the shade of the cave through the heat. When Seth moved on, up the mountain, the big brown kenya he decided to name Hunter and her pack moved on with him.

He was nearing the crest of the mountain and so far he hadn't seen anything that would have caused the lights he had seen from the window of the anhabit. He decided to head to the left, back to the side that faced the Coray's. Hunter seemed reluctant to go left. She yapped and tried to lead Seth in the other direction. "Sorry, girl. I have to go this way," he explained and started to walk. To Seth's surprise, she and the others followed anyway.

The Keeper and his pack hadn't traveled to the left for long before he saw it. The Corays had built a whole village on the mountainside. Dozens of obviously temporary structures stood around a central fire pit. People moved back and forth between the cloth structures, involved in their daily routines. A small lake at the far end of the settlement was filled with playing children. The place was busy with life.

Seth moved out of hiding to the path that led down the hillock where he stood to the village below. Hunter growled and whimpered.

"Come with me, Hunter," he called to her.

She growled again, this time baring her teeth, then she dug in the soil and lay down.

"All right. Stay. I'll be back." He started on the path followed by Strat and the gray kit. Hunter yapped and jumped on the kit. Strat stopped. Seth looked back at Hunter. She looked at him, whimpered, then waked in a tight circle.

"All right. I'll wait here. But only for a little while."

She danced from side to side happily.

"I suppose you're right. I should wait until night fall." Seth agreed. He and the pack returned to the safety of the woods.

Chapter 25

"Come to order, Carlafs." The Exoltaire Touchea stood at the head of the oval table in the middle of Lumdon Hall. There was an empty chair to her right. "Where is Pouchetia?"

"I've sent someone for her. She should be here soon," another at the table said.

"Good."

"Touchea, what's the matter? Why have you called us to Council at such an odd time?" Breyan asked with concern.

"I'll tell everyone at one time, Breyan. Don't be alarmed. There's no danger."

"Pouchetia is here," a voice called from the doorway.

The Exoltaire Pouchetia Coray walked into the hall without stopping to acknowledge the High Exoltaire's presence. Instead she went straight to Tammeia.

"The Keeper you sent me is missing!" She said as she stared coldly at the Regime. "What did you send him to do? Run away to sabotage my Habite!"

Tammeia didn't have the words to answer.

"Well, Sheen woman, where is he!" Pouchetia demanded.

"Seth is gone? I don't know..." Tammeia trailed off into thought.

"What did you send him to do? Tell me, Sheen!" she demanded again.

"Send him? Not I. It's your people who are plotting against me!" the Regime cried.

"Tell my where he is or your Alana will die!"

Tammeia's eyes turned red with passion. "You will not touch my child or I'll..." She turned to Breyan. "Did you hear her? She threatened to kill my daughter! How does she get away with such things?

"Eisen!" Tammeia called to her consort who stood just outside the hall's doors. He came quickly. "Mount some riders for distance. Go to Pouchetia's bring back our people. Bring back my baby! Quickly! Go!"

"Wait." Touchea waved her hand in the air and everyone stopped and stood silently. "There'll be no one leaving and no one dying." She lowered her hands. "Pouchetia, will you sit and calm yourself?" She paused.

"Now, Ladies," Touchea said in a quiet voice, "what's your problem?"

"Her..." "She..." "people..." "Keeper!" Both women tried to talk at once. Touchea put her hand out to quiet Pouchetia and told Tammeia to start.

"Her people attacked two of my Carlafs at knife point. They tried to kill them," Tammeia finally got out.

"If my people wanted to kill them, then they'd be dead," Pouchetia snapped.

"Exoltaire, watch your place." Touchea pointed a stern finger at her. "You will both stop all hostilities now."

"But I'm not plotting against Pouchetia. I've not been hostile towards her or her people," Tammeia said.

"Then where's your Keeper?" Pouchetia sneered.

"I don't know!" Tammeia shouted back.

"Tell me, liar, or Alana will suffer," Pouchetia said coldly.

Touchea placed herself between the two women. "No. Alana will not be touched. Tammeia is speaking the truth. She doesn't know where the Keeper is." The High Exoltaire sat down at the head of the oval table. "Now if you can stop acting like spoiled children then I can get on with this meeting."

Tammeia first, then Pouchetia took their places at the table.

"Welcome, daughters of the sky..." Touchea sang the opening prayer and the meeting began.

"Our Netrin friends will be arriving sooner than we had expected. Due to an error in how we interpreted Netrin time, there was a slight miscalculation. The Netrin sky vehicles are very close. They'll be landing here within a day's time."

"One day!" Breyan Exclaimed. "That's more than seventy days sooner than expected."

"What about my crops? They're still growing in the field that was chosen," another Exoltaire said.

"Yes, my field is full of crops too," another said.

"And the people aren't ready. Surely they can't go now." Pouchetia added.

"I am aware of all these problems. But it seems the Netrins have their own ideas of what would be an ideal time to go."

"Where are we going to put them until we're ready?" Breyan questioned

"Not in my Habite. Not for that long," a woman said. Other voices echoed in agreement.

"Yes, Carlafs. It's obvious they can't stay with us for that long. They would learn too much about our system of realms. It could make them quite a threat in the future. But until our people are ready, they'll have to wait somewhere." The High Exoltaire looked at the woman on her left.

"Maldreya, how long before your trainees are ready?"

"Do you mean thoroughly ready or just marginally ready?" the woman replied.

"Ready enough to survive."

"Fifteen days at least," she said but she didn't seem sure.

"Can everyone accomplish the same in this time?"

A mumble broke out, but there were no direct objections.

"Then, Carlafs, we'll set the departure date for the morning of the sixteenth day, provided our Netrin friends comply. If any of you cannot make this deadline then see me well before it." Touchea put her hand over a polished red control stone that was embedded in the table. The doors to the hall closed and locked with an audible click. A warm red glow emanated from the walls.

"Now, on handling the Netrins..." For no real reason, Touchea spoke just above a whisper.

Chapter 26

Jgar sat on a large, smooth stone near the remains of the last night's fire. Sharl was searching the edges of the clearing for some green plants to feed the equis. Rovear slept on the ground near Jgar's feet. Jgar didn't wake him even though Sharl urged him to. Rovear had led the equis on foot a long way during the day before and then kept watch when they stopped. He needed the rest.

Something caught Jgar's eye. He looked up to see what it was. A silver and yellow streak moved steadily towards rising Kai's bright disk. It overlapped the star and moved across it leaving a heat wave trail that appeared to cut the sky just above the horizon. He watched it for quite a while. By the time Rovear woke up, it was just a faint distant glow.

"Ah, Rovear, you're awake."

"I think I am." He stretched. "Yes, I'm awake."

"You missed it. I think I just saw a comet."

"Where?" Rovear scanned the sky.

"It's gone now."

The Exoltairetive opened a pack and pulled out a rag.

"Looking for food, Rovear?"

"No." He wet the rag with the mineral water and gave it to Jgar. "Here, wash your arm."

"Actually my arm feels fine." Jgar flexed it slightly.

"You should be wearing the sling I made you. You're going to pull your stitches out like that."

"You sound like an old lady," Jgar teased.

"Who's an old lady?" Sharl interrupted as she walked over to them.

"Don't worry. It's not you, little girl," Rovear laughed.

"Don't think so much or yourself, Rovear. After all you can't even find the camp," Sharl snapped back.

"I'll find the camp. It's not far away," he paused to think, "in that direction." He pointed to his left.

"Well, let's go then." She walked off to get the equis that was grazing on the plants she'd gathered.

"In time, Sharl. Why don't you take a nap? You'll feel much better after some sleep. Children need lots of rest," Rovear said with a grin.

"What, and have you fools leave me here!" she said loudly.

"There's nothing I would like more," Rovear sneered under his breath.

"Look, Rovear, Sharl. There's another comet. And still another." Jgar pointed to the sky wildly. "Look, at least three more!" he exclaimed.

"I don't know if they're comets," Rovear said with doubt.

"What else could they be?" Sharl said with worry.

"I don't know. But they don't have the kind of tails comets have," Rovear said uneasily.

"Well, maybe it's a meteor shower," Jgar said.

"Maybe?" Rovear echoed.

They watched for a while then with no answers, they got ready and moved on. All three traveled on foot with the equis trailing behind.

They had walked until Kai faded to dark and Sola was setting when Jgar turned to Rovear. "Tell me the truth. Are we lost?"

"No. I just need some time," Rovear answered after taking a deep breath.

"What good will that do?" Sharl snapped.

"Once it's dark..." he began.

"We become a three part feast for the handra-can," Sharl interjected sarcastically.

Rovear gave her a hard stare. He knew when he first met her he wouldn't like her, and now he was having doubts if he could stand her at all.

"Once it's dark," he repeated with added formality. "I will be able to tell by the stars which direction will take us back to camp."

When darkness fell Rovear read the stars and plotted the night's journey. The sky was alight with yellow and silver streaks but Rovear had seen so many of them that night, they no longer impressed him. With the coordinates set in his mind, the Exoltairetive set off, the equis in tow, with Jgar and Sharl upon its back. After a while, they rounded the hill and saw the fire of their camp.

"Jgar, wake up. We're there." Rovear patted his leg.

"Where?" He opened his heavy eyes.

"At camp. It's just across the field."

Jgar jumped off the animal. Sharl startled but didn't say anything.

"Get on Jgar. You can ride in," Rovear urged.

"Then you get on, too. We'll all ride in. The field will be crossed quicker at an equis' pace."

Rovear agreed. He pushed Sharl back and climbed on in front of her.

"Excuse me, Sharl," Jgar said as he urged her to slide even further back. She was too tired to protest and moved back again. With a little difficulty, Jgar mounted the equis between her and Rovear. Sharl leaned forward on his back. She was still drifting in a shallow sleep.

"Sharl, wake up." He pushed her back rather harshly. "We're near the camp."

When she was awake, they decided to head full canter to the camp. Sharl grabbed Jgar's shoulders tightly. Her touch bothered him.

"Jgar! Something doesn't feel right!" she yelled over the roar of the equis' hoof beats. "Jgar! Tell Rovear to stop!"

"Nonsense!" he yelled over his shoulder.

The equis galloped as fast as it could across the field. It stumbled a stride, jerking the riders forward. There was a rustling of movement from the right. Jgar heard a string snap then the sound of ripping flesh and of a projectile hitting then piercing bone. The equis fell on its side and slid. Its ear wrenching cries of agony echoed in the night air.

Jgar lay on his back in the dirt, Rovear near him. Sharl lay dazed on the other side of the equis. The animal wallowed and howled.

"What happened?" Sharl screamed.

"A trap, I think!" Rovear yelled back. Sharl got to her hands and knees then began to stand up.

"Don't move Sharl!" Jgar shouted. "There may be more traps. Let me check it out first."

She quickly and carefully sat down.

"Look at this, Jgar." Rovear drew his attention to the dying animal. He pointed to the ends of a long thin projectile that stuck out of the equis on both sides. Blood was everywhere.

Jgar peered through the darkness. "Clear across," he murmured.

"Faithful beast," Rovear said as he slit the animal's jugular vein. It died quickly.

Rovear pulled at the arrow shaft. It didn't move. "Here, help me with this," he said.

Jgar joined him. They pulled at the back end of the arrow. It still didn't move.

"It must have teeth. Maybe we can get it from the front and pull it though." Jgar took off the sling that hung loosely around his neck and wrapped it around the arrowhead then pulled. The tip of the projectile snapped off. Jgar examined it as closely as he could in the dark. "It's a Torta weapon."

"What?" Rovear was lost in his thoughts and didn't hear him.

"I said, this is a Torta weapon."

"Torta? Then it's from camp."

"Yes," Jgar said with a calmness that didn't reflect his true feelings.

"They too, must have met the handra-can," Rovear said quietly.

"I'm going to project to camp and find out if everyone's all right and if there are any more traps. If there are, I'll find out where they are." Jgar readied to leave his body.

"No." Rovear grabbed him hard to break his concentration.

"Why? If there are more traps we have to find out where they are."

"You can't leave your body," Rovear stressed the word can't.

"Hey! What about me!" Sharl still sat obediently where Jgar had told her to.

"Wait, tell me why soon. First I have to get to her," Jgar said to Rovear then turned his attention to Sharl.

"Sharl, crawl over here. But be very careful of any cords or vines you might come across," Jgar instructed. "Go slowly. We know the land on this side of the equis is safe. Come this way."

Sharl put her right hand in front of her and shifted her weight onto it. The she followed it with her knee. She moved her left hand and knee. Again she lifted her right hand, found good ground and put it down. She followed it with her knee, then again, her left hand and knee. Once more she lifted her right hand and reached forward. Her fingers found a fine cord at about knee height.

"Jgar! Rovear!" she called, her voice shaking. "There's a cord here. It's another trap I think."

Rovear looked at the dark form that was Sharl and followed with his eyes to where he figured the cord must go. There were only trees at the other end.

"No way of telling where the actual trap is," he mumbled.

"Sharl, can you fit under it without touching it?" Rovear squinted to see her better.

"I don't know," she answered. "Maybe I should spring it. Do you think if I lay down, it'll pass over me?"

"With your luck it will, Rovear." Jgar teased, hoping to relieve some tension.

"With her luck," Rovear replied dryly.

"No, don't touch it. Try to slide yourself under it." Jgar strained to see her. It didn't help. "Be very careful not to touch it."

Sharl lied down on her back, held her breath and slowly pulled herself under the trip cord.

"Are you past it yet?" Rovear asked. It was impossible for him to tell. The night was too dark.

"I think so, but I'm going to stay this way until I reach you."

"I'm going to go get her." Jgar walked to the edge of where he felt it was safe. Sharl was still eight or ten paces away from him. He felt around at the ground below his feet. No trip cords. He took another step forward and felt around again. "Still no cords," he thought with relief. He did this five times before he felt he was close enough to grab her.

"Give me your hand, lady. I'll pull you to where it's safe."

Sharl cautiously raised her hand as high as she could. Jgar couldn't reach it. He leaned forward. She inched toward him and he managed to grab her fingertips and hook them with his own.

"Hold tight. I'm going to pull you in." The Regimitive took a deep breath and pulled Sharl towards him. He heard a snap before he felt the tug of the cord. Jgar threw himself to the ground. Sharl screamed.

"Jgar, are you all right!" Rovear yelled almost immediately.

"I didn't see that one," he answered. "You're all right, aren't you?" He asked Sharl as he helped her to her feet.

"I think it grazed me," she said quietly. "On my head, I think?" She wobbled. Jgar grabbed her arm to steady her. "I can walk by myself. You almost got me killed!" She pushed him away and stomped off then stopped abruptly. "Are you sure there are no traps on this side?"

"At least from where we are to where Rovear is," Jgar answered.

Sharl nodded. As she walked to where Rovear was, Jgar noticed her dark shadow was not quite steady.

"We're going to have to stay here until daylight," Rovear announced. "We can't take the chance that there are more traps."

"Agreed," said Jgar.

"Yes, agreed," Sharl echoed.

"Are you sure you're all right?" Jgar was concerned.

"Yes, it only skinned me."

"Let me see." Rovear stood close to Sharl. Even so, the night was dark and he couldn't see any detail in her face. "Here, put my hand where it hurts." Rovear had appointed himself the group nurse. She put his hand on the left side of her head.

"Does it hurt?" he asked as he poked the spot.

"Yes, but not terribly."

He rubbed the area with his index and fore finger, then rubbed their tips over his thumb. They felt dry. He put them to his tongue. There was no taste of blood.

"You'll be all right, Sharl." He pulled his hand away with a jerk. "Just don't touch it. Let it heal."

"I'm going into the bush to get some fire wood," Jgar announced.

"No you're not." Rovear stopped him.

"We have to build a fire." Jgar pulled away.

"Jgar, think! If this field is full of traps then those woods are suicide!" Rovear said with force.

"We have to have a fire," Sharl uttered, her voice still a bit shaky.

"We can burn..." Rovear looked around him but found nothing useful. "We can burn the equis."

"Be serious. You can't set the equis on fire. And even if you could, the smell of meat will attract every animal in the brush," Jgar remarked.

"Then what do you suggest we burn, Jgar?" Sharl questioned nervously.

"I don't know. I guess we'll have no fire tonightm," Jgar answered.

"Then we'll take shifts watching so the other two can rest." Rovear sat down.

"I'll watch first." Jgar sat near him.

"No, I will. You try to sleep," Rovear said.

"Well one of you can watch. I'm going to sleep." Sharl lay down and closed her eyes. Not long later, she was sound asleep.

"Can she sleep anywhere?" Rovear broke the night's silence with his question.

"It would seem so." Jgar put his arm around Rovear's shoulders. The closeness he felt for Rovear grew with every day. They were, Jgar thought, truly brothers. "I don't know how after nearly getting killed, she sleeps so soundly. Somehow she can put the day's events out of her head. It's like there's nothing real to her." Jgar looked up at the stars.

"Maybe she'll get a good taste of reality in the morning," Rovear said smugly.

"Why?" Jgar eyes opened wide.

"The arrow,"

"Yes?"

"It didn't break the skin, but it pulled out quite a bit of her hair."

"Will it be noticeable?" Jgar asked with concern.

"I sure hope so," Rovear laughed.

Jgar laughed too. "Maybe she'll learn that beauty is something easily stolen. I look forward to seeing her face when the others notice it." His chuckles faded.

"Do you think the others are all right, Rovear?" Jgar was looking directly at him but couldn't see any facial details.

"Well someone had to build that fire," he said then turned away.

"I'll go see." Jgar closed his eyes.

"No! You can't!" Rovear's words were quick and sharp.

"Don't worry. I will be right back."

"No. It's not worry." Rovear took a deep breath and let it out slowly. "Jgar, when my Carlaf heard your people were coming she set up a kind of defense system against internal attack. She made it impossible to take to the projection planes from anywhere other than the confines of a building. You can only travel from one anhabit to another anhabit. You can't leave or return to any other place."

"Why?" Jgar questioned.

"So that your people will always be under a watchful eye. So they can't plot or scheme to attack us."

"What happens to those who try to project?"

"They become nonexistent. They die instantly," Rovear said bluntly.

"And no one warned us?" Jgar was getting upset.

"It wasn't necessary. What would any of your people be doing outside of an anhabit's limits?"

"They'd have no reason, normally," Jgar said quietly.

"Correct. So Pouchetia didn't think it was necessary to bother anyone." Rovear fidgeted.

"Or get herself in trouble with the Council," Jgar added crossly.

"Or that," Rovear affirmed meekly.

Chapter 27

Under the cover of darkness, Seth and his pack headed down the mountainside. He made sure to stay away from the well-worn footpath so he wouldn't be seen. It was a dark night and odds were good he wouldn't be spotted anyway, but he didn't want to take the chance. He walked slowly and carefully in the low shrubs.

Candlelight glowed through the cloth walls of some of the village's structures. The others were dark. A roaring fire towered out of the center pit of the camp. Hundreds of people sat round it. Most of them just talked. Some were singing.

Before the pack broke from the cover of the brush, Seth stopped. "Hunter," he called in Keeper's tongue. Hunter listened carefully as Seth spoke then she darted into the dark. Seth had to cross the lit part of the village before he could find a place to hide. The fire pit wasn't far to his right. No doubt someone near it would see him and he didn't want that.

"Yoelwooo! Yoelwoooo!" Hunter howled at the top of her voice. "Yowlwoooo! Yoelwooooo!" She edged closer to the village perimeters yapping and howling all the while.

"Yoelwooo! Yeolwooo! GRRRRRR! Yeolwwoooo!"

"That kenya is awfully close," a blonde man said to the woman who sat near him.

"Yoelwoooo! Grrrrrr, yoel, yowlwoooo!"

"You're right. It is very close," the woman replied.

"I'll be back. I'm going to see about it." The man got up and walked away from the fire. The night was dark and his eyes were used to staring into the bright flames of the campfire. Unadjusted as they were, they were useless to him. He made loud rustling noises in the brushes. "Any kenya with half a mind is afraid of people. This should scare it off," he thought confidently.

"Grrrrrr." The growl came from behind him. He turned but he didn't see the kenya. Hunter, with her eyes naturally equipped to see in the dark, saw him though. She jumped at the back of his ankle and tugged. He yelled out as he fell to the ground. Hunter retreated at full speed into the woods.

The man's cries drew all eyes in his direction. People ran to the woods to help him. Seth slipped by unnoticed.

"It bit me, then ran!" Hunter's victim repeated with disbelief as they brought him into a tent for treatment.

After an unsuccessful search of the brush near the village, everyone calmed down and all was again quiet. As the night went on the people petered back to their tents until all but a few were left. Seth ventured from his hiding place to check out the surroundings.

A small group of men remained awake, watching the fire.

"Camp watchmen," Seth concluded. "I'll have to be careful they don't see me." The Keeper stood in the shadows, thinking of what these people could be doing in the hills and trying to find the best approach to find out, when the decision was made for him. Someone lit a candle in a tent behind him. Its light went unnoticed by him, but it silhouetted his figure perfectly.

"You. Come here," one of the men called from the fireside when he noticed Seth's outline against the tent's bright backdrop. "It's all right. Come here and share the fire," he called again.

"Hum..." Seth mumbled. His first reaction was to turn and run. If these men where Exoltairetives, they would be consorts to Pouchetia. Maybe they would recognize him.

"Come on. The fire feels good...um..." the man paused waiting for a name.

"Nyllative," Seth answered. He hoped his station would be enough. The Keeper took a deep breath and decided there was only one way to handle the situation. He walked with confidence to the fire.

"Well, Nyllative," the blond man said. "What keeps you up at this time of night?"

Seth tried to say as little as possible. "Not tired," he replied.

"Artin, make sure first thing in the morning I tell Kasha she doesn't work her consorts hard enough," he laughed.

"Yoelwooo!" A howl came out of the distance.

"There's that kenya again," the man said. "I wonder what's wrong with it?"

"It must be mad," Artin replied.

"It must be a Sheen," a third Exoltairetive laughed. "After all, what other kind of creature would bite and run before its opponent had a chance to fight back?"

"Only a Sheen is that low," Artin said. Seth held his tongue.

"I can't wait until we get rid of them altogether. The world will be all the better." Artin spat on the ground. "If I had my way, we'd kill them all tonight."

"Patients, brother. Have faith in your Carlaf," the first snickered. "She'll kill them all, in good time."

"Starting with the hag Tammeia and her people," the third added.

Seth shifted uneasily. The Exoltairetives sensed his uneasiness. "What's wrong, Nyllative. Your stomach too weak for death?" Artin asked.

Seth didn't answer.

"We'll have to make sure this man draws first blood." He turned to Seth. The fire light reflected off the Keeper's black hair. He was amazed that the Corays didn't take notice of it. But by some stroke of luck they didn't. Maybe they thought he was wearing a hood of some kind to keep warm against the cool night air.

"Soon we'll ride down from these hills, brave Nyllative and stalk my Lady's anhabit by night. When we reach the pen where she keeps those Sheen animals, we'll kill them in their sleep.

"Except you, brother," the man laughed. They were obviously making sport of Seth. "You'll wake the hag child, Tammeia's blood, and you'll cut her throat and watch her die. Then you'll be strong." The Exoltairetives laughed hysterically. "I'm sure Pouchetia would give you a grand reward for such a great deed." Everyone but Seth laughed uncontrollably. Seth just walked away.

"Do you think he believed us?" Artin said between laughs and breaths.

"No, I don't think so," one of his companions laughed. "If he does, we'll hear from Kasha in the morning."

"Besides, even if he does, who in their right mind would punish us for talking about killing Sheens." The thought was ridiculous and the men laughed some more.

"Kill my people," Seth muttered to himself. "They will not!" he repeated over and over again as he retreated into the woods.

He was greeted by Hunter, the two kits, Strat and Noir. "Hunter," He patted her in a friendly way. She lay at his feet. The kits wrestled playfully in the dark. "Hunter," he repeated, "what would you do to another kenya that was going to kill your kits?" He spoke mainly to himself. Hunter cocked her head. Since he spoke in common tongue she didn't understand.

"If another pack was going to kill your kits, Hunter my friend," this time he spoke in Keeper's tongue, "what would you do?"

The kenya jumped to her feet and yapped with barred teeth.

"Yes, my friend, you're right." He stroked the tuft of hair between her ears. "You are very right." Seth and the pack disappeared into the darkness of the deep woods.

At daybreak, Seth was up cutting wood and fashioning arrows. He found a smooth stone and worked his knife to a fine sharp edge. The pack ate fresh meat Hunter had caught and slept most of the afternoon in the shade of the trees. As night began to fall, Seth was just finishing fastening sharp pieces of bone from the afternoon's kill to his arrows.

The fire in the village wasn't at full burn yet and the people, for the most part, were in their shelters. Seth spoke to Strat then he and Noir took off down the hill. There was some commotion in the village. A few minutes later Seth saw two burning dots running in different directions.

"Good boys!" the Keeper cheered. "Run!"

Strat held the log he had stolen from the fire tightly in his teeth. Its flame blew back on his tender ears. The taste of charcoal burned on his prehensile tongue. When he reached the large tent that Seth pointed out to him, he dropped the log as close to it as he could. The cloth wall lit up with blue and yellow flames. Strat ran around the flaming structure and out of the village. He didn't run up the hill where he had come from. Instead, he ran up the opposite bank, just in case he was followed. He would rejoin the others later.

Noir dropped his log and ran. The structure where he dropped it burst into flames. A woman and two small children ran out screaming. They blocked his path. He darted around them. A burning figure let out an echoing yell and fell in front of him. He jumped over the thing. The flames singed his belly fur. There was a building if front of him. He was blocked.

He jumped to the left. Several people with knives and sticks ran after him. A knife flew by his ears. He heard it slash the wind, but it missed him. He ran in an uneven zigzag. Each time he turned he looked for a way out, but there was nowhere. In front of him was only the lake.

He reached the water's edge. To the right, tents burned in brilliant yellow flames. To the left, men ran toward him. From behind, came more people with knives and sticks. He went the only way he could go. He dove into the water.

Kenya are not good swimmers and Noir was no exception. He swam well enough to keep his head above water but with very little speed. The men were coming. He kicked his legs faster and faster but he moved forward slowly.

"Splashing in the water! They are coming!" The kenya's heart pounded with fear. His pursuers were beating the surface with their sticks. Noir tried to swim faster but it only caused his head to go under water. He struggled to the surface. There was a dull slap on his hindquarters and he plunged under again. Someone had hit him with a stick. His feet touched bottom.

Traction — his feet had traction. He began to run under the water. It was slow, but it was faster than swimming. He pushed off with his hind legs, bounded forward and wiggled to get his front end back down again. As if in slow motion, his paws hit the muddy bottom. He pushed off again. This time he came up to the surface for air. In that brief moment when his head was above water he tried to look back at his perusers but he couldn't see them. All he could see was the splashing behind him. He dived back down. His front paws hit bottom, then his hind paws hit. He gave a kick to push himself forward. A knife was through him before his hind paws even left the muddy bottom. His blood oozed to the surface.

Hunter stood a quarter way up the hill. From the protection of a nearby tree, Seth shot arrows at anyone he could get in his sight. He already killed seven men and women and wounded many more. Hunter yapped and jumped feverishly. "I know," Seth called down to her. "It's time." He jumped out of the tree and ran, knife in hand, into the panic stricken, burning village.

The first person Seth met was one of the Exoltairetives from the night before. The man swung out at Seth with a heavy staff. Seth dodged it, came in close, and slit the man's throat. The Keeper grabbed a flaming log from the fire and lit two or three more tents before the rest of the camp's defenses knew he was there. They ran after him, their clothes still wet. Seth threw the burning log at them. They jumped back in surprise. He grabbed the dead man's staff and swung it madly. Hunter attacked the men from behind. They turned to face the new attacker. Seth seized the opportunity and swung out hard with the staff, crushing the back of one man's head. He struck at another and missed. The sound of screaming and the smell of burnt flesh and hair was sickening. Seth's eyes watered because of the acrid smoke bellowing from the burning tents. He began to cough. They were on him in a second's time. Hunter ran off, up the hill into the woods.

The Corays decided not to kill him right away. Instead, they were going to beat him then bring him to Pouchetia for questioning. Besides they had to get the village under control before they had time to deal with him.

The Village burned around them causing a roaring that was almost unbearable. Suddenly, there was a brilliant light above them. It pierced the smoke and made the flames from the burning tents seem dull. Soon it was apparent to Seth that the sound he heard wasn't the fires around him roaring, but whatever that thing was above them.

The Corays dropped their weapons; their mouths open in awe. Even Seth stood there dumbfounded for a moment, eyes wide, looking up. Then it dawned on him, and he realized no one was guarding him. They were all distracted by whatever it was. He took off up the hill.

He managed to get to the top of the rise and into the shelter of the thick brush before they noticed he was gone. A small group of men and women ran after him, but the course they chose took them well away to the left.

The brilliant, yellow light that was over head minutes ago now blazed and burned over the face of the mountain, between it and the Exoltaire's anhabit. Seth covered his eyes with his hands and squinted out between his fingers. The sky in front of him was blinding yellow - white. He looked up as high as he could. Behind the light was something black and silver. The silver was as bright as the light below it and the black as dark and absorbing as the night sky could ever be. It was if Kai were falling to the ground.

Seth was distracted by a rustling near him. "Damn, they found me," he pulled out his knife. "Strat," Seth said with relief. It was only the kenya. The animal approached with its head low and its tail between its legs.

"Strat, friend." Seth pulled the kenya near and hugged him. "You did well for me." He rubbed the animal's side. "I'm glad to see you, friend." He spoke some of his thoughts in Keeper's tongue, others in common tongue. "Do you see that light?"

The animal wouldn't look where Seth pointed. The light and noise obviously scared it.

"That light is direct from heaven. That light saved me to finish my quest." He noticed how scared the kenya was, so he offered it his lap. Strat was rather large and heavy for Seth's lap, but it made both feel more secure.

"They'll regret the day they decided to kill my people," Seth said. "They'll pay for trying to kill my pack," he repeated in Keeper's tongue.

The animal looked at him. It could see the fire that burned in the man's eyes. Seth still stared at the sky and the black and sliver object with the glowing yellow bottom as it got closer to the ground on the other side of the mountain and out of his sight. He watched it until it was only a glow over the mountain's ridge. He still had no real idea what it was, but it didn't scare him.

Strat's lips rolled back revealing his gleaming white teeth and he let out a low steady growl.

"I knew they'd find me," Seth said to himself. "Come, Strat. Let's get away from here. We don't want to meet a Coray empty handed." He picked up his staff and left as quietly as only a Keeper can. His pursuers never even knew he had been there.

Chapter 28

"Alana, tell me where Seth is," Palray pleaded. "If you don't tell, Pouchetia will hurt..." He cleared his throat. "She'll be very upset. You know what your mother said. We have to cooperate with the Corays. We all have to be good. You don't want her to hear about this, do you? So just tell me where Seth is and I promise no one will tell her."

"I don't know where he is," the child replied.

"You must know. You saw him last," he urged her. "Don't you remember? Think."

"I don't remember because I don't know," she insisted.

"Was he in the play room?"

"Ummm." She rubbed her arms nervously.

"Well, was he?" Palray insisted she tell.

"No," she whispered.

"The meal room then?" he questioned.

"No!" she said with agitation and began to cry. "No! I don't know! Stop asking me."

"Alana, if you refuse to tell me, then Pouchetia will find him first. And when she does, she might hurt him for hiding," he explained calmly.

"He's not here," she whispered.

"I know he's not here. Where is he?" Palray said with agitation.

Alana struggled in her mind. Should she defy what her heart told her to do? She didn't feel she should tell.

"Little one, tell me. I won't tell anyone," he said with a forced sense of calmness.

"No one at all?" Alana looked at Palray with uncertainty.

"No one," he promised.

"Seth's gone," she said quietly.

"I know he's gone. But what I need to know is where did he go." The frustration showed in his eyes.

"He's just gone." Alana couldn't explain more.

"Is he in the house?"

"No!" Alana snapped sharply. "I said he's gone!"

138

"Did he say anything before he left?" He turned her to face him directly.

"No!" She pushed by him. "I don't think so."

"When did he leave? Which way did he g..." Palray stopped short because Alyx walked into the room.

"I think he's in the kitchen," Alana lied. "I'll go and see." She trotted out the door.

"Who?" Alyx asked.

"Un...just one of the Torta boys," Palray answered. Alyx scrutinized him with cold eyes, then headed out to follow Alana.

"Alana," Alyx called.

"What?" she said without stopping.

"Who are you looking for?" He caught up to her.

She paused to think. "Gabriel."

"Gabriel, huh." Alyx grabbed her arm. "Come with me, Sheen child. I think my mother would like to talk to you."

"Don't touch me." She struggled and pulled free. He caught her again and dragged her down the hall. Her screams drew the attention of everyone in the area.

"What's the problem, Alyx?" The man with red hair stopped him.

"She knows where the Keeper is. She was telling another Sheen but saw me and ran," he explained and let Alana go. She brushed off her clothes and tried to look imposing.

"Come here," the man said. Alana obeyed reluctantly. He picked her up. She struggled a bit but she knew it was useless. The man brought her to see the Exoltaire Pouchetia.

"Carlaf, this Sheen child knows were the Keeper is." He put Alana down. Her shaking legs could barely support her. The Exoltaire sat facing a window with her back to Alana. Alana felt some relief that she didn't have to face the woman.

"Where is he then?" Her voice sounded surreal in its even tone.

Alana didn't answer.

"She didn't tell me. I thought you would best enjoy questioning her," the man said.

"Yes," Pouchetia whispered. "How nice." She turned slowly. Alana felt as if the floor below her was a moving, bending mass. Her spine felt like a tower of blocks ready to collapse. She held her muscles tight to stop the flow of fear, but it was no use. Her stomach turned and its contents welled up in her throat then settled back down.

"Well, scion of Tammeia, tell me. Where is he?"

Alana felt the heat of Pouchetia's burning gold eyes. "I don't know," she said meekly, her voice cracking.

"Liar!" Pouchetia struck the child with the back of her hand. Alana fell.

"Get up!" she said.

Alana didn't move.

"Get her up!" she commanded. The man picked Alana up. "Hold her, will you please," the Exoltaire said sweetly. "I don't want her to move."

"I'll give you one more chance." She stroked Alana's soft face, then pulled her hand back with a quick jerk. "Tell me!" She said and swung forward hitting Alana squarely on the side of the face. The red headed man held fast. Alana bled from the nose and mouth.

"He's gone," she sobbed.

"Where?" Pouchetia drew her hand back to strike again.

"I don't know," the child said meekly.

Alana flinched as Pouchetia's hand made contact for the third time. The child screamed and cried hysterically. The man shook her to stop her from struggling. Pouchetia grabbed Alana's face from under her chin. Alana's blood ran down the woman's arm. The child froze with fright.

"No more games Sheen demon." The Exoltaire put her down and pulled a thin sliver knife from a sheath on her calf. "You will tell me. Where did he go?"

"To...to.." Alana shivered. Her words were broken with tears. "Ho...home...He has...g...gone home."

Pouchetia tried to confirm what Alana said by touching her mind, but the mind of a child is inaccessible to an adult. Her attempt failed. "If you are lying again!" She drew a deep breath and released it slowly.

"Give me her hands," the woman commanded.
The man with the red hair held Alana's arms tight, palms up to Pouchetia. The Exoltaire placed the knife flat side down on Alana's bare wrist. "You have made me angry and I don't tolerate

children who make me angry." She slid the knife over Alana's wrist. "You, Alana sheen," the woman turned the blade so now the sharp edge rested on Alana's wrist, "I do not like. You're as worthless as the filth that bore you."

Alana looked at the shining knife's edge. Then at Pouchetia's burning gold eyes.

"Afraid of death are you?"

Alana tried to say something but couldn't utter a sound.

"Your death, for me, will be a sweet taste indeed."

Alana closed her eyes tight.

"That's right. Close you're eyes. Don't look. You don't have to see death to know it's come." She tightened her grip on the knife. Alana screamed and tried to pull away. Pouchetia drew the knife across Alana's fingertips, slow and deep.

Pouchetia nodded and the man let go. Alana stood in shock. Her tear filled eyes wide, looking at her bleeding fingers.

"Don't think you have won, little girl. Your life is still under my will and your death will be at my hands. I promise you." She turned back to the window.

"Bring her to her people, then assemble the women of the Habite," she said.

Alana didn't wait for the man to bring her back. She ran out the opened door.

"The Keeper has escaped," Pouchetia addressed a room full of women with light hair and their consorts. "He may be headed back to Tammeia's or he may have gotten lost trying. Whatever the case, I want him found and killed. I don't care how many of you it takes. I want him dead by night fall."

"Do you think he ran towards our camp in the hills?" Renia asked. "We'd have a lot to explain if Council found out we were keeping the Sheens away from our children."

"I don't think he'd run that way. He was going home. He would have headed in the direction he came here from," the Regime Dalta said.

"She's right. He's running in the other direction," Pouchetia agreed. "Who had the consort duty of gate watch that night?"

"Jerami. He reported no unusual events."

"Then, how did the Keeper get though?" Pouchetia demanded.

"If I may," Renia interrupted, "we sent three supply wagons to the gate area yesterday, after nightfall. He may have smuggled himself aboard one of them."

"Very possible. Dalta, get a group and investigate it."

"What were those wagons carrying anyway?" Pouchetia asked Renia.

"One carried gorlifm cloth. The other two carried some empty crates to carry back our share of the gate house's harvest."

"The cloth was made at the hill camp?" Pouchetia asked.

"Yes, even though the facilities are crude at best, they're managing to keep up one third of their quota for this time of year," Renia paused a long quiet pause. "Are you sure he didn't run for the hills?"

"Really, Renia. If you were a dull Sheen Keeper, where would you go?" Pouchetia said.

"And if he does find the camp?" she asked.

"If he does, it doesn't matter. How will he report to Council? If he tries to leave his body, he will be destroyed," the Exoltaire said with a smile.

"You know, he's probably tried already." Renia smiled.

"Then I want his dead flesh." The Exoltaire grinned back at the Regime. "Just to make sure." Pouchetia turned sharply. "Dalta?"

"Yes," The woman replied.

"Has the messenger from the hill camp come in today? It's the fourth day," Pouchetia asked.

Dalta checked a list she held then answered, "Yes. He came in this morning."

"Just to make certain, ask him if he's seen anyone. Make sure he's aware that the Keeper is loose." Pouchetia took a breath. "Now, if you would all take a look at this map." She pointed to a chart laying across the table top.

The women of the Habite gathered around the table to plan. They laid out a pattern of search for Seth that completely excluded the high hills and mountains.

When they where done, Pouchetia rolled up the map and spoke, "You all know what to do. Now go. I don't want that Keeper to see another day." Pouchetia dismissed the women.

"Oh, Renia," she called to the woman who was about to leave.

"What?" The Regime turned back.

"Even though I gave you the Cragin Plains and the foot hills of the Illu-Danchant Mountains, make sure not to go into the upper elevation. It's the birthing season for the handra-can and they will hunt by day to provide for their young this time of year. Keep yourself safe." She smiled a wicked smile. "If that Keeper make it to those hills he's as good as dead. Not even a Keeper can tame handra-can."

"There wouldn't even be any pieces of him left to find," Renia said. They both laughed and walked out together.

Chapter 30

"Eisen," Tammeia walked briskly into the story room, "come here. I need you."

Eisen put his book down. "Sorry, friends. I can't read today. Maybe we can finish it tomorrow."

"Awh," a few voices complained until another man picked up the book. "I'll read it." The group settled back down. Tammeia and Eisen exited the room and closed the door behind them.

"What's the matter?" he asked anxiously.

"Eisen, you have to get a group of your best people and ride to the Coray's. That wretch, Pouchetia, has threatened my child once too often."

He looked puzzled. "But what about what Touchea said?"

"Don't worry about that. Go there and bring her home."

"So," his gaze softened, "the Council has said she can come home."

"No. I don't care what the Council said. I want her home, now."

Despite the respect Eisen had for his Carlaf's decisions, he had to doubt her judgment lately. Ever since this whole thing started, she had been verging on depression again. "Alana will be fine. There's nothing Pouchetia can do to hurt her." He tried to sound reassuring.

"She never said she would hurt her. She claims she'll kill her!" And it's not below her to do it!" Tammeia's eyes welled with tears. "Please, please Eisen, believe me. She's in great danger. All our people over there are in danger. Go and bring them home."

"Love, I think it would be better to wait until Jgar returns." Eisen knew that no one was more soothing to Tammeia when she was like this than Jgar. Maybe if he could get her to wait until Jgar returned, Jgar could talk some sense into her. Eisen continued, "After all, he knows the way. He'd be the best choice to go." He put his hand on the nape of her neck and stroked softly. "You're tired. You need some rest."

She ignored his touch and his comment. "If you leave now, you'll see him on the way," the woman said. She pulled away from him absently. "Take only a few, but the best you can, and go. Tonight."

"But what do I tell the Corays?" he questioned. "What do I say when I get there?"

"Say nothing. Don't let them know you're there. Never let them see you. The wind goes places light cannot."

"But how?"

"Eisen!" she raised her voice sharply. "You will go and you'll find a way to do my will. I won't let my baby die for the sake of that evil woman!" She threw her hair back over her shoulder. "And you will do it now!"

Eisen nodded submissively. "Alright, but please pray for us. When the Corays find us we're dead."

"You seem certain they'll find you."

"Without a guide to show us the way through the Habite, we'll be found for sure," he said pointedly.

"And your solution?" she asked.

"Please, let's wait for Jgar. He knows the land behind the wall. He'll be the best one to lead us in."

Tammeia sighed. "When is he due?"

Eisen thought for a brief moment. "In eight or nine more nights, I suppose."

"Then ride out and meet him. That will save at least eight night's ride for him. And my Alana will be home eight nights earlier."

"If we do get through unnoticed. How am I supposed to get Alana out?" Eisen asked.

"You will." She kissed him on the forehead. "You must. Now go. Start your ride tonight," she said. "Please ride quickly."

Eisen nodded and walked away, he obviously lacked Tammeia's enthusiasm.

"What is this? My own consort refusing to heed my wishes!" She exclaimed in frustration as she walked slowly and lethargically down the hall. "What does it matter anyway?"

Despite his better judgment, Eisen assembled riders and readied to head off to Pouchetia Coray's Habite. They left after the day's heat and rode at a quick, even pace all the rest of the day and into the night. The band consisted of three men, Eisen, Raata, (who Eisen chose because of his agility with weapons and his steadiness on his feet), and Quetan, (who Eisen chose for his speed and ability to think as fast as he ran).

They had only three animals between them and five bags of supplies. What they didn't have was any idea of what they were going to do. But Eisen was bound to Tammeia's words and wishes, as were the other two men, and it would be a long ride, so they did have time. Time enough, Eisen hoped, to plan.

Chapter 31

"Jgar, wake up it's morning." Sharl shook him lightly. He opened his heavy eyes.

"Good morning, Sharl." He looked around. "Where's Rovear?"

"He's disconnecting the traps that lay ahead of us."

"What traps?" Jgar rubbed his eyes and shook his brain awake. Then he remembered where they were. "Rovear!" he called. There was no answer.

"Rovear!" he called again. There was still no answer.

"How long has it been since you've seen him?" Jgar peered far into the distance.

"I don't know. Maybe since Sola came up," she said.

Jgar looked up to the orange disk. Sola was already a third into the morning sky. "He's been gone a long time. Hasn't he?"

"Yes, but he said he would be," Sharl said without concern.

Jgar headed toward the brush. He paused between steps and looked around carefully just in case there were any traps. Before he entered the brush, he stopped and checked everything again. He didn't see any trip cords or unnatural placements of shrubs and branches. It looked pretty safe. He took a deep breath and walked cautiously to a rise in the forest floor. On the other side of the rise he found Rovear. The Exoltairetive's body lay distorted in a crouched position over a low limb.

"Rovear!" Panic over took Jgar and he ran to his friend.

"Damn!" Rovear snapped.

Jgar stepped back with surprise. "I thought you were dead."

"Dead?" Rovear's eyes rolled back and he shook his head. "I was trying to catch a phefer. I've been stalking it all morning." He jumped down from the limb. "It's long gone now."

"I'm sorry. I didn't know. You did look dead, you know." Jgar said.

"You will be sorry. It was your breakfast," Rovear teased with a smile.

"Do you think it'll come back?" Jgar peered into the woods.

"Never mind that. Look over here." Rovear lead Jgar to an area full of young trees. Many of them were pulled back, tied down and loaded with arrows. "If the equis would have, by chance, made it past the trap that killed it, we would be dead now."

"This must be their last line of defense." Jgar ran his hand over the trunk of a sapling that was pulled back taunt. "Do you think we can spring it without any problems?"

"It wouldn't be hard to spring. I'm surprised the wind hasn't blown it loose already." Rovear turned to face the clearing. "Sharl! Take cover! Stay low!" he shouted.

"I will!" a distant voice called back.

"Let's do it." Rovear pulled out his knife. "Now." He sliced a vine that held the central tree. It jutted up to vertical, flinging its deadly cargo into the open field. There was a series of snaps and creaking of wood as the other trees followed in suit.

"There, that should do it." Rovear sheathed the knife.

"Did you see anyone at camp this morning?" Jgar looked through the trees at the clearing.

"No," Rovear replied without feeling.

"Did you try to call to them and tell them we're here?"

"I was going to, but then I discovered this trap. You wouldn't believe it, there were six different release cords for it. I figured it would be better if I took care of it first." Rovear pushed some saplings aside. "Come on, let's get out the these trees."

"And to camp," Jgar added anxiously.

"To camp," Rovear echoed.

"Do you think it's safe to move on now?" Sharl shouted to the two men coming from the trees.

"It should be. But stay behind us just in case," Rovear answered.

Jgar turned toward the camp. "HEY!" he yelled at the top of his voice. "HEY! Is anyone there?"

There was no reply.

"Save your breath," Rovear picked up what was left of their supplies. "At this distance they can't hear you."

"Have you seen anyone yet, Sharl?" Jgar peered toward the camp but saw nothing.

"No," she said. She ran her fingers through her sable hair in lieu of a comb. Jgar noticed the bald strip over her ear. It ran forward to her brow leaving only red skin and stubble. He wondered if she noticed it yet. Even though the hair from the top of her head hung over and partly covered it, the strip showed vividly. For a fleeting moment, Jgar thought it looked like some hunger-crazed animal had grazed across her hair, mistaking it for weeds. He chuckled to himself.

"Your thoughts?" Rovear questioned the laugh.

"Never mind." He turned this gaze sharply to the side.

Rovear followed it to Sharl. "Let's get on our way," he said with a shrug, then beamed a smile at Jgar.

They walked close together. Rovear lead the way looking for traps and trip cords, Jgar and Sharl not more than one step behind him. They came to a strip of brown dead weeds that stretched to the brush on one side of the field and to a cliff drop on the other side. It was too wide to jump over.

"A trap?" Rovear turned to Jgar.

"It would seem so," Jgar confirmed.

"What now?" Sharl kicked her foot around in the high weeds.

Jgar pulled on her hair very lightly. "I wouldn't do that, lady."

She pulled her foot back.

"What about the woods, Rovear?" Jgar tried to see through the trees but the undergrowth was too thick.

"Maybe," he answered slowly.

"I think there's someone at the camp!" Sharl exclaimed.

"Hey!" Sharl yelled. "Hey!" she yelled again this time in unison with Jgar.

"Torta and Sheen People!" Jgar shouted and waved his arms in a frenzy. "Is anyone there!"

"Hello!" Sharl yelled at the limits of her voice.

There was someone moving. A figure appeared from the tent. It was bent over and crumpled. It seemed to be covered with dark clothes or maybe it was dirt. It was impossible for them to tell from that distance. The figure waved its arms. Rovear strained to see who it was. The figure only had one hand.

"Hey you!" Rovear called.

"No! Don't...tr..p!" the figure in the camp yelled. His weak voice lost on the wind.

"Trap!" Sharl gasped, echoing what she had heard.

"We Know!" Jgar yelled back. "How do we get around it!"

The dark figure waved his arms wildly.

"Around! How do we get around! Get past it!" Jgar shouted.

The figure's mouth moved but Jgar couldn't hear what he said. He only caught slight sounds on the wind. "Can you hear him?" he asked Rovear. The Exoltairetive shook his head no.

"No..cli..f...NO!" Was all they could make out from what the man screamed.

"We can't hear you!" Jgar called back.

The wind shifted a bit. "Dagor... trap... do..ot.. edge.. tr."

"Dagor?" Jgar turned to Rovear. "Dagor. What's dagor mean?"

"He said matadagor. It's a matadagor trap," Rovear replied calmly. "We'll never be able to cross it."

"Then how do you propose we get to that side?" Sharl questioned in her usual, sarcastic tone.

Rovear shrugged. "Maybe through the trees?"

"We're going into the woods! We will be there soon!" Jgar called to the man.

"No... mat... ag..r trap... n.. th.. trees!" The figure jumped up and down with frustration. "Wait... proj..tion!" The figure shouted and collapsed.

"What did he say?" Rovear looked at Sharl

"Something about the trees and projection," she answered.

"No!" Jgar screamed. "No, do not project! Do not leave your body!" The wind shifted again and blew his words back into the pit of his stomach. "Do not project!"

The figure moved no more.

"It's too late," Rovear said quietly. He put his hand on Jgar's shoulder.

"This is your fault!" Jgar grabbed Rovear's arm and pulled it back with a quick twist. "You and that vile witch you call a Carlaf." He twisted Rovear's arm until the pain showed on the Exoltairetive's face. Rovear pulled himself free but did nothing to really defend himself.

"You killed them all! All of them!" He swung at Rovear's face. The Exoltairetive closed his eyes and braced himself for the blow. Jgar's fist hit hard, but Rovear still didn't strike back. Instead he put his hand back on Jgar's shoulders. "Please, brother," he whispered.

"Don't call me brother. You who sprang from poison to deceive me into defying the orders of my Carlaf and leaving her people to die."

"I have not deceived you," Rovear said evenly and sincerely.

"You have deceived me! You're the one who insisted we come to these forsaken hills and then insisted I leave my people here alone to die. But what should I expect from a Coray. The most evil of all the creatures to walk in daylight!"

Rovear swallowed hard and turned his eyes away. He didn't feel it was the right time or place for a fight.

"And you're a coward too!" Jgar bellowed. His eyes were red with anger. "If you won't fight me for the honor of my dead, then I'll kill you were you stand."

Rovear still said nothing.

"Kill him, Jgar! He's done us nothing by harm!" Sharl shouted, feeding Jgar's rage.

Rovear still stood silently.

Jgar ran at him and threw his full body weight into the Exoltairetive's mid-section. Rovear flew backwards onto the ground. His arms wrapped around Jgar's shoulders. "Don't do this, brother. Calm yourself," Rovear gasped, half his breath lost in the fall.

"You're as much a coward as you are stupid! And as evil as your lady is ugly!" Jgar struck out, hitting Rovear up and down the sides of his body. He threw punches wildly. Rovear struggled to hold Jgar back, but didn't try to hurt him.

"Kill him, Jgar!" Sharl cheered.

Rovear broke away and got to his feet. He tried to put some distance between him and the enraged Regimitive.

"Look at him run, Jgar!" Kill him! Kill him!" Sharl screamed.

Jgar ran and jumped towards Rovear. He knocked him flat. Rovear's face made contact with a round rock just under the ground's surface. He clawed forward to the cliff edge in hope of finding a handhold. His vision was blurred. Jgar sat astride his back with his hands tight around Rovear's neck.

"Now you will meet your death. I only wish it was one as horrible as the one my people felt.

Rovear gasped for breath. He found a handhold on the loose rock and pulled it out of the ground. The Exoltairetive tried to turn to see the Regimitive. He couldn't focus his eyes. All he saw was a Sola browned image in the corner of his peripheral sight. Rovear gasped for air again. He was unable to breathe at all.

"Kill him, Jgar! Do it! Kill him!" Sharl laughed and jumped with excitement.

In a last ditch attempt to breathe, Rovear swung the rock haphazardly over his head. The limit of the backward rotation of his arm made it impossible to grab and hold Jgar but maybe he could knock him off.

Rovear barely heard the three thudding impacts of the rock against Jgar's face. Jgar rolled off of him and staggered away. Rovear dropped the rock and tried to catch his breath. He gasped, swallowing more air than he was inhaling. His head spun as he looked up and saw Jgar staggering away. The side of the Regimitive's face was covered with blood and dirt.

"Jgar!" Rovear reached up. Jgar didn't see him. "Jgar!" he called louder. Jgar staggered back and forth, oblivious to the world around him. Rovear rolled over and tried to stand. "Jgar. Brother. Can you hear me?" Rovear's throat pounded with each breath he drew. It felt as if his throat was somehow turning inside out and back again. There didn't seem to be enough air around him. "Jgar!" he called again. With difficulty, he stumbled to his feet.

Without warning, Sharl jumped on his back.

He grabbed her arm. She was light and even in his present condition he was able to brush her off easily.

"If he's not capable, I'll kill you!" She pulled the knife away from him and jumped back before he could react, then ran at him. His eyes couldn't focus on her. He backed up one step. She plunged the knife at him and missed. He grabbed her hand.

"Let me go, Coray!" the woman screamed.

Rovear was silent.

She lunged her weight forward trying to cut his arm and free herself. "You won't get away with this. Jgar will kill you!"

"You are very foolish." Rovear tried to focus on her small, dirty face. "Very foolish, indeed." He made a tight fist with his free hand and hit Sharl with all the force he could muster. She flew backwards to the ground, dropping the knife at his feet. When she landed, she hit with a hard thumping sound that somehow satisfied Rovear. She didn't move.

The Exoltairetive tried to take a deep breath, but choked instead. He spat out the bloody mucus and steadied himself. After a moment, Sharl's unconscious body was in focus, the camp was in focus, even the confusing mesh of the matadagor trap was in focus. He remembered Jgar, staggering. "Where is he?" Rovear thought in a near panic. He turned around, looking in every direction, but didn't see Jgar.

"The forest!" Rovear jogged with labored breath to the forest edge. He didn't enter it, though. The matadagor trap was in the woods too. It was certain death to enter there. He decided, instead, to peer over the low bushes and trees. He found several dead animals, but no Jgar.

Rovear ran back to the clearing, then sat down to catch his breath. The heat was beginning to rise and his already difficult breathing was becoming almost impossible. He wiped his hands across his forehead and stared into the distance. He still didn't see Jgar.

Then the thought hit him and he ran to the only other place where he could possibly be — the cliff's edge.

The drop at the end of the field was particularly steep at the point where Rovear stood. It petered out to a hill then a gentle slope in the distance. It seemed to go down forever, and a sense of vertigo grabbed Rovear, causing him to step back from the edge. When his head and stomach settled he returned to the rim.

"Jgar!" He looked down the cliff's depths. "Jgar!"

"Rovear," a cold, low voice came from the field in back of the man. Rovear turned slowly. Sharl stood behind him. Her cheek was swollen and red. She held the knife that Rovear neglected to pick up after his struggle with her.

"Sharl!" he scolded, "Be still. I'm looking for Jgar. We can settle this later."

She lunged at him. His reflexes told him to jump back, but his intelligence knew that behind him was a long drop. He blocked the lunge. The knife nicked the palm of his hand. He pulled it back quickly.

She lunged out again. He jumped to the side. The blade shaved some hair from his arm, but didn't cut him.

He kicked out at her, in much the same way he'd done with the handra-can. She dodged to his left. Before she could jab at him again. He kicked out at her arm. The knife flew in the air. It landed near the cliff's rim. Rovear grabbed it.

Sharl looked unsure. "Kill me, Coray. It's a well known fact that your kind take pleasure in killing women." She tried to look strong but her voice was shaking.

Rovear walked slowly toward her. She began to run. He was on top of her in no time. He held her to the ground in such a way that she could barely move.

"Go ahead. Have your way with me before you kill me. You know you want to." Her eyes were wide with fright.

"I surely don't want your flesh. I'd rather be consort to a kenya!" he laughed loudly, then lowered his voice. "And no matter how badly I want your blood, it's not mine to take." He grabbed her by the hair and thought for a moment.

With little difficulty he rolled her on her stomach with her arms placed under her so she couldn't move, then he put all his weight on her back. Convinced she couldn't move, he grabbed her hair and started to knot and braid it. Then he began to cut.

He made four strong, long ropes from her hair and bound her hand and foot. He threw the others over his shoulder. As he walked to the cliff's rim to resume his search he turned and looked back at Sharl. She was a sorry sight with her dirty swollen face and her close cropped hair.

He left the water within her reach. She would need it. The heat was rising.

"I'll kill you!" She sneered.

Rovear ignored her. "Jgar!" he called.

"Here!" a voice replied.

"Jgar, brother, I'm coming." Rovear took one last look at Sharl, then hurried down the cliff side.

<h1 style="text-align:center">Chapter 32</h1>

All over the world the sky lit up in bright yellow fire as the black and sliver sky vehicles landed. In many fields, crops burned. In some, unknowing and shocked workers died. The vehicles, seventy-three in all, had arrived. One of them landed in the very field outside Tammeia's anhabit.

"Tammeia, the sky ship is here," one of her consorts said. He fidgeted with excitement.

"Yes. I know." Tammeia heard the loud rumbling of the sky vehicle's engines. She would have had to be deaf not to. Even then she would have felt the shaking of the ground under her feet. "Has anyone emerged from it yet?"

"No." He reached into a closet and pulled out a long white flowing cape. "They haven't signaled us either." He draped it over her shoulders and smoothed it out until it hung delicately to the ground. Tammeia opened a drawer and took out two chains of silver. She placed one around her neck and the other around her waist. Her consort took out a third silver chain. It was very long and more than twice as thick as the others. He clipped it into her hair, underneath where it didn't show, then he took a soft brush out of his pocket and shaped her hair into a flowing black waterfall of silk. He took the silver chain and wrapped her hair tightly with it all the way to the bottom. He checked it to make sure it was even, then he clipped the loose end of the chain to itself.

Meanwhile, Tammeia put a silver and white ceremonial knife and sheath on her calf. Her feet were bare.

"Your shoes, Tammeia," her consort said. He pulled a pair of loosely made sandals out of the closet and put them on her. They tied just above her ankles. The Regime made a face. She didn't like shoes, but in these formal occasions they were expected of her, at least by the Netrins. Their kind wore clothing and shoes all the time, no matter what the weather.

A few more preparations and Tammeia was ready to meet her guest. She mounted a dark brown equis. Its presence felt strange to her. It lacked the sense of unity she was used to feeling with her usual mount. But the night black mare was gone. Alana had taken that with her.

Two of the Lady's consorts, Joric and Talock, sat astride similar animals. At Tammeia's signal, they rode out of the padding to greet their visitors.

Tammeia's first sight of the sky ship caused her to shudder. It didn't seem real, black and silver against the sky. The ground around its base was singed and blackened. The vehicle gave off a blasting heat that radiated toward Tammeia and her consorts. They had to stop a great distance from the ship. She wanted to get closer but the heat was over powering. There was a far away hissing sound.

"Tammeia, will you go from here in projection?" Joric asked.

"No. It may be deemed an intrusion." She thought for a moment. "It seems their vehicles need time to settle. Joric, stay here and wait. Talock and I will ride back. It there's any change consult with me immediately.

He nodded his understanding. Tammeia prodded her mount and headed home.

"Talock, watch my body. I have to talk to Eisen." Tammeia said.

Talock rode up along side of her and placed his arm around her waist. She handed him the reins of her equis and leaned into the crock of his arm. Her eyes closed then her body went limp.

She projected toward the Habite's limits. She knew she would pass over Eisen long before she reached them. Tammeia made a picture in her mind's eye of Eisen. Even before she could finish the visualization, she was upon him. Without warning, Tammeia entered his mind.

"Eisen."

"Lady?" he thought to her.

"The sky vehicles have come. Hasten your ride. The time is growing ever shorter."

"Yes, my Carlaf," he thought the loudest he could, but he couldn't hide his true feelings. Tammeia began to get angry.

"Eisen, do my will or be warned not to return!" she commanded then ripped her consciousness away from his as fast and as violently as she could. His mind spun with great pain.

Tammeia didn't return to her body right away. Instead, she took to the realm of absentenial projection and to the warm comforting light of Lumdon Hall.

The hall's doors were locked but Tammeia knew the key. She put her hand over the golden knob and sang three perfect notes. The doors glided back on their hinges and she entered, making sure to close them behind her.

The hall was as quiet as heaven, and in her solitude, the Regime felt that she was indeed in heaven. Tammeia ran her hands over a dark wood column, letting her fingers feel each groove, examining each carved notch. She didn't look with her eyes but her hands could feel the story of the column. She stared dreamy eyed into the distance, not focusing on anything. Daydreams ran through her mind. Dreams of her and Alana sitting at the Council table. "Mother and daughter, leaders of the Council," she said to herself. "And how beautiful my daughter will grow to be. One day her child-like ways will be transformed into perfection. Someday, Alana will have consorts of her own and a Habite that commands much land and great power," Tammeia dreamed. "My daughter will have everything she wants. She'll have..." Her thoughts ended abruptly to avoid thinking of where Alana was now, or where she was heading.

The Regime began to walk the perimeter of the hall. Only six out of the ten columns were carved. The sixth was only carved from the ceiling center to where it evened off, perpendicular to the floor. Tammeia wondered what history would fill this beam. What names would become immortal in its pulp and varnish? It would surely mention the journeys. But what will it say? Who would it blame or praise?

Tammeia wondered if generations of the future would bring their children into the hall to gaze upon the pictures on the sixth column. And if they did, would they laugh. The irony made the woman shudder. She had been asked to give up her future so that someone else's future can look upon her grief and laugh. Tammeia cried.

Chapter 33

"Hunter!" Seth called out, his face lit with joy. "I thought you weren't coming back."

The kenya ran to him. The kits trailed her with their tails waving so frantically their whole hindquarters shook back and forth. Hunter whimpered a welcome. Seth rubbed her head and neck heartily.

She grabbed two of his fingers in her mouth and wrapped her prehensile tongue around them tightly. Then she pulled him back, his fingers still in her mouth. He laughed and tried to swing her around, but she let go and jumped on him. They rolled and wrestled in play. It didn't take long before the kits were involved.

Seth tired out long before the kits did, and it took some time for him to calm them after he found exhaustion. "Kits," he said in Keeper's tongue, "until I return to my own, you're my family. Never have I had better." They cocked their heads. His words were odd. After a moment, they ran off in play together. Their mother, Hunter, stretched out at Seth side.

"Hunter," he greeeted.

She looked up at him.

"I have to continue into these hills. My journey will take you far from your hunting grounds. I will understand if you don't care to come."

She lifted her head and placed it on his lap. Strat walked over and sat on Seth's other side. Soon the kits settled themselves and the pack took an afternoon nap.

After they awoke, Seth left the camp with Hunter and the pack at his side. He was glad she'd chosen to go with him. He would've missed her had she stayed behind.

As they traveled higher and higher into the hills, food was becoming harder to find. Seth felt it would be better if they kept on walking through the heat and the night. The sooner they crossed the barren hills, the better. Hunter felt the same way, he was sure.

By morning Seth was exhausted. He had walked half the night with the two kits slung over his shoulders. Even so, the hills were crossed without trouble. He saw no one and was seen by no one, though many times during the night, Seth felt eyes watching him. And several times Hunter and Strat began to howl and yap in warning, but nothing came of it.

As the day grew lighter, they found a crack in the rocky face of the hill that formed a small cave further in. They made it their den. After a short sleep, Seth climbed the cliff face to have a look around.

In the not so great distance, he saw a large gaping ravine. It stretched for what seemed like forever. A road cutting through the blue-green grasses led to a large wooden bridge that spanned the distance. He looked as far as he could in both directions. The bridge was the only visible way to cross the ravine.

Seth recognized where he was. "That's the ravine we crossed on the way to Nylla Christance's anhabit," he said to hunter. He was amazed by how far he had traveled. The route the Corays had used to take them to the main house must have made a grand loop around the hills he just crossed. The Keeper looked out over the barren plain on the other side of the bridge. The heat was still to come. That plain would be dry and cracking soon.

"Not a good time to go on," he mumbled and climbed down to the cave.

When he arrived, Hunter and Strat were gone, but the kits were still there. He greeted them playfully and decided to rest and wait for Hunter and Strat to return with dinner. He just started to doze off when he was startled by the sharp sound of equis hoofs. The Keeper poked his head out for a look. There were riders coming down the road below.

"Renia?" A man called to the Regime riding in front of him.

"What?" She pulled back on her equis' reins and rode along at his side.

"We should continue this search later. The heat is rising and the Cragin plain will be difficult, if not impossible to cross during the heat this time of year."

"Yes, I know," she said. "We'll go back until the heat is over. Tell the others."

The man nodded then waved his arm in a beckoning motion. "Come on everyone! Back to Christance's!" he called to the riders. They all turned and started back.

"Wait!" The Regime Renia pulled hard on the reins. Her mount stopped immediately. "On the cliff side. I see something."

Seth pulled back quickly.

"Probably nothing, lady," her consort said. He saw nothing.

"Or probably the handra-can," someone else added worriedly.

"Probably the Keeper!" She motioned for them to dismount. "See. In that crack in the rocks. Go and check it out."

Her consort headed toward the rock face and started to climb. Seth's heart pounded hard in his chest. The thought of fighting this man made his stomach turn. He knew that if he were found he would have to kill the man and his companions, and the chances of doing that were slim at best. Seth didn't even have a weapon handy.

The Coray man climbed closer. Seth felt like the beat of his heart would echo through the rocks and give him away. The tan kit lunged out of the crack and nipped the man's hand then darted back into the cave. It didn't even break his skin. The man reached in after it.

Seth contemplated jumping out to strike the man but instead he pressed himself up against the farthest part of the cave wall.

"Renia, Dalta!" the man called down to his Carlaf and her companion. "Is this your Keeper?" He grabbed the kit by the skin of its neck and haunches, and hauled it out of the cave. The animal struggled a bit but couldn't really move. Seth stayed motionless.

"Let it go!" Dalta called. The women began to laugh. The Regimitive dropped the kit and climbed back down the rock face.

"Let's go," Renia called to the riders. "It's getting hot out here."

When Seth was sure they were gone, he emerged from the cave. Hunter and Strat came out of the surrounding landscape without a catch. After a long silence, Seth spoke. "Hunter, Strat, kits, let's get going. We have work to do."

Chapter 34

The terror of the day just past was too much for Alana's mind to understand. She cried all afternoon and refused to eat. Many people asked her how she cut her fingers so severely, but she never answered them.

The cuts were deep enough to warrant a stitch or two in each fingertip and the mender who worked on her doubted she would ever be able to feel properly with them again. He bandaged her hands with ribbons of gauze, wrapping them like mittens. When Alana got back to her room she sat still and silent in the corner. No one could ever know what was in her mind. When Gabriel came to see if she would go out and play, she screamed with fright and ran away.

The next morning the pattern continued. In the afternoon, Alana slept. Her dreams were filled with burning gold eyes and shinning thin blades that came closer in a warped distortion of reality. Their presence robbed her of her breath. A frigid crackling laugh rang her eardrums like great iron bells. Its sound got louder and the eyes she saw in her dream got hotter until they burned right though her. Alana tried to wake herself. She tried to find reality. Suddenly it stopped.

She was somewhere else. She was in a different dream. One she had a hundred times before. It was one that was familiar. Even though the dream usually disturbed her, she felt safe in its pattern.

She was floating above a ravine. A great wooden bridge crossed it. Alana knew what came next, she was sure of it — equis, large black equis.

This time there were equis, large and black as any the child had dreamed of before, but something was different. There were riders on them; six women and nine men. They were riding hard and fast. They were in a great hurry to get somewhere.

Alana's heart pounded. The dream had changed, and her security was lost. The equis galloped below her toward the bridge. "No!" Alana screamed to them. "The bridge is not safe. NO!"

They didn't hear her. The animals sped onto the bridge as fast as fire. The pounding of each racing hoof turned into a crackling sound. Alana had to reach them. She had to tell them. But like always, she drifted up. The harder she tried to get down, the faster she pulled away. The pounding was lost in an incredible screech and overpowering thunder of the bridge as it crumbled into the Ravine's depth.

Alana begged to close her eyes but they wouldn't shut. The ground below her pulsed with yellow and purple. It pulsed in her mind until there was nothing left except the color. Then it was gone.

She was in the woods. There was a long stone wall off in the distance. It was the limits of Exoltaire Pouchetia's Habite. Alana had to get out and get back to her mother. She tried to get to the great wooden gate. Her ghostly dream-hand felt the warm wood. It felt soft and fragile. She pushed on it with all her might, but it barely moved. She pushed again and she awoke in her room.

"Alana, child. What's the matter?" Palray picked her up. The little girl said nothing.

"What's wrong, Alana?" he questioned gently. "Your sleep was restless." He brushed her hair back away from her moist eyes. "Are you hungry?"

Alana nodded.

"Good." He reached into his pocket, pulled out a small paper covered roll and unwrapped it. Alana sniffled a bit but watched patiently. Inside the wrapper was a stick of candy made from sweet berry juice. He offered it to her. "Have this until I can get you some supper."

She reached to grab it in her mitten like bandages, but it fell to the ground and shattered. Alana cried out loud and ran from the room.

"What happened?" a Torta boy said, covering his ear because of the child's sudden scream.

Palray shrugged sadly and picked up the shards of sweets then threw them away.

Alana's run brought her back to the fence and the definite boundaries it represented to her. She tried to wipe the hair off her face, but it stuck to her tear-wet cheeks. Strands of it worked its way into her mouth. The mittens were clumsy and encumbering.

They aggravated the child until she could no longer control her anger and she unwrapped them in a fit of fury, pulling them and untwisting them frantically. She shook her hands wildly until the last shreds of gauze fell to the ground. A feeling of frustration overtook her and she fell to the ground in a limp type of crossed-legged sit. Her fingertips were red and raw with brown threads in them. They showed traces of the yellow-green herbal medicine the mender had smeared on them. She tried to wipe back her tears. Her skin pulled pack at the knots of the stitches, exposing the wounded flesh to her salty tears. The pain was only momentary but severe. During that moment of pain, Alana decided. She had to run.

She was small and would fit through the fence without effort. She ran to it and slipped through. There was a sharp buzzing in her ears and she felt like she was slipping into a dream state but she managed to shake it off. She was on the other side of the fence and free from Pouchetia and her evil consorts. She knew what to do. "Now I have to go into the hills and find Seth," Alana said out loud.

She knew he went for the hills. She didn't know how she knew, she just did. Alana looked out at the horizon. The hills were behind the anhabit, so she set her course around the building to find Seth.

Chapter 35

"Taresse!" Jerami shouted as he entered the anhabit. "Where is Taresse?" he asked a passer-by.

"In the dining hall," the other answered.

Jerami nodded then ran to the dining hall.

"Taresse," he said through heavy breaths, "there was a disturbance at the gate. The alarm was tripped."

She opened her eyes wide. "I hope you sent someone to investigate it. It may be the Keeper trying to get back in."

"I sent Talton. It was his day to watch the gate." He made a bitter face. "I watched it again last night."

Taresse ignored the remark and headed out. She was stopped at the door by Palray. "Lady Coray, have you seen Alana?"

"No," she pushed by him. "I'm in a hurry. If I see any Sheens I'll send them to you." She hurried to the yard.

"Did you find anyone?" she questioned a man on an equis.

"No. But I've only completed half of my boundary search." He offered her an arm up on the animal. She accepted. "I haven't checked out the side toward the hills yet. The Netrin sky vehicle is there and it's very hot. Besides, since that thing arrived, the area's been heavily guarded. No one would get through unnoticed.

"Have the guards been warned?"

"Yes, of course."

"Then let's go." She kicked the animal's sides and it galloped off parallel to the fence.

Chapter 36

Hunter panted heavily and saliva dripped from her tongue as she trotted down the hillside to the road below. The kits kept a faithful distance behind her. Seth walked up ahead with Strat at his side. The man looked behind him every so often just to make sure the riders weren't coming back. Once he was on the bridge there would be nowhere to hide.

The Keeper took his first steps onto the bridge. His feet barely made a sound on its giant wooden beams. The kenya's sharp digging nails clanked and scratched high tones behind him. He walked for sometime. The bridge was longer than it looked from the cave above. From its center, he looked to both sides. The banks of the ravine were far away and the parallax effect made the bridge seem thin where it met them. He stopped and sat with his legs hanging over into the gaping ravine below.

The chasm was more like an incredible large crevasse in the world's surface. Its shining sharply cut walls merged somewhere below. To the Keeper it seemed like gaping jaws, ready to grab him from the bridge and swallow him whole. He stood up and continued his walk to the other side.

It was the peak of the heat by the time Seth and the pack stepped foot on the opposite bank, and Sola's rays were hot on the man's face. He wiped the sweat from his brow and looked around for shade. There was none to be found. He looked over the great expanse of the bridge, then across the barren heat cracked plain ahead of him. The Keeper contemplated going back across the bridge to the cave. "This place will give us no protection from the heat and no place to hide from the riders when they return," he said to his companions.

The kits whined in discomfort. Hunter dug as fast as she could in the dry, hard ground. Loose dirt flew into the air behind her, hitting Seth's back. He turned to see what was happening. She was trying to dig a den to hide her kits from the heat. He bent down to help her when he noticed the cliff's drop. "It doesn't go straight down. There's a ledge that passes beneath the bridge. We can find shade from the heat and shelter from the riders there." He motioned to Hunter. She stopped digging and followed him.

Even though the air was stale and hot, the shade was cool relief. Strat dozed, Seth stroked one kit's back and the other's head, while Hunter stared far into the cloudless sky. Seth wondered what she was thinking. Did she regret her decision to follow him? The kits hadn't eaten in several days. Their occasional cries for food kept Seth very aware if it, as he was sure Hunter was — very aware.

From where he sat it was impossible to see into the ravine's depth and the opposite bank seemed an eternity away. The bridge above him was wide enough to accommodate at least four riders abreast. Where it ended on the opposite back, it was merely a ribbon of dark color.

He looked at the bridge's construction and was amazed. The entire bridge was held up only by simple "V" shape side-beams that came out from the ravine's walls and joined to the support bars that ran the bridge's length. He peered into the distance. It didn't seem logical that such a large bridge would be built with so little structural support.

"It must be the bare minimum needed to hold it up. The Corays certainly know little about building bridges," he thought out loud to no one who would care. "This bridge is so poorly reinforced," he directed his words to Hunter who didn't understand them, "that a simple flaw in the building materials, say from weathering, would cause it to collapse." He pointed to the distance. "If someone wanted to knock this thing down, all they'd have to do was..." His eyes opened wide with excitement. "All I'd have to do was find a way to cut through that pole."

He checked his supplies. Yes, he still had his knife in his hip pouch. He was all set.

The Keeper descended the ravine wall to where he could easily jump to the pole. Hunter yapped nervously as Seth climbed the pole's length to about a quarter way from where it met the bridge. He didn't dare look down. Even though the beam was heavy and easy to grip, Seth knew the height would make him dizzy. All he could think of were the open jaws ready to swallow him. He cleared his mind of the thought and began to cut away at the pole.

Chapter 37

"Jgar, my friend, are you hurt?" Rovear approached him cautiously. Jgar stood leaning against the cliff wall, his face brown with dry blood and dirt. He closed his eyes as Rovear approached. "Jgar." Rovear reached forward slowly, ready to pull away at the slightest indication that Jgar would attack him again. "Let me help you." He put a hand on Jgar's neck and tried to examine the bloody side of his head.

Jgar pulled away. "Please don't touch me. I'm in shame."

"Nonsense," Rovear said. He felt a hard lump under Jgar's hair but it didn't really seem too serious.

The Regimitive flinched with pain. "You should leave me here to die. I've done nothing but harm to you." He opened his eyes but kept his gaze away from meeting Rovear's. "I've done you a great evil. You who I called brother."

"You've done no wrong. Come on, I'll help you out of here."

"Let me die. I'm ashamed," Jgar protested.

"Pity is your only shame. Besides you were right. The death of your people is on my head. But I assure you, Jgar, it was a flaw in my judgment, not a wish of Pouchetia's or anyone else that these things happened." He reached out to the Regimitive. "Here, Jgar, tie this rope around you. It'll help support you for the climb up." After Jgar had tied it securely around his waist, Rovear checked it then tied the other end around his own. There was not much room in between them but they didn't need much. Rovear stayed at Jgar's side and helped him up the hill.

Once on top, he took the rope off and untied Jgar. Then he untied Sharl's feet but not her hands.

"Get up Sharl, come on. I know a way around the Matadagor trap." The Exoltairetive pulled her by the arm.

"Is that necessary, Rovear?" Jgar asked dully.

"Maybe not," he replied. Rovear yanked her again. "But maybe she'll learn this way. At least she's not going to be able to do us anymore harm."

"Kill him, Jgar!" Sharl screeched. "Don't let him live for this!"

Rovear looked at Jgar. "See what I mean."

"All men will find death some day," Jgar said in answer to Sharl's cries.

"All women too," Rovear added. "Now. Move!" He forced her to the cliff's edge and gave Jgar the end of the rope that bound her hands.

Jgar took a good look at the ropes. They were sable-brown and soft. He looked at Sharl. Her head had less hair then his own. "Rovear?" he gasped and turned in bewilderment, the rope in his open palm.

"We needed some rope," Rovear said with conviction. "Besides, I think the fashion suits her."

"You're a crude man," Jgar said, not knowing whether to be shocked or amused.

"She's a crude woman," he replied.

"She's a hairless woman," Jgar shrieked with unwilling laughter.

Sharl could say nothing. Her heart was feeling nothing but hate.

"So, where are we going?" Jgar rubbed the lump on his head.

"To that edge." Rovear pointed to a rim in the cliff wall. "Then past the trap and up to the camp."

"Why? They're all dead there," Jgar's words dropped to near silence.

"I know," Rovear answered, "but maybe they have left some clues as to why."

"It's simple, why!" Sharl intruded. "Because you left them alone in a land infested with flesh eating animals."

"For that I'm truly sorry. I really believed they were safe. I feel their pain," Rovear said sincerely.

"Don't feel pain. You couldn't have known. None of us did," Jgar said with an understanding he'd lacked before.

"Oh, let him feel pain. I wish he felt death!" Sharl screamed. "Jgar, you're a fool. He kills your people and you still believe his lies."

"I assure you, I'm not lying," Rovear said.

"Will you have us believe the words of a murderer?" she protested.

"That's enough!" Jgar exclaimed. His voice rang through the surrounding hills. "Today I will believe him. He's my brother."

Sharl fell strangely silent.

They climbed down the ridge, passed the trap and climbed back again. They made it to the camp before the full of the heat. Like they suspected, there was no one left alive in camp. Only two lone equis grazed warily on some surrounding vegetation. All the other animals had run off or been killed days ago.

"Stephen," Jgar said without expression.

"What?" Rovear walked closer.

"This is.. was Stephen." Jgar turned the boy's body over. The hand and wrist of his left arm were gone. In its place was a shoddily wrapped stump. "His mother, Marlisa Torta died on the journey in."

"I remember," Rovear spoke just above a whisper.

"I lied to him twice," Jgar said with glazed eyes. "I told him his mother would live. Then I told him he would be safe." Jgar cleared his throat. "It seems I can't be trusted."

"Please, don't do this to yourself. You shouldn't blame yourself. The fault lies with me and my Carlaf's paranoia."

Jgar looked at Rovear with curiosity.

"There are three shallow graves behind the tent. Maybe three of four died from the handra-can attack, but the rest lie dead in the tent. Victims of my Carlaf's mind trap." Rovear lowered his eyes. "It's I who should feel shame."

Jgar said nothing, but his eyes burned with inextinguishable anger. He didn't attack Rovear again. His anger wasn't for him. It was for Rovear's Carlaf. He was angry at her for all that had happened. He was angry about the death of his people and about the pain in his arm, head and heart. But most of all, he was angry at her for the pain he saw in Rovear's eyes. He hated her for what she had done to his bother.

"Come. It's getting too hot to stand here. We should get some rest," Rovear said.

"I'm not staying here. This camp reeks of death, and it'll be worse in the heat. Do you want to die of disease?" Sharl bit her lip and wrapped her arms around herself. Without her hair she felt naked.

"She's right, Rovear," Jgar said meekly. "I'm fine to walk. We can take the camp's water and equis, and continue through the heat." he paused. "Where will we continue to?"

"It's less than one day's ride to Nylla Christance's anhabit." Rovear picked up a container of water. "That's the anhabit we started from. We can go back there and get new supplies."

At that moment the fact hit Jgar. They had been in the hills for what seemed like an eternity, yet they were barely a day away from their starting point. It seemed so ironic. They'd be well beyond the Habite's boundaries now if only he hadn't been so curious. "Then, we'll go back there," he finally said.

"Once I'm there, I promise I'll go directly to Pouchetia and make her lift this evil mind field," Rovear vowed.

Jgar nodded. The three grabbed containers of water, mounted the equis and set off back to Christance's anhabit.

Chapter 38

"Lady," an icy female voice echoed in the emptiness of Lumdon Hall. Tammeia turned. Pouchetia stood at the hall's doors. Her eyes ablaze with hate. "I received news from the people in my hill camp. It seems that they were attacked by a Sheen man and a band of wild kenya." She walked closer. Her voice raising with each step and syllable. "He burned the village," she paused. " He murdered several of my Consorts! Many of my people! All totaled, two hundred and fourteen Carlafs, consorts, and children dead! Nearly one hundred more injured!"

Tammeia fumbled backwards away from the burning eyes.

"You should be proud of your Keeper! It seems he even managed to ESCAPE!" Pouchetia shouted. She aimed the charge of her thought energy at Tammeia and released it. The Regime's muscles tightened and contorted in pain, then relaxed. She fell to her knees.

"But there shall be no escape for you." The Exoltaire struck her again. Blood oozed from Tammeia's ears and nose. She stumbled backwards away from her tormentor, unable to strike back. She couldn't even muster enough power to protect herself. Tammeia struggled to her feet.

Pouchetia made the motions of striking her again, but didn't. Tammeia flinched, her eyes shut tight. "Just like your ignorant child," Pouchetia laughed. Tammeia opened her eyes. "Close your eyes, Tammeia. Close them so you won't see your death coming. But I assure you, you'll feel it." She readied to strike again.

"My child! What have you done to Alana?" Tammeia screamed out. She backed up against the oval conference table.

"Not enough, yet," Pouchetia said in a cold voice as she readied to strike out again. "Not nearly enough."

She struck out. Pain seared through Tammeia's being. Her back slammed hard against the table.

"Don't hurt my baby. Please don't hurt my baby," Tammeia sobbed through her pain. "She's only a baby. Don't hurt her."

"I will do what I please." Pouchetia's psychic strength lifted Tammeia into the air. The pressure that the Exoltaire put on the Regime's body was unbearable. Tammeia cried in high tones of pain.

"What of the children your Keeper killed?" With her words, Pouchetia made the Regime's body raise higher. "What of the babies who were burned alive in their cribs! What of the charred burnt remains of what were once my people!" She pulled her power away sharply. Tammeia fell to the table. There was a loud snap. The Regime's ears buzzed with pain, her limbs were unmovable.

"Don't struggle," Pouchetia said. She moved closer. She grabbed Tammeia's arm and gave it a quick jerk. The Regime screamed out.

"You see, your back is broken. You're dying," Pouchetia laughed. "I never miss." She let her go.

"Do you have anything to say before I send you to eternity." She pretended to be listening.

Tammeia's clinched teeth conveyed nothing but her pain. Her eyes were the dull red eyes of the dying. Pouchetia pushed her off the table into the open table center. Tammeia was beyond the point of reacting to pain. She didn't scream.

The once dormant amber stones that rimmed the table started to glow a bright orange. Pouchetia struck out at Tammeia again. Nothing happened. Maybe Tammeia was dead.

The stones glowed brighter and Lumdon Hall filled with a high pitched humming sound. The orange glow reached up to the halls ceiling and folded over itself coming back down and covering Tammeia in its light. It glowed and danced around her distorted body. The humming turned to a buzzing that got louder and louder.

Terrified, Pouchetia ran out of the hall.

Chapter 39

The Exoltaires, Touchea and Breyan, sat in Touchea's room discussing their plan to handle the Netrins. After a short time they had all the details down and were ready to greet their guest.

"Then it's settled," Touchea said with confidence. "I've already sent Pouchetia to ready the hall. Our Netrin friends should be comfortable there for a little while, anyway."

"How long do you think it will take?" Breyan ran a long blue comb through the other woman's hair.

"Not long. The sooner they leave, the better."

"I must tell you something," Breyan bit her bottom lip nervously. "I told Tammeia to send her Coray trainees home. They won't be on the mission."

"Why did you do that?" Touchea turned and faced Breyan.

"They tried to escape. They even tried to kill some of her people."

"Then, it's begun," Touchea said evenly.

"Yes, that it has," Breyan replied.

<h1 style="text-align:center">Chapter 40</h1>

Jgar, Sharl and Rovear had the Nylla Christance's anhabit in sight before the heat of the next day, and arrived before it got very hot. Christance saw them coming and met them at the door.

"Rovear!" she said with surprise, "Jgar and..." she paused to look at the Dominion's lack of hair. "Sharl, what's wrong? We thought you would be long away by now."

"We had a problem, mother. The handra-can..." Rovear started to explain.

"Don't tell me you went into the mountains. Didn't you know that it's the handra-can hunting season." She shook her head slowly. "Where are your injured. I'll send someone to get them."

"There are no injured," Jgar said quietly. No one else said anything for a long moment.

"I have to go to Pouchetia's now and take care of what we discussed," Rovear said to Jgar. He motioned a good-bye.

"Wait, I'll go too." Jgar made ready to follow.

"No, you can't."

"What? Another mind field?"

"Well. Yes," Rovear replied reluctantly. "There's a fence around the main anhabit. It's just an alarm in the physical realm, but in projection it's a barrier that can't be passed unless you've been keyed to it."

"Show me how to get past it."

"I can't," Rovear explained. "If the barrier doesn't know your mind pattern it will destroy you."

"Oh, I see. Another one of your Carlaf's paranoid protections," Jgar sighed.

"It would seem that way," Rovear sighed too.

"What about our people?" Sharl questioned. "Their minds aren't tuned to your fence."

"Like I said before, on the physical plain, the fence only serves as an alarm. And a very poor one at that. It's tripped by everything. Even low flying birds." He shrugged. "I'll return soon." He sat his body down and left it.

"Come on. Let's get you rested and fed." Christance led them away. One of her consorts took over Rovear's flesh and followed with them.

Jgar felt odd eating with a stranger who looked like Rovear. He tried to ignore the stranger and the situation, but it was difficult. Somewhere in between his food and his bath, Jgar heard talk of riders from Pouchetia's anhabit arriving. They were sent to kill someone. He didn't know whom, but he hoped it wasn't him.

Chapter 41

When Rovear arrived, Pouchetia was alone in her bedroom. She seemed a bit pale. "Carlaf," Rovear greeted her as he entered her mind.

"Oh, Rovear," she said without much expression. She left her body and entered the realm of absence. He followed. "Are the Sheens on their way?"

"Well, no."

"No? Why not? I don't want them running around here. I have enough problems!" she snapped.

"They're not running around, Pouchetia. There are only two left alive," he said quietly.

"What happened?" She didn't seem shocked or upset, just surprised.

"They were destroyed by your mind field."

"What! You let them take to projection. Council will have my head! When they find out that I..." She raved.

"No," he interjected quickly. "I didn't let them. They did it while I was away."

She thought for a few moments. "Take their bodies to the hills. We will tell anyone who asks that the handra-can ambushed and killed them."

"Their bodies lie in the hills already."

"Good," the Exoltaire said.

Rovear wanted to explain to her why they were left alone in the hills but decided not to. She didn't ask him and she already seemed upset if not disoriented.

"Lady, remove the mind field," he suggested quietly.

"Yes, yes. You're right," she replied. "Council will never have to know it existed." She motioned a few odd ways and stared at the floor with her hands on her forehead.

"It's done. Go now and bring the bodies to the nearest anhabit. Make sure they look like victims of the handra-can."

"We're at Nylla Christance's. I'll tell her to send someone to get them."

"My riders should be at Christance's soon. Tell them to go to Nylla Valties and get more riders. The search has turned to the hills and mountainside."

"Search?" Rovear asked curiously.

"Yes. In the hills behind the anhabit and the mountains beyond it," she said absently. She didn't tell him more. "Go now." Pouchetia pushed at him with her mind and sent him into projection.

There was something wrong. Rovear was sure of that, but what exactly was wrong, he had no idea. He didn't resist her push and returned to his body.

The rest of the day, Pouchetia thought of the orange beads in the center of the oval table. What were they for? What were they doing?

Chapter 42

Alana ran as fast as her legs could carry her around the anhabit. It was a large building and before the hill was even in her sight, she had lost her strength and was at a slow somber walk. She kept her mind off the length and strain of the walk by singing some songs. By the time she rounded the bend to the field that led to the hill, she was singing the same line over and over. "...She will ride to the sky on the equis of shining black and she'll never come back. No, she'll never come back."

It was getting hot. Alana wiped her forehead with the back of her hand. She didn't stop to realized that it wasn't even near the heat of the day, so there had to be another reason why it was so hot. Not until she rounded the corner, then she knew why.

A great black and silver tower stood in the distance before her. It hissed and steamed like some deranged animal ready to charge. Alana's limbs weakened and her head shook back and forth with jerks. She tried to reason, but she'd never seen anything like it before. Was it some kind of monster? Was it going to pounce on her and eat her? She had no idea. The hissing grew louder and faded away then grew louder again in a rhythm that sounded like breathing. Alana took a deep breath as the sound faded and held it, letting it out slowly until the hissing was gone. She stood mesmerized, breathing in time with the ship's eerie rhythm.

The rhythm compelled her to walk towards it. She took her first cautious steps in the black and silver tower's direction, her hands out in front of her in an effort to look friendly.

"It's a very large animal," Alana concluded. "Seth said to always approach a strange animal hands open. Especially large ones." As she got closer, the heat grew more intense and a wind started blowing at her face, whipping her hair back.

"Hey, Look!" a guard yelled to his companions.

"What's that child doing?" another asked.

"I don't know, but she'll be killed." The first man kicked his mount to get it to gallop to Alana, but the animal faltered. It didn't want to get any closer to the strange vehicle. He kicked it again, this time much harder. It bolted forward. The guard bent down as he rode pass the child and scooped her up under his arm.

"No, no, no!" Alana kicked and screamed. "I only wanted to play with it."

He rejoined the other guards at the fence and dismounted. "She only wanted to play with it," He said then put her down and laughed. "Go back to your mother, child. That thing is far from a toy."

Alana looked up at him. Her dark eyes shined like onyx. The man was taken back by them. He had never seen such dark eyes before.

"My mother is far away. Will you take me to her?" the child asked with innocence.

He picked her up again. His heart filled with tenderness and compassion for her. By the color of her hair, he knew she was one of the travelers and that her mother was probably one of them too. "Sure," he said with a smile. "What's her name. I'll find her for you."

"Tammeia," Alana replied.

"Tammeia," the man puzzled. It never occurred to him that she could mean Regime Tammeia Sheen. "Does anyone here know a woman called Tammeia. She's one of the visitors."

"I know of a Tammeia from Council," another answered.

"Alana!" An equis cantered on the other side of the fence. It stopped and Taresse dismounted. "Alana, what are you doing so far from the anhabit?" The woman was only lightly scolding.

"I... I.." Alana stuttered.

"She wanted to play with that." The man who found her pointed at the Netrin sky vehicle.

"I only wanted to pet it," she said meekly. "It wanted to play with me."

"That's silliness. The sky vehicle isn't alive. It's not a pet." She motioned and Alana climbed back through the fence. Taresse grabbed the child's hands and pulled her up on the equis. They felt callused and blistered but Alana didn't seem to be in any pain.

When she arrived back in her room, Palray hurried to get her. "Where have you been?"

"I saw a big, big animal," Alana answered. "It was so big it could touch the sky." She stood up on her tip toes and reached as far over her head as she could.

"Your hands? Where are your bandages?" He took her hands in his own and examined them. A few pale, red marks on each were the only indications that they were ever injured. Even the stitches had dissolved and fell off.

Alana looked at her fingers and shrugged.

"The Coray's have very powerful menders," Palray remarked with amazement.

Chapter 43

Seth had been hacking at the support beam for what seemed like time unending, yet he had only cut a small groove in the hard, seasoned wood. Frustrated, he climbed back to the pole's base.

The heat had been over for a while, yet the riders had not returned. Maybe he had time to find another method of destroying the bridge. There were no suitable materials around him to make a hatchet or an ax of any kind, and his knife was getting dull quickly. He pulled a flat stone out of his hip pouch, spat on it and used it to sharpen his blade.

Strat made his way as far down the cliff's edge as he felt safe doing. With Seth's help, he joined the Keeper at the beam's base.

"What's next, Strat?" The man asked absently as he stroked the yellow animal's neck. "What's next?"

Seth returned to the task at hand. He had to get the blade very sharp. Strat sat by him and gnawed at the wooden pole's end. Before Seth was finished, Strat had pulled away a sizable chunk of the pole's wood.

"If only I had some kindling, I could try to light the bridge on fire," he said to Strat in Keeper's tongue.

The kenya looked around his front paws. Splinters and strips of chewed wood surrounded them. He picked some up and dropped them on Seth's lap.

"Thank you," Seth said absently as he felt the damp wood, "but it probably wouldn't work away."

Suddenly the Keeper realized something. "Where did you get this stuff? There aren't any trees around here." Seth focused his tired eyes on Strat. The kenya put its tail between its hind legs in shame and crouched at the pole's end. Seth eyed the chewed and splintered beam.

"Strat!" he exclaimed.

The animal cowered in fear.

"You're wonderful, Strat!"

Strat poked his head up, still a little unsure.

"You did good, Strat. Very good!" Seth praised in Keeper's tongue.

The kenya jumped up with joy.

"Strat, my friend," Seth said with seriousness, "I need your help."

It was difficult, even for a Keeper, to convince the kenya to climb the beam over the ravine, but somehow Seth did it. The animal's legs were clumsy climbing the upward tilt of the pole, but Seth was behind him, slowly and carefully guiding him to the notch he had started with his knife.

"Go ahead, Strat. Rip it." Seth showed him the place and the kenya put his jaws as far around the pole as he could. Its eyes turned to look down.

"No. Don't look down, Strat!" Seth ordered.

It was too late. Strat dug his nails into the wood and crouched as low to it as possible. His body was quivering but otherwise still. Seth reached up and patted the animal's back. He tried to smooth the animal's neck hair that was sticking up tight in fright. "Relax, Strat. Calm yourself, brother kenya. I won't let you fall," Seth repeated. After some time, Strat relaxed and began to chew at the wood.

Chapter 44

"Mother," Rovear greeted Nylla Christance, "are there riders here from my Carlaf's?" He flexed his body. It had been a long time since he had been free of it. He almost hated to come back. It felt so closed and alone to be in a body again.

"Yes. Four Carlafs and four consorts," she explained as she watched him put on a clean robe and helped him tie it.

Rovear reflected for a moment over how much she, his mother, still babied him even though he had been in a lady's service for almost half his life. He sighed.

"Pouchetia wants them to ride out to Valties' and get more riders. I'm to tell them they have to search the hills." He ran a comb through his freshly washed and still damp hair.

"Oh, so the Keeper has run to the hills. That could be a problem. He's gone mad, they say." She shook her elderly, yet still attractive head. "But if he's in the mountains, he's not coming back."

Her son heard her words but didn't stop to wonder what Keeper she spoke of. It just passed through his ears, never settling in his mind.

Rovear handed his mother the comb. She motioned for him to turn around, which he did, then she gave him the motherly look of approval. He nodded then walked briskly out.

Renia and Dalta headed the group of riders that were looking for Seth in that area. Rovear knew them well. They were both High Regimes of Pouchetia's command. They met Rovear as he was leaving the room.

"Renia, Dalta," he greeted their surprised expressions. "I bring news from my Carlaf."

"What news?" Renia looked concerned.

"Pouchetia wants you to ride to Valties' and gather more riders. The hills are where the search will center."

"The hills." Dalta's face went pale. "What's happened?"

"I don't know. All she said was get riders and search in the hills and surrounding mountainside."

"Come on, Dalta. We have to go and assemble the riders right now." Renia took a deep resigning breath.

"Pardon me, Ladies, but I lead travelers to the gate. There are only two of them. Since you're going to the gate anhabit to get riders, can you leave them at the gate with food and equis for the return trip to their Habite? I would take them myself, but I feel Pouchetia needs me now." The worry showed easily in his eyes. "It won't add any time to your ride."

Rovear didn't have any idea what had happened in the hills behind his home, but he knew that almost all of the main house's residents were camping in those hills. From the start he knew it was a mistake to send them away. He knew in his soul that it was sure to cause more trouble than leaving them to interact with the Sheens. Maybe Pouchetia was truly afraid that some of her people would learn to like the Sheens as he had learned to like Jgar. "But there's no arguing with Pouchetia," he thought with a sigh. "When she feels threatened or in danger, she always goes to the extremes." He knew his skills could be put to better use back home, calming Pouchetia and trying to soften her sharp fits of extremes, than as a tour guide for Jgar and Sharl. Besides, after what had happened to the group he felt uncomfortable in their presence. It was time for him to go home. He needed to.

"All right, Exoltairetive," Renia nodded. "If Christance will supply the necessities for them, then we'll bring them as far as the gate. But no further.

"That's all I require." Rovear motioned the customary thank you. "When shall I tell them to be ready?"

"We'll ride as soon as their supplies are ready," Renia answered. Rovear agreed and trotted away.

He found the Sheen Regimitive in the main meeting hall. "Jgar," Rovear said with slight sorrow. "I've been called back to do my Carlaf's bidding. She had provided for you and Sharl. You're going to ride out with the Regimes, Renia and Dalta, and their group."

"The group of riders," Jgar's mind darted, but he said nothing out loud. "They were sent to kill someone."

The Regimitive took a deep breath. "Why are these women here? Don't they come from the main anhabit?"

"Yes," Rovear whispered. He looked around. There were people all over the room, probably listening. He pulled Jgar to the side. "They were sent from my Carlaf's to track down and kill someone."

"Who?" Jgar squirmed a bit.

"A man gone mad, I was told."

"No one I know, I suppose?" Jgar dared to ask another question.

"No, I doubt it." Rovear gave him a hard stare. "If my Lady wanted anyone to kill you, I could have left you on the cliff or let you rot of infection," he said with a smile. "Maybe Pouchetia would have rewarded me for doing to. You do belong to Tammeia, after all."

"I get your meaning, my brother," Jgar said slightly embarrassed by his own lack of trust.

"Brother is the important thing," Rovear said. He reached out and took Jgar's hand. "We are brothers. Consorts to the last of our blood. No matter what fate our Carlaf's intend for us, we'll never let it come between us."

Rovear and Jgar hugged.

"I may never lay my hands on you again, but be assured you'll always be in my thoughts." Rovear squeezed him tightly then broke the embrace.

"And you in mine," Jgar whispered.

A far away voice echoed through the hall. "The riders are ready to go."

"I'll say good-bye now." Rovear patted Jgar's back. "When I see you again, if I ever do, it will be a wonderful moment for me." He smiled.

"For me too," Jgar said as he left the room. He looked back only once as he ran down the hill and Rovear was gone.

The Corays had provided them with an equis drawn wagon and provisions enough for the trip home. They headed off. Four riders in front, and wagon with Jgar and Sharl aboard, and four more riders in back.

Jgar looked to his side. Sharl's head was draped in a shawl, only her face showed. He looked away.

"What?" Sharl said.

"Oh, nothing," Jgar replied. He turned and looked behind him. She followed his gaze back to Rovear's mounted figure riding in the opposite direction.

"I'm glad he's gone too," she said.

Chapter 45

Strat had been chewing and pulling at the pole for so long that boredom caused Seth to feel sleepy. Strat had managed to gnaw slightly more than half way through the beam and with the help of Seth's knife, the slice was getting larger, slowly. Maybe by morning they would have cut through enough that the support would collapse.

"But what then?" Seth thought. "We'll have to get to the banking quickly."

But that was far away. For now he was only concerned with collapsing the bridge before the riders returned so he could make his escape safely.

He went back to the cliff shelf. Hunter was gone, but the kits were not. She was out searching for food again. He hoped she would make a kill this time. Strat perked up his ears and stopped chewing.

Seth listened for a moment and heard a far away sound. The riders were coming back. His plan had failed. Seth scrambled back up the pole to Strat.

The first equis steps on the bridge were hollow sounding but soon there was a low rumbling sound. "Must be a wagon," the Keeper thought.

As the riders continued across the bridge it began to shake. Seth dug his knife as deeply as he could into the wood to provide himself with a hand hold. The riders were at a trot. Their animals moved in a steady continuous rhythm. The bridge shook more and more.

Strat let out a quiet yap and dug his claws into the wood.

The riders neared the center of the bridge. The beam Seth and Strat were on shook harder. Strat's nails slipped. He clawed wildly for something to grab on to. He even tried to wrap his tongue around the huge pole, but it was no use. He plunged into the ravine below.

"Strat!" Seth reached out as quickly as he could. By a stoke of luck, he caught the animal's hind leg. Strat's free fall body weight pulled hard on the Keeper, causing him to loose his delicate balance. He tried desperately to regain it but the bridge continued to shake and he slipped.

The riders passed over the bridge, unaware that below them, Seth hung with one hand from a knife dug into the beam, and a yellow colored kenya hung from his other.

Chapter 46

"I don't like that bridge," Sharl said as the wagon rolled across the massive wooden structure.

"It's been there for more than three generations," Dalta told her.

"Don't be afraid of its shaking," Renia added. "I was told it's made to shake like that so it will absorb shocks and not fall."

Sharl sighed. She didn't care why it shook. She was glad she would never see that bridge again.

When the party got to the gate, Jgar and Sharl were let out. Jgar remarked about the gate's size. It took four men with equis to open it enough for the wagon to fit through.

There was a misty rain falling and Jgar remembered that it was misting the same way when he first saw the gate. He looked at the field ahead of him, sighed and snapped the wagon reins. The equis picked up the pace. Jgar waited until they were far away from the great wall and the Habite behind it before he spoke. "Well, it's home we go," he said with false enthusiasm. He wasn't looking forward to telling Tammeia about what had happened in the hills. He would also have to stop at the Torta's Habit. His stomach turned at the thought.

"How do I tell them I left their loved ones alone to die? How do I justify bad judgment when it's caused people to lose their lives? They must already know something's wrong. Like Rojer, some of the men must have had Carlafs who died on the journey. If they didn't break from their bonds to the women at the time of their deaths, they would've gone into a fever. But maybe," his thoughts rambled on, "without news of death, the fevers would be attributed to something else."

Jgar kept thinking about it all through the night and the next day. By the next nightfall, he was tired of thinking. Even so, sleep was hard to come by. He couldn't lie still and quiet anymore. Before long, he found himself walking in the dark. In the distance he saw a flickering of fire and made a mental note of where it was. The next morning, after they ate, Jgar and Sharl headed to where he had seen it. After a while, something appeared on the horizon. Soon it was apparent it was riders.

"Jgar! Do you see them?" Sharl pointed with excitement. "They look like our people!"

Jgar squinted. They did look like Sheens. He hit the equis' hindquarters and its trot turned to a canter. Sharl waved her arms above her head.

"It looks like Eisen!" Jgar shouted with excitement. He urged the animal to run faster. The wagon bumped and shook wildly.

"It is Eisen!" Sharl shouted. She jumped up in her seat. "Oooooh!" Sharl coupled over and fell to her seat.

"Sharl are you all right?" He pulled back on the reins. The animal slowed then stopped.

"I'm all right. I..." She put her hand on her head. "I think I'm coming down sick."

The approaching riders recognized Jgar and Sharl.

"Jgar! Jgar Sheen!" Eisen called.

Jgar waved his sash in the air and the riders picked up their pace to get to him. They stopped along side of the wagon. Jgar and Eisen embraced. All four men greeted each other. Then greeted Sharl. The welcomes complete, Jgar turned to Eisen. "Eisen, how are you?" Jgar greeted.

"I'm well," he answered.

"And Tammeia? I miss her."

"She misses you, I'm sure."

"Well, how is she? How's she handling all this?" Jgar asked.

"We'll talk later." Eisen looked at the Dominion. "What's wrong with her?"

"She's coming down ill. I'm on my way to get her home." He took a breath. Quetan and Raata were silent.

"Where are the others?" Eisen looked confused.

"I'll tell you when we're alone." Jgar glanced at Quetan and Raata.

"Don't' worry about them. They can be trusted." Eisen said and smiled.

"I know that. But the Lady," he said under his breath and motioned towards Sharl. Even though Sharl knew the reason it was a good excuse, and Eisen believed it.

"So, tell me, brother. What brings you out here?" Jgar said changing the subject.

"I have a mission. Tammeia's sent me to retrieve Alana." Sharl moaned.

"Are you all right, Lady Dominion?" Eisen asked.

Sharl felt odd being addressed with respect again. Her head spun. "I just need some rest," she said with her hands still on her head.

"I think it's best she returns home right away," Eisen said.

"Yes. Then, good luck on your quest. I'll move on now." Jgar waved a reluctant goodbye.

"No, don't go, Jgar. It's very important that you ride with us. You've been inside of the Coray's Habite limits. You know the way."

"Someone has to return with Sharl. She would be near to useless to us if she were well, but sick she's totally worthless."

Sharl tried to make an indignant face but only became sicker.

"What exactly is this mission? Do they know that you're coming to get Alana?"

Eisen shrugged. "Let's talk away from here." He and Jgar walked away from the group.

"Jgar, you remember how Tammeia acted when she lost her first girl child?"

Jgar nodded.

"And how upset she was when we first moved to our Habite."

"Yes. Yes," he said impatiently.

"You remember, she felt that everyone was going to hurt her."

"Yes!" Jgar said with force. "Get to the point!"

"She's much the same now. It's just too much for her that Alana is being taken away."

"But that's only natural. Alana is her only daughter. Even I feel the pain of parting with her," Jgar said.

"I too. But Tammeia is convinced that Pouchetia will kill Alana," Eisen explained.

"Maybe she will," Jgar said coldly.

"Why do you say that?" Eisen was shocked. "Are you losing your mind too?"

"Because I know of Pouchetia. She's a wicked, vile woman. Just as Tammeia has said."

Eisen rolled his eyes in exasperation. "You know as well as I that the Council wouldn't send our people, including Alana, to Pouchetia's Habite if the Exoltaire could not be trusted."

"And what makes you so sure?" Jgar asked boldly.

"Pouchetia is a woman bound by the Council. She is bound by her honor." He began to walk further away. Jgar followed. "After all you're free and well, and you are consort to..."

"Eisen," Jgar cut in. "Pouchetia killed the rest of our return party."

"I don't understand." Eisen fell silent for moment. "She what?"

"She killed them. She enforced a mind field that destroyed each of them when they exited their bodies for the realms if projection."

"All of them?" Eisen's shock showed.

"No," Jgar answered dryly. "As far as I know, only the return party."

Eisen looked blankly at Jgar. "There is no mistake?"

"None, Eisen. Even her own consort admits to it."

"Than this is a matter for Council."

"Council will be told, I assure you. But if your mission is one to be performed in secret, then it would serve you best not to tell anyone yet."

"And you suggest?" Eisen lifted his eyebrows with curiosity. His mind was busy trying to absorb what his ears had just heard.

"I know some things about Pouchetia's Habite that could be invaluable. It will help us to retrieve Alana and the rest of our people. Then we can tell Council. That way Pouchetia won't have our people to lay her wrath upon."

"Is that all you plan?"

"Eisen, Council will surely give Pouchetia what's due her." He smiled a toothy grin. "And when they do, I'll make sure to be there to watch."

"Jgar, your heart is bitter."

"Maybe so. But it's a bitterness brought on by the evils done me."

Eisen didn't reply. What could he say?

"If we can get as far as Pouchetia's anhabit undetected it will be easy to get Alana." Jgar pushed a few stray hairs out of his eyes. "I'll tell everyone about how to do it as we ride. Come on, let's get back. We're wasting time." Jgar and Eisen returned to the others.

<h1 style="text-align:center">Chapter 47</h1>

Breyan and Touchea entered the Council hall together.

"Are you sure Pouchetia knew she was supposed to ready the hall?" Breyan asked after she noticed that the place was unchanged.

"Yes, I told her myself. Her consorts confirmed her leaving to do so." The High Exoltaire looked around her. Lumdon Hall was still set up for the usual Council meetings. She had asked Pouchetia to dissolve the powerful rings of mind energy that encircled the hall and to cover all of the control stones, so the Netrins wouldn't have anything to use against them, just in case. But none of these things were done. In addition, the Council table was a wreck. Its chairs were scattered everywhere. "It would seem she never got here."

Breyan looked at the rug below her feet. She gasped, her hand over her mouth, at what she saw. There was a trail of blood leading to the oval table. "Touchea!" Breyan was horrified. She pointed to an unconscious figure in the center of the table.

Touchea ran to the table. "Breyan, come quickly," the High Exoltaire called.

Breyan hurried to her side. "Tame!" Breyan cried out when she saw her daughter's body. She ran around to the center of the table. "Tammeia." She cradled her daughter's head in her lap. "My beautiful Tammeia," Breyan cried.

"Wait." Touchea looked closely at the Regime. "She still breathes."

Breyan put her hand near the Regime's mouth. "You're right. Quick, call a mender."

"I don't need a mender," Tammeia mumbled.

"Child, Child. What happened? How do you feel?" Breyan stroked Tammeia's forehead.

"I'm fine. I guess I must have fallen asleep." She lifted her head. "How did I get..." Then she remembered.

"Pouchetia attacked me. She broke my back. I can't be alive." She looked around joyfully puzzled. "But it appears that I am."

"What happened?" Touchea looked concerned. "What did Pouchetia do?"

"She attacked me. She said that she was going to kill my Alana. Then she left me to die." Tammeia looked around her. "I remember. She pushed me off the table. I landed here. The pain was incredible. I know I was dying." She was confused.

Her mother examined her but found nothing wrong. She even wiped off some of the dried blood but there were no cuts or scars underneath it. "You're unhurt now."

"It must have been the beads." Tammeia ran her hand over the orange beads. "They must have a strange power. I remember an orange glow."

"It's said they have powers unrecorded. But I've never seen them restore life before." Touchea walked around the table.

"Yes, they have many powers. The first generation Council was very wise," Breyan added.

"Huh?" Tammeia stood up. "I don't understand."

"The beads did indeed save your life, daughter. Unfortunately, the next time you choose to tangle with Pouchetia, they may not be so near."

"Help us get this hall ready for our guests. Then go home. The Netrins will be ready to leave their vehicles before the darkness falls," Touchea instructed, changing the subject.

Breyan looked at her with mild surprise, then looked at her daughter again. "She's right Tame. We better get to work."

The High Exoltaire broke the rings of mind energy that spun through the hall. Tammeia physically covered any control stones or other points that emitted power. Breyan followed using her own power to hide or disguise any emanations the stones gave off. By the time they were done, the hall felt helplessly empty.

<h1 style="text-align:center">Chapter 48</h1>

Seth hung motionless and silent, his face in a hideous grimace that showed the strain. He was dreadfully aware that the knife couldn't hold forever. He had to make some kind of effort to get back on the pole, and for that would need both hands. He thought of Strat. The animal was very large and its weight pulled Seth's arms from their sockets. He was sure that the kenya was still alive. Its whimperings were very clear. If only Strat was in shock or dead of fright, he would let him go.

Seth had to make a decision and make it quickly. His joints couldn't stand the strain and pretty soon it would be too late for both of them. He tried to start a slight swinging motion, maybe he could gain enough momentum to get Strat to the pole then pull himself up. The knife started to slip. He stopped then kept dreadfully still.

"Yoowoo!" echoed in the depths below. Hunter had returned. She was at the base of the pole.

"Hunter," Seth tried to yell but his words were barely audible. "Come here. Help us," he said in Keeper's tongue. His teeth were clinched tight with strain.

Hunter took a few steps onto the pole. The kits on the cliff shelf above whimpered and howled. Hunter turned to them and jumped off the pole, back to the cliff's edge.

"Hunter! Please!" Seth strained. Strat let out a high tone screech. His body twisted one quick revolution. Seth groaned as pain burned through his shoulders.

"Easy, Strat," he whispered.

"Hunter!" the Keeper cried again. His voice cracked. "Help us, Hunter. Come over here and help me pull Strat up."

Hunter walked in a tight circle, all the while yapping nervously. Seth fell silent. He put all his concentration on his arms. He told himself they were solid bands, that he felt no strain and there was no pain. It didn't work for long. He closed his eyes tightly and again contemplated dropping Strat to save himself.

Finally, he decided he had to save himself. If he held Strat any longer, they would both die. When he opened his eyes to say goodbye and apologize to his kenya friend for what he had to do, Hunter was on her way up the pole. Her tongue hung out in a nervous pant. Her tail was low between her legs.

"Hunter," Seth said. Strat began to whimper louder. "Easy Hunter. Good girl." Hunter edged her way closer. "Good, my friend," Seth said in an easing tone. When Hunter reached him she dug her claws as deeply as she could into the hard wood.

"Are you steady, Hunter?" Seth asked. The knuckles of his hand that held the knife were white with strain. Hunter was starring at them. Maybe she was contemplating biting him and sending him to his death.

"Are you steady, Hunter, old girl?" he repeated.

She tried to look down at him.

"No! Don't look down, Regal Lady." He looked her in the eyes, making sure she wouldn't look down. "Are you set?"

She wagged her tail cautiously.

"Good." He looked down to the ravine's endless depths, then he looked at Strat. "Hold tight, Hunter. I'll try to lift Strat to where you can grab him."

Hunter tightened her grip.

Seth took a breath and began to lift Strat. His face turned red as blood, and sweat ran off him like rain. He lifted Strat to about his chest. The animal's weight was tremendous. Seth held his breath and put as much force as he could into his shoulders and arms. Pain seared through him. There was a creaking sound as the knife began to slip. Seth tried to regain his grip on the handle as it slipped forward.

Hunter stretched her neck. Her teeth neared Strat's hindquarters. The knife slipped again. Seth adjusted his grip once again. This time two of his fingers found the blade. It dug deep. Hunter grabbed Strat by the skin of his hind side. When Seth was sure she had a good grip on him, he let go of the kenya's leg. Hunter faltered forward, but held her grip. Her sharp teeth pierced Strat's skin. Red blood oozed over his yellow coat.

Seth swung forward. He managed to pull himself up onto the pole. The Keeper leaned forward and helped Hunter pull Strat to safety. The three descended the pole to the cliff shelf.

They settled themselves down. Strat licked his wounds, and Hunter licked Seth's hand. Her saliva stung. He looked down at his hand. The tip of his smallest finger had been severed off in the struggle for safety. It seemed strangely comical to him. The ravine's jaws had managed to get at least a taste of him. He gave his hand back to Hunter's mothering care. Her saliva had a healing property. It wouldn't cause his finger to grow a new tip, but it would stop the bleeding and guard from infection.

He thought about the futility of his effort. "I should have known," he said in Keeper's tongue. "One man can't collapse a bridge of that size." Hunter gave him a hard look then returned to the job of cleaning his wound. Seth watched the kits eat the rodent Hunter had caught earlier. He was hungry but there was barely enough for the two of them.

Chapter 49

A long silver shaft on the side of the sky vehicle turned and a door opened. By the time Tammeia arrived, three dark figures were descending the black ladder that was lowered from the door.

The three figures drew some kind of weapons that didn't have blades, but were no larger than knives. The regime looked closely at her new guest.

All three were men. They wore their hair closely cropped and their bodies were clothed completely in tightly fitting dark garbs. What made them look so different to Tammeia was their facial hair. All three had hair growing from their cheeks and chin. Tammeia looked at her smooth faced Consorts. The thought of men with facial hair disgusted her.

"Welcome," she said finally.

"Thank you," the man in the middle replied.

"I'm to take you to the Council hall. You will meet with the Exoltaire Touchea there."

The man on the left mumbled a translation. The man mumbled back. "Take us then," the interpreter replied.

They followed Tammeia to her anhabit where she offered them drinks that she had laced with a mild sedative. When she was sure of its effects, she pulled their minds out of their bodies and brought them to Lumdon Hall.

The trip to the Council hall didn't take long. Soon after leaving their drugged bodies, the mind of the Netrins became clear and sharp again. By the time they entered the hall, they were wide-awake and very unaware of how they got there.

"Regime Tammeia Sheen," Touchea greeted.

"Welcome, Sarjon." She bowed to the Netrin. Her consort handed the men robes. Their projection selves were bare and the Netrins felt uncomfortable naked. Tammeia was shocked by the amount of body hair their guests had. She was glad they were given robes. It was below her station to stare, but it would have been hard not to.

The hall was filled with people. Everyone had arrived before Tammeia, including Pouchetia.

Pouchetia stared at the Regime. Her eyes glossed with disbelief. Tammeia strode by, trying not to show how nervous she was.

"Welcome to Tigrin and to Lumdon Hall," Touchea greeted. All seventy-three translators mumbled at once. "We are presently preparing suitable quarters for your people. I trust you'll be comfortable here until our people are ready to go."

Another mumbling ran through the hall. Heads turned. One man spoke in words that sounded like gibberish.

Breyan translated before the Netrin translator spoke. "He said, thank you but his people can't stay. They want our people to board immediately. They will be leaving as soon as each site is aligned correctly."

"Our people are not ready. We misunderstood your instruction. We didn't expect you for some time yet," Touchea addressed the man who spoke.

"We're sorry. Our ships are set to work a certain way. To upset their time sequence would mean disaster for our missions," the man's translator said. "Our planet needs the resources badly. We can't afford to waist even one ship."

Touchea looked at Breyan and several other Council women. The man said something else. Another man spoke in reply to the first. The interpreter said nothing. Touchea looked at Breyan.

"He said if we don't send our people now, they'll leave without them." Breyan took a deep breath. "The other one said they should. We're only trouble."

The interpreter spoke. "Our ships are automatic. That is to say they are preset and cannot be changed."

Touchea swallowed hard. "Very well then," she announced. "Dispatch our people to them now."

Again there was a mumble in the crowd. This time, it was from her own people.

Chapter 50

Alana slept heavily that night. Her long afternoon walk had made her tired — too tired to dream. However, as morning came she did dream.

The first dream was a restful happy dream of childhood. She was playing in a field with some of her friends. They were running and racing. She was having a wonderful time. She raced through the field, trying to catch Gabriel. He jumped over a log. She followed, leaping after him. Instead of landing on the other side, she floated up and flew over him. She flew faster and faster until she saw the bridge under her.

It was the dream of the equis again. The riders were coming. She could not bare to see it all happen again. She broke away and tried to head for home, but the big wooden gate blocked her way. She had to get past it to get away. She pushed with all her might. The gate creaked. She pushed again. This time it opened just a little, but it had to open more. She pushed and pushed until it opened just a little more. Then it swung closed with a resounding boom. Alana woke up.

Chapter 51

Eisen sent Raata back with Sharl, then he, Quetan and Jgar rode, keeping a quick and steady pace to the Coray Habite boundaries. They spent more than half the day trying to open the heavy wooden gate, but it wouldn't budge. When night came, they made camp near the gate and the next morning they were out at daybreak trying to open it again.

"What's on the other side of this wall, Jgar?" Eisen questioned. He was surprised that they were trying to enter in daylight.

"More of this barren plain, and further in, some trees."

"Are there any anhabits close by?"

"None. A desert area separates this from the livable part of the Habite. There's one woman's anhabit along the wall, but it's far enough to the right of here that we should get by unnoticed. Aside from an occasional guard, I think the only time there are people around this part of the wall is when they harvest the plants that grow in the rainy season. I guess the Corays have a lot of faith in their defenses."

"And it's no wonder. How do you think we're ever going to get past that damn wall?" Eisen scoffed.

"Brothers, look." Quetan pointed. The great gate was moving. Its hinges creaked.

"Damn, someone's seen us. They're coming out," Eisen said. The gate moved outward a crack.

"I'll check." Quetan carefully poked his head through to the other side. The gate creaked again and he pulled out quickly. "There's no one there?" he said. His confusion showed on his face.

"Are you sure?" Jgar didn't believe it.

"It must move with the wind," Eisen reasoned.

"Are you a fool, Eisen?" Jgar laughed. "How could a gentle breeze open something we ourselves couldn't budge?"

"Whatever the case, the gate is opened," Quetan pointed out. With his words, the three men raced through it before it closed again.

After riding a while, they came to a crossing of four roads in the forest. "Now which way?" Eisen scanned the horizon.

"This is the way." Jgar kicked his mount. It ran and the others followed.

At Valties' anhabit along the wall, Dalta and Renia had gathered two more women and five more men to ride back to search the hills. There had been a delay because Renia's mount tripped and fell. In the process, she injured her knee. Since she was the only one certain of the trails through the Illu-Danchant Mountains, and that was the shortest way back to the hills behind Pouchetia's, they had to wait the afternoon for a mender to heal her sufficiently enough for her to ride again. The Regime and her group passed the gate not long after Eisen, Quetan and Jgar entered.

Chapter 52

"Pouchetia," Touchea gained the attention of the Exoltaire. "Can I speak with you?" She asked cordially.

"Yes, what is it?" Pouchetia said reluctantly. She believed she knew what the High Exoltaire was going to say and she was determined to deny it all.

"Your affairs with Tammeia Sheen are your own. How you wish to settle any disagreements is also your own concern, but if I find out that you have killed the Sheen child, Alana, then I will be forced to take your life in return."

"I haven't killed the child."

"Then promise me that you won't." Touchea motioned for Pouchetia to give her the sign of honor.

Pouchetia grabbed the other woman's hand so she would know what she said was true. "I will not kill her," she promised.

"Good. Now go and get your sons ready for the trip." Touchea motioned for her to leave, and Pouchetia disappeared into the realms of projection. After she was gone, Touchea sat down in her seat at the Council table. She looked at the Wall of Exoltaires, at the countless pictures of past heads of Council. "Ah, sisters. How can our children be so heartless?" She thought for a moment longer then got up and walked out of the hall.

<h1 style="text-align:center">Chapter 53</h1>

Seth and the pack stayed under the bridge, recuperating and resting for quite some time. Finally, Seth stood up. "Let's get going, Hunter. We have to find some game." The Keeper took a deep breath. He didn't even know how long it had been since he'd eaten last, but it was quite a while. His stomach growled as if to remind him. "No sooner time than now," he said.

When they came out from hiding, the field was cool and stable. The heat was long over.

"If we're lucky, we'll find the forest before the Corays find us," Seth looked down at Hunter. "If they catch me, don't stay and help. Run away as fast as you can. Save your kits." He sighed. "But it won't come to that," he said hopefully as he turned to take one last look at the bridge. It seemed to mock him, laugh at him. Seth had never hated anything, living or not, as much as he hated that bridge.

"Come on. Let's get going." He shook his head with disgust.

The pack walked till the night began to darken the sky, yet it seemed as if they barely moved. Eventually, there was a hint of trees in the distance and they had yet to come across anything to eat. Seth squinted and tried to see clearer. There was something else there.

"Riders!" His heart skipped a beat. He looked around, but there was no shelter. "Run, Hunter! Hide your kits!" he yelled in Keeper's tongue. The four kenya took off. Seth didn't see where they went.

A hundred plans ran through the Keepers mind. All of which were either impossible to complete in the time available or just impossible. There was nowhere for him to hide. But it didn't really matter, they would have surely seen him by now. Maybe he could spring an attack on them, but he had no real weapon. His knife was still in the bridge support. All he had was his staff.

The riders were getting closer. Still, Seth couldn't make them out. None of them looked like a woman, but it was starting to get dark and the light of setting Kai came from behind them, silhouetting them and hiding any defining features. He prayed they didn't have any long-range weapons or he was as good as dead.

The riders slowed down and pulled up close to each other. They stayed still for a moment then rode on again at full canter. Seth gripped his staff tightly, ready to use it.

As the riders got closer, the Keeper thought they looked familiar. He was sure he knew who they were.

"Jgar? Eisen!" he called out before he realized how unlikely it was that the riders were who they appeared to be.

"And who are you, consort?" a familiar voice called back. They didn't recognize Seth yet or maybe they just didn't know him.

Seth's heart pounded, he verged on panic. "Never mind, consorts, I mistook you for someone you're not," he called back to them, hoping they wouldn't ride any closer. "I'm sorry I bothered you. I'll be on my way."

Hunter and Strat watched from a safe distance. They were too far away to hear the words Seth spoke and even if they did, they wouldn't have understood.

The riders continued to get closer.

"Seth?" Eisen called out. The Keeper kept his head low. He didn't look at who addressed him, nor did he reply.

"It can't be Seth," Jgar said.

The Keeper recognized his voice. "Jgar?" Seth looked up and smiled. "Eisen! Quetan!"

Eisen jumped off his mount and ran to hug Seth. He was glad to see his good friend again. Seth pushed him playfully. Eisen pushed back. Soon they were wrestling like young boys.

"Eisen!" Jgar shouted. There was a sound of struggle and low growling.

"No! Strat!" Seth yelled in Keeper's tongue. "No! They're my friends!"

Hunter was in a frenzy, tearing at Quetan's neck.

"No! Hunter Stop!" Seth grabbed her by the ear. "Stop! They're friends!"

Her frenzy slowed and then stopped. Strat trotted over to Seth. He had knocked Jgar off his mount but hadn't hurt him.

Hunter looked up at Seth. Even in the darkening light, he could see her face was red with Quetan's blood.

"Oh, Hunter." Seth shook his head slowly and turned away from her. He felt for any signs of life in Quetan. "He's dead," the Keeper said quietly to Eisen. "My friends were only defending me." He began to nervously stroke Strat's back. "They misunderstood our little brawl."

Seth looked at Quetan's lifeless flesh. "I suppose we should bury him. It wouldn't be right to leave his body out on the plain to picked apart by birds."

Eisen drew a slow deep breath. There was a long moment of cold, still silence.

"It's all right, Seth. Tell your kenya that it's forgiven. We understand," Jgar finally said, breaking the silence like the breaking of glass.

"But they killed Quetan," Eisen rumbled under his breath.

"Many fatal accidents have happened on this soil. One more won't matter much," Jgar said without feeling. "We can forgive them. They did what they did out of loyalty. That makes Quetan's death more meaningful than any of the others. It can be forgiven."

Eisen nodded but didn't reply verbally. His eyes showed his true feelings though his voice spoke no anger.

Seth chose a spot and was digging Quetan's grave. He thought about how Hunter continued to tear at the man's neck even after he told her to stop. It made him uneasy. Did he trust the pack too much? After all, they were still wild animals.

Seth dug alone for a while. Eventually Jgar and Eisen joined him. The three men dug long into the night. The digging was slow because the soil was hard and because they had only their hands as tools. Jgar carried a knife, but he wasn't about to dull its sharpness by digging with it.

When the grave was deep enough, Seth walked back to get Quetan's body. When he picked him up, he realized that a good portion of the man's flesh was gone. He laid Quetan in the grave and quickly covered him with dirt before the others found out. Now Hunter's behavior made sense to Seth. "She wasn't defending me," he realized. "She was just making another kill."

When they rode out the next morning the kenya followed, each with a full round belly.

Before the heat of the next day, the great ravine and the bridge were in sight.

"Do you see that bridge?" Seth pointed. "That bridge is a stubborn lady. I nearly lost my life trying to make it fall," he laughed. "As you can see, I didn't succeed."

Hunter and Strat yapped. Seth looked behind them. "Jgar, Eisen! There's a band of riders coming!" They turned to look. The fifteen mounted Corays looked like a moving wall across the plain.

"Hurry! Get going!" Eisen shouted and kicked his mount.

"I know the way!" Seth shouted out. His equis took the lead. They raced down the hill to the bridge. The kenya kept close behind.

The stocky Sheen bred equis were no match for the sleek, tall Coray animals. The Corays were gaining on them fast.

The gray kit howled and stopped dead in its tracks, exhausted.

"Keep going!" Seth shouted to the others. He gripped his saddle pad tightly, reached down with his free arm and scooped up the kit.

The Corays crowned the hilltop. One of them had a bow, and arrows flew by Seth's head.

"Go!" he yelled and kicked his mount with all his might. The Corays were still gaining.

Jgar and Eisen reached the bridge. The equis' steps rang hollow and loud.

"Hurry, Seth!" Jgar called back, but his words were lost in the thunder of the running animals.

Seth bent down and grabbed the other kit. Now he had one under each arm and the equis reins in his teeth. "Come on Hunter! Run!" he shouted. Seth kicked and kicked urging the equis to run faster. Hunter ran as fast as she could. Arrows flew by Seth's head.

"Yaaahwooo!" The kit under his right arm had been hit. Seth was too tense to drop the lifeless body.

Jgar and Eisen were almost at the other end of the bridge when Seth reached it. The bridge creaked. Seth remembered the damaged support beam and the gaping jaws of the ravine below. "Don't fall now," he said to himself. "Not now!"

Jgar and Eisen were off the bridge. Hunter and Strat ran behind Seth. He was less than half way across when he heard an incredible hollow thunder as the fifteen Coray riders reached the bridge.

"Faster! Faster!" he screamed to the equis in Keeper's tongue. The animal huffed back. Seth remembered the lifeless kit under his arm. The dead weight was useless and slowed the equis. He tossed the kits' body over the bridge's side.

Hunter saw the kit fly into the ravine and jumped after it, not realizing until she herself was plummeting to her death, what she had done. Hunter was dead of shock before her body followed the kit's into the bubbling fluid below.

The Coray's were nearing the center at the same time that Seth saw the end of the bridge and the dusty soil after it. The bridge creaked under the strain. The equis pounded a steady hard rhythm on its timbers. Seth heard a low rumbling and resounding crack. The bridge in front of him pulled away from the solid ground.

The equis jumped. Seth held on as tight as he could with one hand. He slipped, and the other kit fell. It bounced off the cliff's edge and into the endless gap.

Seth lay low on the equis' back. It's front legs found the ground. Its back legs didn't. The animal struggled to pull itself up. Seth hung on for his life. Strat flew past him, making the wide distance with relative ease.

The equis managed to regain its footing and made it to safety. There was an incredible screeching sound that panicked the animal and it reared up. Seth, too, was shocked by the ear wrenching sound. It was the sounds of cracking and snapping. Sounds of screams and unworldly thunder. He covered his ears and closed his eyes. He didn't see the massive bridge give way and fall apart as if it were made of kindling. He didn't see the fifteen Corays, including Pouchetia's High Regimes Renia and Dalta, fall to their deaths. He didn't see anything.

<h1 align="center">*Chapter 54*</h1>

"Pouchetia, Love." Rovear entered her room. "Several of Renia's and Dalta's consorts are inflicted with death fever. I called menders presently to detach them from their blood bonds, but I fear the women are dead."

Pouchetia's eyes opened wide. "The Keeper's struck again."

A man ran into the room. "Lady! Lady! News from Nylla Christance's. The great bridge has collapsed. It's feared your riders were crossing it at the time."

"Find that Keeper!" She yelled. "KILL HIM! NOW!"

The man ran out. Rovear stayed where he was.

"How could the Keeper be responsible for the bridge's collapse?" Rovear dared. "He couldn't destroy that bridge without some very strong tools."

She ran her hand through his soft yellow hair. "He did, my love. He did. And he shall die for it."

"Do you want me to go to the bridge to see if I can find any sign of him?"

"No. No, my consort. You've been away too long already." She untied his robe. "I prefer that you stay here with me."

Rovear wasn't confused by her sudden change of attitude. She often handled her stress in unexpected ways. He knew she was not only trying to deal with murders of her people, but she also had spent the morning saying good bye to her sons. He wondered if she had heeded the Council's wishes and performed the ceremony that would permanently bond her sons as consorts to Tammeia's daughter Alana. He didn't ask though. He knew she wouldn't want to talk about it, no matter what she decided to do. So despite all the horrors that happened that day, he followed her to bed and afterwards, he rested at her side.

"It's all Tammeia's fault," she said breaking the calm.

"What?" Rovear looked amused.

"This is all Tammeia's fault. It's all because of that witch."

"I'm sorry, Carlaf." Rovear cocked his head. "But what are you talking about?"

"Renia and Dalta's deaths, the destruction of the hill camp, everything is her fault." Pouchetia sat up. "I wish there was some way I could get my revenge on her. Some way that would hurt more than simple death." The Exoltaire neglected to mention her earlier attempt on Tammeia's life. "I'd like to send her child's corpse to her and watch her heart break, but Council has absolutely forbidden it. I must let the child live to go on the mission."

Rovear sat up behind her and rubbed her back lightly. She threw her head back in an attempt to relax. "Be assured her heart bleeds with pain," he said. "After all, once the sky vehicles leave she'll never know if Alana still breathes."

Pouchetia sat straight up. "That's my answer."

"Huh?" Rovear watched her get up and walk to the window. She stared out at the black and silver sky ship.

"When that ship leaves tonight, Tammeia will have no way of knowing?"

"Knowing?" Rovear asked.

"After the ship's left, I'll tell her I've struck a deal with the Netrins to have them kill Alana. Tammeia will have no way to check if I'm lying. Even is she doesn't believe me, she'll always have that doubt. It will drive her mad," Pouchetia said with a grin. "And when I'm satisfied that she's suffered enough, I kill her." A feeling of giddiness filled her and she giggled.

A bell rang in the distance. "Come on, Rovear. It's time to go."

"All right," he said. He took her hand and they hurried out of the room.

The Sheens, Tortas and Corays alike, were assembled outside the anhabit's limits. Pouchetia and Rovear rode out to watch them board the sky vehicle. The Exoltaire had no last words for the group. Anything she had to say was already said.

Her son, Alyx, wore the same stone face as his mother. He held his younger brother's hand. Gabriel's face was lined with tears. Pouchetia gave them one last look. Somewhere on the other side of the world, her third and eldest son was leaving in a similar vehicle. She looked at the Sheens.

Palray held Alana in his arms. The child whispered in his ear. "Where's Seth? He promised to come back?"

"He's forgotten us, child. But don't be upset. We have a great adventure in front of us and he's missing out on it."

The Netrins loaded Pouchetia's people aboard. She stood and watched until the ship began to hiss and rumble.

"Quick, everyone. Into the Cavus!" Pouchetia called above the sound. The crowd followed her underground and the Cavus doors were closed and secured. Soon there was a roaring echo from above, and the ground shook. One of the cavus' walls crumbled slightly but it didn't collapse.

"Good bye, may babies," Pouchetia whispered to herself. "Fare you well."

Rovear put his arm around her to help ease her pain. She pushed him away sharply. "There will be cleaning and repairs to do on the building and land," she announced to her people.

No one moved.

"NOW!" she shouted. The people scattered.

Chapter 55

"Breyan?"

"What, Touchea?"

"It's time."

"I know." Breyan lowered her head. "It just seems so drastic. If only there was another way."

"But there is no other way. These times are just beginning, and our children have a long trek ahead of them. Their pain is no longer our own." Touchea put her hand on the other woman's shoulder. "Our job is almost complete."

"Yes," Breyan said with a forced smile. "It will be a well needed rest."

"That it will." Touchea returned the smile. "You take the side facing Sola. I'll take the side that Kai shines on. Make sure that you destroy them all. None of the homeless minds can survive. There can be no consciousness without a body remaining, for they would only be a hampering in the plan."

"Yes, I know," Breyan said and bit her bottom lip. "Wisdom is always a child born of a difficult labor."

"Yes, the child of a long and terrible struggle. Be here come morning."

Breyan nodded and the women left.

That night the sky was hot with death. The morning came too soon for both Exoltaires. When Breyan arrived, Touchea opened a bottle of ancient viltar nectar. Breyan held a crystal glass filled with the powerful liquid. It was the first time her lips would touch the wine.

"Are the others of the Council taken care of?"

"Yes, Breyan. I watched the last pass on not long ago. That is with the exception of Tammeia and Pouchetia. The prophecy will take care of them. Their lives and deaths are in its control."

Breyan held back the tears.

"The first generation Council was all wise, dear Breyan," Touchea said with a solemn but still friendly smile.

The High Exoltaire raised her cup. "To the growth of our society and the coming of age of our people."

"To the future and our children's, children's child." Breyan raised her cup.

"To you and whatever eternity brings you, my dear friend," Touchea toasted.

"And you, beloved Exoltaire," Breyan offered in return. The woman drank from their cups.

Touchea sighed. "The time is now." The Exoltaires held hands and disappeared into nonexistence. At that very moment, somewhere in the world the skies burned with fire, the clouds cried boiling rain and the lightening struck the soil again and again.

Chapter 56

Pouchetia looked at the sky. There was something wrong, but the feeling was so obscure, so vague that she just couldn't place it. She put it out of her mind and turned her thoughts back to her revenge.

"Rovear, go to Tammeia and tell her that I want to talk to her. Say that she's to meet me in Lumdon Hall as soon as she can. Tell her I promise she won't be harmed. Be sure to tell her that," Pouchetia said then paused. "Tell her I promise, by my word of honor as a woman of the Council, that I only wish to talk to her. Go tell her now." She grinned and cracked her knuckles one at a time.

"And if she doesn't want to see you?"

"Of course she'll come."

Rovear nodded and took off into projection.

Not long after Rovear delivered the message, Tammeia left her body to meet with Pouchetia. She opened the door to the Council hall carefully. Her knees were watery with fear. Why she had taken Pouchetia's invitation, she didn't know.

"Come in, Tammeia." Pouchetia stood in front of the orange beads. If she were to attack, there would be no sanctuary for the Regime.

"What do you want?" Tammeia asked boldly.

"I have some wonderful news for you." The Exoltaire smiled a friendly smile. Tammeia's stomach turned.

"What's your news?" The Regime braced herself for an attack. She had purposely left the door behind her open, just in case.

"It's just that your worries are over. You'll never have to worry about your sickening little girl again."

"What!" Tammeia's eyes opened wide. "What have you done to her!" She readied to strike out at the Exoltaire.

"Calm yourself, Lady Sheen. I only did what was necessary. I couldn't stand to see you worry about her for a moment longer. That's why I had the Netrin's ship fixed to fail."

"You would never! Your sons were aboard that vehicle," Tammeia fumed with anger.

"Of course not. I just had her sleeping chamber, let us say, adjusted. Somewhere in space, sometime very soon, Alana will wake up in that small box with little air and no food or a chance to live." Pouchetia laughed. "Maybe she'll try to sustain her life by eating her own flesh!"

Tammeia's mouth hung open in disbelief, her eyes dark and wide. "No! You're lying!" she screamed. "You're lying!"

"No, I'm not," Pouchetia said coolly. "Truly, I'm not," she laughed.

Tammeia ran from the hall in horror. It took her several tries before she could project herself.

Chapter 57

The three Sheen men traveled in the woods, parallel to the road. "Look, Seth, Eisen." Jgar pointed to the sky. "They're leaving."

"No," Eisen yelled. "No! They can't leave this early."

"It looks like they have," Jgar said.

"Netrins?" Seth asked.

"Yes," Eisen answered. "It's too late. Let's go home."

"Wait." Jgar took a breath. "I'll check with Tammeia. She can decide what to do."

"Jgar, what about the mind trap you told me about?" Eisen was concerned.

"Rovear promised it would be removed. I guess we'll see if he keeps his word." He dismounted and closed his eyes. Jgar successfully projected to the anhabit of his Carlaf.

"Where's Tammeia?" he addressed a servant who was polishing out a charred spot on the dining room wall.

"She's in her room."

Jgar took over the servant's flesh and headed up the stairs. Tammeia's door was closed so he listened before he went in. She was crying. He opened the door slowly.

"Lady?" he said quietly.

She turned. "Go away. I wish to have some privacy."

"Tammeia, it's me, Jgar," he said.

The woman put out her hand to feel his aura. It was Jgar. "Jgar, did you meet with Eisen?"

"Yes, Carlaf. I know you said that you didn't want us to use projection unless it's an emergency, but the sky vehicle that landed at Pouchetia's Habite has left. Alana with it, I'm sure. Should we return?"

She began to cry again. "Yes. Do what you wish. I don't care." She wiped her face but it didn't help much. "Pouchetia has informed me that she sabotaged the vehicle. The chamber where Alana sleeps is broken. She is dead." The woman burst into hysterical tears. Jgar tried to cradle her to comfort her, but the servant's arms were too short. The body was too small.

"She's gone forever," Tammeia cried.

Jgar's eyes welled with tears. He tried to hold them back but they over powered him. He cried, too.

"She must pay for this!" Jgar banged his fist on the table top.

"It doesn't matter, Jgar," Tammeia sobbed. "It's all over now."

"No! It does matter," he said with contempt. "I'll make sure she pays!" He exited the body and returned to his own.

"Eisen, Seth, we have a new mission." They came closer. "And on this one was cannot fail."

He explained his plan and they began. They rode fast, hard and amazingly unnoticed to the boundaries of Pouchetia Coray's very anhabit.

Chapter 58

"Rovear, don't go yet." Pouchetia walked away from the window. "Stay with me this night. I have a feeling in my stomach that this isn't just any night." She sat on the bed. "And I don't want to be alone."

Rovear took a brush off the table top and brushed the woman's long hair.

"And why will this night be so different?" he asked uneasily. He too felt something strange but was trying to put it off as nothing important. He knew she was missing her sons, he was too, maybe that was it. But there was no use dwelling on it. Instead he decided it was better to do something to keep her mind off it. He put down the brush and urged her gently to her back.

"It will be different," she said.

"I know it will be special." He ran the tip of his tongue over her soft, pale neck.

"Don't humor me, Rovear. I had a dream." She sighed.

He ran his hand over her chest and abdomen. "What was this dream," he whispered in her ear. Her body quaked slightly.

"I was standing, looking at the stars. You were at my side."

"It sounds nice so far." He kissed her cheek and lips.

"Rovear." She pulled slightly away. He retreated to devouring her neck. "The stars were silver. And they were melting."

"Melting," Rovear echoed breathlessly.

"Melting into blood," Pouchetia added. She got up, leaving a slightly aroused Rovear alone on the bed, and returned to the window.

"Come back here, my lover. How dare you desert me?"

She didn't seem to hear him. She didn't move.

"Then I'll follow you. You can't brush me off that easily." He joined her at the window.

"It's all Tammeia's fault," she whispered.

"What does Tammeia have to do with such a beautiful night." He urged her away from the window.

"You don't understand!" she snapped.

"Maybe I don't." He threw himself on the bed. "You had no way to stop what happened."

"They were my people!" she shouted at him. He flinched slightly. She looked into his deep green eyes. "I'm sorry, Rovear."

"Don't apologize." He held out his hand. She grabbed it and joined him on the bed. "Roll over. I'll rub your back."

Pouchetia lay on her stomach, "Tammeia is the cause of this," she said again.

"Enough talk about the Sheen woman." He worked his fingers into her tight shoulder muscles. She purred with contentment. Rovear continued to rub and relax her tight muscles until she drifted off to sleep.

Once she was asleep, her consort, Rovear, yawned and stretched then cuddled up next to her. Despite everything, sleep came easy to him.

"That window, up there," Seth said. He pointed to a second story window on the far corner of the main anhabit. "That's her bedroom."

"Then, let's go." Eisen approached the fence.

"No. The fence has an alarm system," Jgar remembered.

"Yes, you're right," Seth confirmed.

"What kind of alarm?"

"Rovear said that it's a physical alarm. Anything living that crosses the fence will set it off." Jgar laughed. "He said it's constantly being tripped by low flying birds."

"So if we cross it they may think it's a false alarm," Eisen reasoned.

"I doubt that. Most birds don't fly at night, " Seth tied his robe tighter. "Besides, they'll be looking for me. They'd be foolish not to investigate all alarms, even if they're believed to be false."

"What if they find a cause for the alarm?" Eisen looked to the fence's extents.

"Then, they find us," Seth replied.

"Maybe not." He eyed the kenya. "Will your friend do us a favor and create a distraction that will set off a false alarm?"

"Seth whispered in Strat's ear. The animal snorted. He was upset because of what had happened to the pack.

"Please, friend," The Keeper said aloud in words only Strat understood. "This is the object of our mission. This is the strike at the end of our hunt. I need you."

Reluctantly, Strat agreed.

"Whenever you're ready, Jgar." Seth patted Strat on the head. "My kenya brother will comply."

"Well, let's go," Eisen said. He darted forward.

"Wait, Eisen." Jgar reached out and stopped him. "Wait until the window's dark."

The three men and the kenya sat and watched. When the house was almost completely dark, Strat went to work. The kenya jumped on the fence, balancing like a man walking on a rope, his footing slow but sure.

"All right," Jgar whispered. "Go."

The three men jumped the fence and ran.

Inside the anhabit an alarm went off alerting three house guards. They ran to the gate.

"Look there, on the fence!" the gate guard shouted to the men. "It's a kenya."

The four men stood there amused by Strat's balancing act.

Behind the building, Seth, Jgar and Eisen made their way to the area under the window.

"This wall is easy to climb," Seth whispered. "The stones are well defined. Follow me."

They ascended without trouble to the second story window. It was open and they were able to climb in noiselessly.

Strat tried hard to keep the guard's attention. He danced and jumped back and forth on the fence post.

"Look at that kenya. It must be mad," one man said. The others laughed.

"Mad kenya?" another said. "Wasn't the Sheen Keeper seen with kenya?" The man's eyes opened wide. In near panic, he ran for the building. The other men ran after the animal. Strat was long away before they neared.

"There," Seth whispered quieter than death. Jgar looked around. They were definitely in Pouchetia's room. Her name and clan name etched on the glassier of the window made that clear. There were two sleeping figures on the bed. The one closest to them was a woman. It was definitely the Exoltaire.

Eisen fumbled in the dark. A table behind him moved and some jewelry clinked. The male figure in the bed reached for the light.

Jgar's heart pounded. His stomach knotted up. "I won't be caught now," he thought to himself. "I've got to do something."

"UGH!" Jgar screamed out loud. He plunged his knife through Pouchetia's chest again and again. The Exoltaire didn't even have time to scream.

Rovear lit the lamp.

The guard raced up the stairs.

Eisen and Seth jumped out the window. There were guards all around them. They ran.

A club hit Eisen in the stomach, then on the back of the head. He fell lifeless. Seth forced his way past them and cleared the fence. Arrows flew around his head as he raced for the field's edge and the safety of the trees.

"Jgar," Rovear's voice was unnaturally soft.

Jgar looked up. Pouchetia's blood covered his hands and face. The knife he held still dripping with the warm red fluid.

"Rovear. You don't understand. It was my Carlaf's command. I tried to change her mind, but she insisted." He backed away toward the window.

Rovear was silent.

"We're brothers, Rovear. We swore loyalties to each other." Jgar dropped the knife. "You said we would never let the women's squabbles come between us."

There was a pounding on the door. "Lady, are you all right!" the guard called from the other side.

"Go away!" Rovear yelled back.

"Let me go, brother. Friend. You understand. I did just what I had to do."

Rovear said nothing. He picked up the knife and wiped the blood on his cheeks, then looked at his Carlaf, Pouchetia's mutilated flesh.

"Rovear." Jgar put out his arms submissively.

Rovear hinted a smile.

Jgar released his breath slowly. "We'll always be brothers, Rovear. And 'brothers' is the important thing."

Rovear could say nothing. There were no words in him to be voiced, only emotions. With one stroke, he plunged the knife through Jgar's heart.

The Regimitive's eyes opened wide. He fell into Rovear's arms. The Exoltairetive stepped back and Jgar fell forward to the floor, the knife still in his chest.

Rovear looked at the man at his feet. "Brothers," he said with bitter sadness.

EPILOGUE

As these things happened, somewhere in the depths of space, the root of the seed slept, peacefully dreaming of the things only a child could, never knowing what had come to pass.

For more information on this and other
Sweetgrass Press
&
Sweetgrass Fiction
Books and authors, check out:

http://www.sweetgrasspress.com

or

Email: info@sweetgrasspress.com

You can write to Michelle:

Michelle LaVigne Wedel
C/O Sweetgrass Press
P.O. Box 1862
Merrimack, NH 03054

Email to:

mwedel@sweetgrasspress.com